Books by Carol Anne Douglas

Lancelot: Her Story
Lancelot and Guinevere

For Young Adults
THE MERLIN'S SHAKESPEARE SERIES
Merlin's Shakespeare
The Mercutio Problem

THE MERCUTIO PROBLEM

Book Two of the Merlin's Shakespeare Series

Carol Anne Douglas

Hermione

Hermione Books USA

Hermione

Publisher's Cataloging-In-Publication Data
(Prepared by The Donohue Group, Inc.)

Names: Douglas, Carol Anne, author.
Title: The Mercutio problem / Carol Anne Douglas.
Description: [Washington, D.C.] : Hermione Books, [2019] | Series: The Merlin's Shakespeare series ; book 2 | Interest age level: 012-018. | Summary: "The immortal wizard Merlin transforms teenage actor Beth Owens to the character Mercutio so she can save him. The time is the present, and the first decade of the 17th century. The main character lives in Maryland, but she is transported to Shakespeare's England and the worlds of Shakespeare's characters"--Provided by publisher.
Identifiers: ISBN 9781732789944 | ISBN 9781732789937 (ebook)
Subjects: LCSH: Merlin (Legendary character)--Juvenile fiction. | Teenage actors--Maryland--Juvenile fiction. | Mercutio (Fictitious character)--Juvenile fiction. | Time travel--Juvenile fiction. | Great Britain--History--17th century--Juvenile fiction. | CYAC: Merlin (Legendary character)--Fiction. | Teenage actors--Maryland--Fiction. | Mercutio (Fictitious character)--Fiction. | Time travel--Fiction. | Great Britain--History--17th century--Fiction. | LCGFT: Fantasy fiction.
Classification: LCC PS3554.O8235 M47 2019 (print) | LCC PS3554.O8235 (ebook) | DDC 813/.54--dc23

This book is dedicated to
Nell Quinn-Gibney, Meg Quinn-Gibney, Sophie
Marney-Dejanikus, and Claire Marney-Dejanikus. I
am grateful to them for being the girls in my life and
for listening to my stories. I would never have written
this without having known them.

The book is also dedicated to the memory of my
dearest Mandy Doolittle, who encouraged me to
write it.

I also want to dedicate this book to my mother,
Joan Flannery Douglas,
who read stories to me and understood that I always
wanted to be a writer.

The Mercutio Problem is a concept propounded by literary critics who say that a playwright may have to kill off a secondary character whose presence is too strong.

Chapter 1

NO MORE DANGER, NO more killing, no more other worlds this semester, Beth Owens told herself as she walked to her history class.

She didn't want to go through anything more difficult than attending classes at James Dean High School and having good times with her friends. She stepped around a smelly mess of fast food breakfast that some dumb kid had dropped in the hall.

The history classroom would be refreshingly normal, with pictures of Tolstoy, Rasputin, and Lenin from last fall's unit on Russia.

But when Beth entered the classroom, she saw pictures of Henry VIII, Elizabeth I, and worst of all, Shakespeare. Moscow's Red Square had been replaced by a map of London circa 1600. Her heart skipped a beat. She had time traveled to Shakespeare's world—both London in his era and the worlds of some of his characters—the previous semester and she couldn't bear the thought of having to study about that period again.

Now she was going to have to revisit Shakespeare. It was all Beth could do not to run away screaming. But other kids were pressing into the room, so she moved along with the crowd and seated herself at a desk. She couldn't drop out. World history was a required class.

The other students looked more or less enthusiastic, depending on their personalities. One boy she didn't know said, "That Henry VIII was quite a dude." One girl was showing another girl a new bracelet. Beth felt alone. James Dean High featured the performing arts, so she had something in common with many of the other kids, but she felt like they were living in another world because their experience was limited to the twenty-first century USA.

Her friend Arnie Silver came in and sat in the next desk. He was beaming because he was a Shakespeare geek like Beth, but he hadn't time traveled except when she had inadvertently pulled him into Shakespeare's world, and he didn't have the power to remember it well. Like her, Arnie loved to act in Shakespeare's plays in drama class. "Are you happy to see the pictures of Renaissance England?" he asked, probably remembering her enthusiasm for that era just a couple of months ago.

"I can't tell you how happy," she said with a voice full of sarcasm.

Sita Desai, her best friend, would understand why the pictures upset Beth, but Sita didn't take the same history class. Sita and Ms. Capulet the drama teacher were the only people who knew almost all of what had happened to Beth in Shakespeare's world.

Her eyes swelled up at the memory, but she managed to stop herself from crying.

Kevin Connelly, hearty enough to play Henry VIII (or at least the young, fit Henry), walked in to the classroom and whooped. "Shakespeare's time! Woohoo! I can't believe our luck." He loved to act, but he either pretended not to be a geek or really wasn't one.

Mr. Clarke, the history teacher, looking his usual buttoned-down self, came in and shut the door. Although he was barely in his thirties, he was one of the few teachers to always wear a suit—a well-fitting suit that probably strained his budget—and a tie and an immaculate white shirt.

He introduced himself to the students who didn't know him. "I listen to students' suggestions," he said in his Jamaican accent. "Last semester, a student wanted to focus on Elizabethan England, so we'll do that this semester." He smiled at Beth.

Smiling back took all the strength she had. Why did he have to listen to her? Focusing on Renaissance England was what she had wanted then, not now. All she wanted now was to hear nothing about Shakespeare's time for the next few years. She hated to remember how eager she had been when the immortal wizard Merlin first sent her there.

She had directed *Macbeth*, but when she prompted one of the actors about the line "Birnam Wood comes to Dunsinane," the kids playing MacDuff and the other insurgents turned into trees and she didn't know how to turn them back. Merlin, wearing an ordinary sweater and pants, had appeared in the high school auditorium, turned the kids back to humans, and erased everyone's memories of the strange event.

After the play ended, only Beth, Ms. Capulet, and Merlin were left in the auditorium.

"I have a task for you, Beth," Merlin told her. He sat down on one of the auditorium seats near hers. "There is one great lack in Shakespeare's writings. I helped him for a reason. I wanted him to write a play about King Arthur." He paused.

"But there isn't any Shakespeare play about King Arthur," Beth said.

"There is not. Or there does not seem to be." Merlin frowned. "I gave Will all he needed. Knowledge of kings, knowledge of battles. But he used bits and pieces in other plays, and never wrote the one I most desired. Or he did not appear to. There may be such a play, but it may be hidden."

"A lost Shakespeare play!" Ms. Capulet gasped. "That would be incredibly valuable."

"Beyond measure," Merlin said, "especially to me. Not just any play, but the one that was to be his crowning glory."

Beth wanted to giggle, because "crowning glory" in this instance sounded like a pun, but she refrained because Merlin intimidated her.

"If you, who are so powerful, can't find it, why do you think I could? I'm just a teenager."

"People might tell you things that they would not tell me," Merlin said. "You have some magical powers—untried and unschooled, it is true— and you love Shakespeare and learn the lines quickly. You also have some talent for acting."

She learned that over the centuries, Merlin had sent many young people with magical powers to find the missing play. He had discovered that Beth could perform magic, but unfortunately her magical power was limited to things related to Shakespeare and his plays.

Merlin had given her the power of simultaneous translation, so she could hear Renaissance English as if people were speaking in her own form of English and they could hear her as if she spoke in their mode.

She remembered talking to Shakespeare in his plain rented room in Old London, with just a bed, a table, one chair, and a stool. On the wall hung the coat of arms he had pushed for many years to obtain. She could almost hear his voice. She had learned that he had never written a play about King Arthur, and why he hadn't.

He sat on the chair and bade her to sit on a stool—the only other furniture—and share his bread. She cut a piece. Then she asked about his plays.

"It's incredible that you could have created both comedies and dramas, with characters as different as Bottom and Lady Macbeth, or Richard III." She tried to say Richard's name without shuddering.

"But there is not just one villain in the world, one lover, one fool," Shakespeare said. "The world holds not just Bottom and Richard, but Falstaff and Macbeth. Not just Juliet, but Portia. And Lady Macbeth." He drank ale, and his speech became more intense. "They are joined, you see. You cannot have Lear without Bottom, or Bottom without Lear. No fairies without the abyss, no abyss without fairies. No light without

darkness, no darkness without light." His eyes shone as if he were looking on faraway scenes.

Her heart almost burst at the memory.

Beth pulled herself together to listen to Mr. Clarke.

"I realize that, except for watching television shows of dubious accuracy, not all of you are familiar with the Tudors," the teacher said. "I doubt that you even are familiar with the history of Maryland, our own state, but that isn't covered in my World History class. So we'll start by studying the historical background of England in that time. We'll do that as painlessly as possible by looking at Shakespeare's plays *Richard III* and *Henry V.* Ms. Capulet, the drama teacher, will join us for that part of the class."

Beth swayed. No, not Richard, the character she hated and feared. Richard who had insinuated himself into her brain. He had seen her thoughts and even influenced them. When she had tried to go to other places in Shakespeare's world, Richard had pulled her into his incense-filled great hall.

Arnie grabbed her before she fell out of her desk.

"Beth was sick over the holidays," Arnie said. "I think she still has a touch of flu."

Everyone was staring at her, but at least Arnie's words made her weakness sound normal.

"I'm sorry to hear that." Mr. Clarke walked over to her. "Would you like to go to the infirmary?"

Arnie answered for her. "Yes." He helped Beth out of her desk and walked her out into the hall.

Now everyone would think he was her boyfriend. Well, that was the least of her worries.

When they stood in the hall, Beth staggered and leaned against the wall.

"Are you going to be OK?" Arnie asked. "Do you want to go to the infirmary?"

She shook her head. "No, I'm going to see Ms. Capulet. You can go back to the history class."

"If you're sure you're all right." He turned back to the classroom but hesitated.

"I'm fine. Thanks for your quick thinking." Beth pulled herself together and hurried in the direction of the drama teacher's office. Ms. Portia Desdemona Capulet was the one who had brought Beth to Merlin's attention—leading her to see things that haunted her.

Beth passed windows showing the piles of January snow outdoors, but she didn't pause to admire the scene. She passed classrooms where kids were reciting in French and Spanish, but she could scarcely hear the words. She almost ran into some boys who were running down the hall singing songs from *High School Musical*. She passed a mural depicting James Dean and a photo of the school's mascot, a guy in a black leather jacket who was riding a motorcycle. She heard someone playing a trombone when she passed the rooms where kids practiced for the band.

She came to the teachers' offices. Ms. Capulet's door was open, so Beth walked in without knocking.

The office was messy, as usual. There shouldn't be many student papers at the beginning of the semester, but there were stacks of paper. Posters of Katharine Hepburn and James Dean looked down from the walls. The books in Ms. Capulet's bookcase were arranged helter-skelter, with some standing up and some lying on their sides. The office smelled like dust. The teacher sat at her paper-filled desk. Her long, gray hair streamed down her back. As usual, Ms. Capulet wore jeans. A t-shirt worn over her turtleneck said "High school is a stage."

"I was expecting you, Beth. Please sit down." Ms. Capulet sounded as if she had heard someone had cancer. She gestured towards the chair reserved for students who came to discuss their work. "I'm so sorry. Mr. Clarke just told me this morning. I didn't have a chance to warn you."

Beth sat down and took a deep breath. "But that play! How could he have chosen that play by chance?" Ms. Capulet would know Beth wasn't talking about *Henry V.*

The teacher shrugged. "He did. It's an unfortunate coincidence. I know it will bring up horrible memories for you. But I couldn't tell him not to use the play because one of the students had been hurt by Richard III. All I can do is try to support you."

She was with Mercutio in Richard's hall. The king had reached for Beth.

"No! Don't touch Beth!" Mercutio drew his sword.

"Traitor," Richard said coldly, staring into a mirror the others could not see and beckoning to someone.

Tybalt, the character in Romeo and Juliet *who had killed Mercutio, appeared, and in a flash stabbed Mercutio in the back.*

"No!" Beth leapt to Mercutio's aid, but she was too late. Grabbing his arm as he fell, she threw herself on her knees beside him.

Beth forced herself to concentrate on the present. "I'm not just worried about bad memories." Her voice faltered. "I don't want Richard back in my life." Just saying his name made her stomach heave. "He was able to see into my brain. I'm afraid that he could connect with me again."

"We did see Lady Macbeth kill him," Ms. Capulet reminded her.

"But not forever. A famous character can't be killed forever." The pitch of Beth's voice rose higher. "We don't know when or how he could come back."

"That's true. I don't think he can come back to our time, but we don't know." The teacher twisted her hands. "Perhaps we can just arrange for you to miss the class when that movie is shown. Just in case."

"But I don't want to take a class in the history of Renaissance England," Beth groaned.

"I know, but you need this class. Mr. Clarke is so proud of taking you up on your suggestion."

Beth wanted to bury her history book under one of the piles in the office. "I should know better than to say anything to a teacher—ever."

Ms. Capulet flinched. "Let's think how you could get more support. Do you have any friends in that class?"

"Arnie Silver. He realizes that something happened to me in Shakespeare's England, but he doesn't know what. And Kevin, but I couldn't confide in him."

"I think you could tell Arnie a little more. And your friend Sita could switch to Mr. Clarke's history class. I could say she needs to do that because of her focus on playing Shakespearean roles."

"If you can get the history class switched for her, why not for me?"

"When the teacher has specifically focused it on the era you suggested? No way. But I think Sita would be willing to switch if that would help you."

"Yes, I guess so." Beth felt a little cheered, but not totally. She and Sita had had their worst arguments over Shakespeare. Sita had magical powers regarding Shakespeare's plays herself, though she hadn't had the chance to test them, and she resented the fact that Merlin had chosen Beth to time travel, and resented even more that Beth wouldn't tell her Shakespeare's secrets.

"Don't you have another class soon?" the drama teacher asked, looking at her watch.

"Yes. Thank you for everything." Beth rose from her chair and left Ms. Capulet's office. It was time to go to French class.

Beth lingered as she walked down the hall that had a wall of photos of previous school plays. The only photos of her were from *The Taming of the Shrew*, where she had played Kate and Kevin had driven her crazy because he kept on playing Petruchio off stage. She saw the photos of Arnie as MacDuff fighting Kevin as Macbeth, and Sita looking evil as Lady Macbeth. Beth had directed that play. Ms. Capulet had said there was too much magic in Beth for her to play a part in any play in which characters were killed because she might inadvertently get them killed in real life. And there were photos of Kevin and Arnie hamming it up in *The Comedy of Errors*. Beth hadn't been able to act in that play because she was so busy supposedly taking a special studies class in Shakespeare from Ms. Capulet, but she had actually been traveling to Shakespeare's time.

Beth hoped she would have a part in a play this semester: a good part—and not in a play by Shakespeare.

THAT NIGHT HER MOTHER served warmed-over pasta.

"I'm sorry that's all there is for dinner," her mother said. "I have to keep working on the first few lectures for my American History class. I'm not satisfied with them." Her mother, a single mother who was a professor at Eleanor Roosevelt State College, never yelled and hardly ever complained. But Beth sometimes wished that her mother was less focused on her. That was the burden of being an only child. When time travel wore Beth down, her mother had wanted her to stop taking her special studies Shakespeare class with Ms. Capulet. Well, she didn't try to explain what she was really doing.

"It's a fine dinner, Mom. No problem. I need to start studying this evening."

Afterwards, Beth sat down at her computer and opened a file where she wrote the names of her classes. Then she stared around her room. Wasn't that quilt with what seemed like magical symbols looking a little old? Maybe she should ask for one with flowers. She didn't want to be reminded of magic.

Before she had experienced magic, she had thought of it as shimmering lights, ever-changing colors, and the ability to fly—and maybe to disappear at will. She hadn't known that it involved dealing with real characters, some of whom were vicious. Only occasionally did it feel enchanting.

A familiar voice sounded behind her back. "You are just pretending to study. You have not moved to another screen in ages."

Beth felt her hackles rise, like an animal's. She turned.

There was Merlin, dressed in the gown and ruff of a wealthy Elizabethan gentleman. A plumed hat sat on his head and his white beard streamed over the ruff. She could never predict what clothes he might wear. For a one thousand-year-old immortal, he was looking good despite his white hair and wrinkles.

Beth frowned at him. "I told you it was all over," she said. "I don't want to time travel for you anymore."

"But now you are taking a class on Renaissance England," the wizard said, stroking his beard. "That is your destiny."

"That's my class schedule, not my destiny." She didn't try to keep the anger out of her voice.

"You need to return to Shakespeare's time."

That was so Merlin. Not asking, but telling her.

"No, I don't need to. And I won't."

"You could save Mercutio."

Beth winced. She remembered seeing Mercutio laughing and teasing her. She remembered his blood-stained body. She rubbed her eyes, as if that would erase the memory. "He's dead. It's cruel to try to use him to persuade me."

"If I am cruel, so be it." Merlin shrugged. "Mercutio is a character, not a human being. He will live again. You have seen him appear to you on the stage."

"Just on the stage." After Beth's last visit to Shakespeare's world, Ms. Capulet had taken her to see *Romeo and Juliet*, and she had seen Mercutio, not the actor who was playing his part. Of course, Beth had had to leave before he was killed in the play. "That was like a miracle, but it wasn't the same as being with him."

"He will live as he has before," the wizard declared. "Now he is only a character on a page. The question is whether he will live in your time and be able to move among Shakespeare's worlds." Merlin scrutinized her. "I believe that you can bring him back, if you choose."

"Why do you care?" Beth felt her body tense with suspicion. "You didn't care that he died." She glared at the wizard. "You wouldn't be interested unless there was something in it for you."

"Your modern usages of language are most unattractive." Merlin frowned, which altered his always-stern features only a little. "My concerns go far beyond my own welfare."

"That's news to me." She deliberately used another expression that he wouldn't much like.

"You have a limited understanding. But listen to me, as well as you can," he said, implying that her best still wasn't very good. He pointed his finger at her. "You are correct that Mercutio is only one of my concerns. I must speak to you about Richard III."

"Please don't." Beth put her hands up to protect herself.

"I must." Merlin's tone was grim. "You saw Lady Macbeth kill Richard because he pretended he loved her as Macbeth had, and your friends showed her scenes from the Scottish play reminding her of Macbeth's intense but misguided love. But Richard is far stronger than any other Shakespearean character. He was based on Mordred, and carries Mordred's ancient power as well as that vested in him by Shakespeare." Merlin clenched his fists, because Mordred was his nemesis, and had been from the time of King Arthur. Mordred had killed Arthur, whom Merlin had loved like a father.

Beth shivered. "That's a good reason for me to stay out of your business, not to get involved," she said.

"You won't convince me that you are a coward. I know better than that." Even though he gave one of his rare compliments, Merlin did not smile at her. He never did. "Mordred," he repeated. "Mordred survives." He shuddered. "Mordred seems to be immortal."

Beth put her hands over her ears, but she could still hear Merlin's words: "When Richard was killed, he apparently lost his hold on you," the wizard continued. He began pacing the room. "He now is trying another strategy. He is attempting to take over Shakespeare's other plays, one by one, apparently in the hope of forcing Shakespeare to write the play he desires, a play in which Mordred defeats King Arthur instead of dying with him."

"Is that new?" Beth asked. "Months ago, I saw Richard trying to persuade Oberon to join him in an alliance. Oberon just laughed at him."

"Oh, he has been pursuing these ends for a long time, then." Merlin drew a lengthy breath. "Every word you say makes it clearer that though you are a mere mortal, your help is needed."

"I doubt it." Beth wanted to escape to her homework, even geometry.

"Mercutio foolishly worked for Richard, but became disillusioned with that vile king."

"Richard had him killed." Beth couldn't keep the agony out of her voice.

"Precisely." Merlin nodded. "So Mercutio would help me fight Richard. And you could bring Mercutio back."

"How am I supposed to do that?" Beth was afraid to listen, but she did. She didn't want to be involved in any more magic. But Merlin's words made her hope that she could see her friend again. "How?"

The wizard's gray eyes stared into hers. "By being him. You must pretend to be Mercutio. If you do, I believe that ultimately your charade will call to him and bring him back to life."

Beth gasped. "You want me to pretend I am Mercutio?" She stared at the wizard. "That's crazy. I'm nothing like him." She recalled Mercutio's frequent bawdy remarks and his eagerness to fight at the slightest opportunity.

"Oh, I think you could imitate him very well. I could make you look like him, and I am certain that your memory of him is acute. How he spoke, how he gestured."

"I remember him." Tears started to form in her eyes. She could hear him calling her "Moonface" because he saw her as a dreamer. He had flirted with her, but had he meant it? She had refused to kiss him. Now she was sorry she hadn't. She remembered his tales about the fairy Queen Mab bringing people dreams. She could see him showing her the beauties of Verona. And, fatally, pulling out his sword when Richard insulted her. "But remembering people doesn't bring them back."

"Not humans. But it can bring characters back." Merlin looked at her as if she were a fish on a hook. "If you care enough to try."

Beth choked back her tears. "I have to remember that this is all one of your plots. It has to do with Shakespeare, not Mercutio."

"Mercutio has no existence apart from Shakespeare."

"That's not what Mercutio said. When I saw him, he could make up his own lines."

"He tries to run away. They all do. But ultimately they are tied to their playmaker. If Richard succeeds in hurting Shakespeare, that would hurt Mercutio. That would hurt all the characters."

Beth believed Merlin. She remembered the vision he had shown her of how Richard wanted to imprison the women characters and do worse to the men. She saw Juliet, Portia, and Rosalind herded into a prison cell. "I'll think about what you've said," she told Merlin.

"Yes, think. With your limited mind." Though he was not tall, the wizard seemed to tower above her. "Where do dead characters go? Do they wander in pain like Hamlet's father? Is that Mercutio's life now? I don't know. Do you?"

Beth reeled, as if from a blow. She grabbed the arms of her chair to steady herself. "That was unfair," she protested.

"What does fairness have to do with life and death? Either for characters or for humans?" Merlin's lip curled with scorn. "Why do you count your wishes as more important than your friend's life? If I give you a chance to help Mercutio, you should be glad. If I give you a chance to help Will Shakespeare, you should rejoice."

"That would sound better if I didn't know that you bullied Shakespeare the same way," Beth retorted.

"I, as you call it, bullied him. And what did he achieve as a result?" Merlin asked.

"A hit, a very palpable hit," Beth said.

"Ha!" The wizard smiled. "A Shakespearean answer. You will act his part."

"I will." The words burst out of her even though she was afraid.

Merlin almost smiled at his success. "Of course you will. Remember that you must stop carrying your mechanical devices, as you did last year. You can't take a chance that they might be carried to old London."

Beth sighed. She would have to tell her friends again, as she had before, that her mother wouldn't let her use her smartphone. And find an excuse to give her mother, who wanted her to carry it.

Merlin disappeared, and Beth burst into tears. She flung herself onto her bed. Mercutio. She had been trying not to think of how much she wanted to see his face, look into his dark brown eyes, and hear his laughter. She tried to erase from her mind the sight of him lying dead, covered with blood.

She had been angry at Richard before, but now when she remembered Mercutio's death she felt consumed by rage. She wanted to attack Richard like an avenging Fury.

Mercutio. Was it possible that she could hear him laugh again? She felt that she would do anything to be near him again, even if he was in one of his obnoxious moods where he bragged about being the cousin of the Prince of Verona and belittled anyone who wasn't an aristocrat.

Mercutio was grotesquely old-fashioned about women. He scoffed at the idea of education for girls. He couldn't imagine any man wanting to marry a woman in her mid-twenties. He scorned people who acted on a stage. But, after all, he was from a different time, long before Shakespeare lived. Mercutio kept getting in trouble visiting England because he couldn't conceive of a time when the Catholic Church wasn't the only Christian Church in Western Europe. English Protestants saw him as one of the hated Spanish, not as an Italian. Sword and dagger jumped too readily into his hands.

But Mercutio could be tender. He made her laugh until her belly hurt. She would do anything for him. She must be crazy, but she didn't care. Most people couldn't bring back someone they loved. But she could, because Mercutio was a character, not a living being. She couldn't pass up the chance.

I'm ready, Beth thought. Let me be something like Mercutio, if that will bring him back.

Chapter 2

S HE SPUN THROUGH FRIGID air. The wind forced her to close her eyes. She landed with a thunk, but upright.

Beth stood on a heath. Fog swirled around her. She could see thorny plants at her feet, but most of the heath was covered in a veil of gray. She smelled the foul aroma of a familiar cauldron. She gagged and remembered that she had never wanted to ask the witches whether the contents of the cauldron were really those that Shakespeare had enumerated, like a Turk's nose and the finger of a birth-strangled babe. She saw the cauldron's muddy liquid bubble and thought she would rather die than taste it.

"All hail Beth!" three voices cried. And three beings she had come to know appeared to her. Their bodies were green, they were blue, they were gray. They were neither female nor male, but neither were they intersex. They were their own strange lumps of almost flesh, with almost hair and eyes that were not eyes but could see far too much.

Beth had learned not to fear the witches—too much. They seemed to mean well by her. But they knew too much about everyone and everything.

"Hail," she said in reply, hoping that was the right thing to say.

"All hail Mercutio!" they chanted.

Beth flinched. "You're right, of course. Merlin wants me to pretend to be Mercutio."

"Not pretend," the first witch said.

"To be Mercutio," chanted the second.

"You will be Mercutio," the third told her.

"That will be hard for a girl," Beth said.

"Not a girl," the first said.

"Mercutio," the second said.

"Truly Mercutio," said the third.

Beth felt as if she had fallen into a pit. She touched her chin. There was stubble.

Her body was a couple of inches taller than it had been and she had shoulder-length hair instead of her usual short light brown locks. She examined the ends of her hair and could see that it was dark. She wore a green doublet and hose that she had last seen on Mercutio, which was extra creepy. She even wore the boots she remembered seeing on him. And his rings were on her fingers, which looked like a man's fingers on a man's hands. One ring was emerald, another was topaz, and one was gold with the design of a falcon on it. She could hardly bear to look at the hands, which would have been fine if they weren't hers. She had calluses, probably from sword practice, on her right hand. She could feel Mercutio's sword hanging on her back. Her chest felt flat and hairy.

She thought that maybe—did she feel different down there? No, not that. She felt the same, but she intended to put her hand down there as soon as she was alone, just to make sure. But otherwise she was too much like a guy.

Beth gagged, and not just because of the cauldron's vapors. "Merlin turned me into Mercutio. Or almost." Her voice sounded like Mercutio's. Like a man's voice. "Merlin made me a guy. I have stubble. Too gross. I'll kill Merlin."

"Kill him? You sound like Mercutio already. But Merlin is immortal," the first witch said.

"But I don't want to be a guy! I'm Beth Owens! I'm not a boy in a girl's body. I'm a girl. How can I get back to being myself?"

"In your world, you are Beth," the second witch said.

"In this world, you will be Mercutio," said the third.

Beth stared at her hairy hands. "I want to be with him, not to be him. Is it true that my being him can bring him back?"

"Bring him back," the witches chorused.

"But how, if I'm Mercutio, can he come back?"

The witches cackled. "You don't guess?"

"No. How can he come back?"

"When you die," chanted the first witch.

"You die," chanted the second.

"He will come back when you die," chanted the third.

"Die?" Beth gasped. She fell backwards, tearing her velvet sleeve on a gorse bush. "No, that's too much." Her voice cracked. "I don't want to die."

"In this world," the first witch said.

"Die in this world? But not in mine?" Beth asked. She tried to stand up even though her legs felt weak.

"Die as Mercutio, not as Beth," the second witch said.

So, probably not in her own world. But it would be scary enough to die in this world. "I don't want to."

"He died for you," the third witch reminded her.

"Oh." Beth stood there in shock. Yes, Mercutio had died trying to defend her from Richard. But Mercutio was a character, and could live again. She was human, and could die only once. Maybe.

Beth shook her head. "It's too much."

"Too much," the witches echoed. "Too much."

"Tell Merlin," the first witch said.

"That you won't save Mercutio," the second witch said.

"Let Mercutio stay dead," the third witch chanted.

"No!" Beth exclaimed. "I'll do it."

"Beth will do it," the witches chanted. "Beth will die. In this world."

The witches vanished. Even though she saw no one else on the foggy heath, Beth went behind a large gorse bush. She pulled down her breeches. Even though the rest of her looked male… What a relief! She didn't want to be *that* much like Mercutio. She pulled her breeches up again. She imagined being Mercutio even when she had her period. That thought made her smile.

Beth spun away, choking in the fog. She landed on her bed.

I'm crazy, she thought. She leapt up and looked in her mirror. Her face was Beth's face. Her hands were Beth's hands. She was herself. She had never thought of herself as super-feminine, but she combed her hair and changed her slacks to a skirt just to reassure herself that in her own world she was a girl. But if she was mostly male in another world, did that make her intersex or transsexual in this one? Should she put on lipstick? Maybe lipstick was unnecessary, because she wouldn't put it on if she hadn't been worrying. Maybe it was best just to be herself.

Would Mercutio still be attracted to her if she managed to bring him back to life? Or would he be grossed out that she had lived in most of his body? Her head felt heavy with the many questions that occurred to her.

No matter what was troubling her, she had to say good-night to her mother.

When Beth went downstairs, she saw her mother hunched over a pile of college history papers that she was grading. She sat on the faded couch that they had had since Beth was a baby.

"Professor Owens, you're working too hard," Beth said, trying to make her voice cheerful.

"It's not so bad, honey," her mother said, looking up. "Some of the papers are good. But some college students are appallingly lacking in their knowledge of American history. This one thinks the Vietnam War occurred before the Korean War." She rolled her eyes. "At least the paper wasn't plagiarized. I hope."

"Good thing he or she is taking your class," Beth said. She paused. "I've been thinking. I'd like to stop using my smartphone again for a while."

"What! Not again!" Her mother stared at her. "Are you having problems with it? I've never heard of any other teenager who was so reluctant to use a smartphone. You used to love it."

"I do love it, Mom. I just want to be smartphone-abstinent sometimes. Not be too dependent on it."

Her mother raised her eyebrows. "Are you sure it isn't just that you don't want me to be able to reach you?"

"Mom!" Beth exclaimed. "You know you can trust me." The words made her feel as deceptive as Juliet was to her parents. Her mother would have been horrified at her time traveling. "I never go places I'm not supposed to go or get in any trouble." Not in this world, anyway.

She hated lying to her mother, but it was necessary.

"I know that. But it does worry me that you're so intense. You worked too hard when you took that special studies class on Shakespeare with Ms. Capulet."

"Oh Mom, you're hilarious." Beth made her voice sound casual. "How many mothers tell their daughters not to work too hard? Don't worry. I won't be tempted to do that this semester. Especially not in geometry."

"You do have to keep up your math."

"I know that. As an actor, I'll have to calculate the diameter and circumference of the stage."

"You're still peerless at advanced placement clever retorts," her mother said. "Get some rest, honey."

"You, too, Mom." Beth crossed the room and kissed her. "Goodnight."

It could be difficult having a good mother, Beth thought. But she was sure it would be worse having a bad mother. People said that being a single mother was difficult, but her mother made it look almost easy.

Chapter 3

THE NEXT DAY, BETH smiled on her way to drama class. At least Ms. Capulet could be counted on not to choose a play that would hurt Beth. No *Richard III*. No *Romeo and Juliet*.

Beth entered the classroom. It looked the same as it had the previous semester—the dramatic black walls, the poster of Shakespeare, the computer screen behind the teacher's desk, and the dark blue curtains that could be used to turn the front of the room into a stage. The room was odorless, until kids brought in their snacks.

All her friends were there—Sita, Arnie, and Kevin, and many other kids as well. Beth knew some but not all of them. Some James Dean wannabes wore leather jackets. Kevin wore one, too, and had his hair slicked back to look like the Fonz. How retro! Beth covered her mouth with her hand so she wouldn't giggle at him.

Everyone seemed much more eager in this class than in any other. A couple of girls wore so much makeup that she wondered whether they thought they had to be ready to audition for the movies.

Beth wanted to wear make-up too—stage make-up that made her look old or young depending on the part. It would be fun to have fake wrinkles, she thought.

Beth exchanged friendly glances with everyone. She hadn't seen Sita in two days. That was a long time for them. Since then, Sita had had a new haircut, stylish as always. And she wore a new outfit with a spangled top. Sita's parents were doctors and could afford plenty of new clothes.

Beth wasn't sure whether she would tell Sita about what was happening, or how much to tell. Was it better to tell before Sita guessed?

Sita was so sharp that she could figure out when something strange was going on. Beth thought of the first time she learned she had magical powers, when she had inadvertently turned another actor's ears to donkey's ears during a production of *A Midsummer Night's Dream* at a summer theater camp play directed by Ms. Capulet. Merlin, disguised as an old man who had just wandered into the rehearsal space, had given Beth the spell to reverse the magic: "Shakespeare midsummer wild thyme hedgehogs Thisbe"—and the reverse spell to make everyone forget what had just happened—"Thisbe hedgehogs wild thyme midsummer Shakespeare." Everyone's mind was wiped—everyone's but Sita's. Sita had remembered that something had happened, though she hadn't been sure just what. So it wouldn't be long before Sita guessed that Beth was back in touch with Shakespeare's world. And Sita would resent that, as she had before.

"This semester, we will perform a comedy," Ms. Capulet told the class. "By popular request."

Kevin applauded. He was a good actor, Beth thought, but he didn't seem to be as bright offstage as Sita or Arnie.

"How about *The Importance of Being Earnest*?" Beth ventured. Not Shakespeare, please, she thought.

"That is an entertaining play," Ms. Capulet said. "Unfortunately, the seniors are already doing it. Shakespeare is my specialty. I had thought of *Twelfth Night*."

Beth exhaled. At least it was a comedy, and one of her favorites.

"The high school would let us put on *Twelfth Night*?" Arnie blinked. "It doesn't have too much bawdy language?"

"I was thinking of making it an unofficial production, just casting my own students, and of course toning down the language a little," the teacher said.

"Or a lot," Sita murmured.

"It might be fun," Beth said. At least no one got killed in the play. That was all she cared about.

"I hope you'll try out for Viola," the teacher urged her.

"Sure." Beth had no problem with that suggestion. If she was going to pretend to be a guy in the Otherworld, she might as well play the part of a woman pretending to be a man in her own world, too. The parts might be good practice for each other. Being Mercutio could teach her how to play Viola. Or vice versa. Playing Viola could teach Beth how to be Mercutio.

"Why not try out for Olivia?" Ms. Capulet said to Sita.

Sita frowned. Even when she frowned, she looked like a model. "I'm not sure I want to be Olivia."

"Or Feste," the teacher added. "You could be either."

"A deluded girl or a fool?" Sita said, but she smiled. "I'd rather be one of Shakespeare's fools, of course."

"I want to be Sir Toby Belch. Playing a drunkard would be fun." Kevin Connelly stuck out his stomach and tried to look fat.

"You've got the belching down pat. I'd like to try out for Sir Andrew Aguecheek. That's another good comic part," Arnie said.

"Yes, and Duke Orsino, too," the teacher suggested.

"Perfect." Arnie grinned even more than Kevin.

So, Beth thought, she was supposed to be in love with Arnie if he played Duke Orsino. And have a girl in love with her. Very interesting, if a little weird. It would be more fun if she were bisexual.

Amelia Hansen, a quiet blonde girl who had just joined the class, said, "I want to try out for Olivia if I don't have to wear make-up. I have chemical sensitivities."

Another girl giggled. She fell silent when the teacher looked at her as if she had insulted someone's mother.

"You don't have to wear make-up," Ms. Capulet said. "We try to accommodate everyone. In fact, no one will wear make-up. This is a high school production, after all."

"How can you be an actor if you can't wear stage make-up?" Kevin asked.

"I don't expect to be a professional actor," Amelia said. "But acting in high school would be fun."

Beth couldn't picture Amelia as Olivia. Shouldn't Olivia be a little harsher, more self-absorbed? Amelia had such a soft voice.

"Who will try out for Malvolio?" Ms. Capulet asked.

"I will." Frank Wilson, a heavy black junior, stepped forward.

"This is a sophomore play," the teacher told him.

"I know, but you put on the best plays. The registrar let me sign up for your class." Frank grinned.

Beth could hardly admit how uncomfortable she was at having a black guy play an unsympathetic part, let alone that of a servant, even a steward. Not to mention a character whom the other characters hated and abused.

She could see from the other kids' faces that they also were uneasy at this casting. Including Sita, Asian American though she was.

Frank looked around the room and smiled. "I guess you'd all rather I played Sir Toby Belch. No thanks. I don't like the way Malvolio is treated in the play, and having me play the part will heighten the audience's discomfort—as well as yours. That's a good thing. People should be uncomfortable about Malvolio. That's what makes this play more than a story of love and mistaken identities."

"I want to try out for Maria," said Lupe Gomez, a new girl in school.

Beth squirmed. She could see that Kevin squirmed also.

"Wouldn't you rather try out for Olivia?" he asked. "You're so pretty."

"Olivia is a wuss. I've always wanted to play Maria. She's tough, and she's funny." Lupe rolled her eyes. "Two people of color playing the servants. How terrible. How too much like real life."

"Enough discussion," Ms. Capulet said. "It's time to audition." She passed out copies of the script. "You first, Sita."

"When that I was and a little tiny boy, with a hey, ho, the wind and the rain . . . ." Sita sang. Her singing voice was better than Beth had guessed, and appropriately androgynous for this part.

When the auditions ended, Ms. Capulet said, "You have all judged your skills well. You have the parts you wanted. Now learn your lines and try to develop your character's perspective. As actors, you have a perspective on the role, but you need to feel the character's perspective, not just yours."

Several kids shifted in their chairs.

"That's Stanislavski's terminology," the teacher said. "I'll explain it to you individually if you need more discussion. Just try to figure out your character from the inside out. What is your character feeling, regardless of what he or she is saying?

"There's something else you need to do," Ms. Capulet added. "If you're in any scenes with Amelia, please do not wear cologne or any other product with a strong scent. That includes not using scented soap or shampoo."

Beth almost never wore perfume, so that didn't sound difficult. She'd have to ask her mother to buy something besides lavender soap.

Beth corralled her teacher after the other students had left. "I've never played a man before, except in class exercises. Then you told us not to worry about seeming like men, just to think about what the character wants and what the character's social position is. But I'm going to be playing a woman posing as a man, so shouldn't she make some obvious attempts at trying to look like a man, maybe more obvious than if I were playing a male character?"

Ms. Capulet nodded. "You've got the right idea. She's playing a young man, so she wouldn't act like a dominant male, but she would probably exaggerate some gestures just a little."

"Thank you," Beth said. In other words, Viola as Cesario would be more subdued than Mercutio.

BETH SAT IN HER bedroom, memorizing Viola's lines and trying to imagine pretending to be a guy. She wondered whether she could visit *Twelfth Night* to better understand the play.

With that thought, she spun through gleaming lights and incense. Her head ached. She knew she had landed in the place where she least wanted to be: Richard's great hall. She looked like Mercutio, but she still felt just like Beth.

Richard III was as alive as ever. Why didn't someone else have to die to bring him back? Beth wondered. She seethed at the thought that he was alive while Mercutio was dead.

Richard sat on his golden throne, his boar pennant hanging behind him. The hundred and some torches reflected in his walls of many mirrors almost blinded her. As usual, he had incense burning as if he were a god. And as usual, Beth choked on it. She disliked the smell of incense, especially his. Just hearing his name was enough to nauseate her, and his incense only worsened the nausea. Amelia must feel that way often. It was a good thing that she wasn't the one who had to be with Richard.

Beth remembered that Merlin had said Richard had used her memories to make his hall look like the one in Kenneth Branagh's movie of *Hamlet*, only grander. She wanted to get Richard out of her mind.

Richard was still handsome. One shoulder was slightly higher than the other, but that did nothing to mar his looks. He wore an ermine-trimmed purple robe that brought out the color in his blue eyes.

"I can't be killed so easily. Doesn't that delight you, dear Beth?" he said, leering at her.

"I'm thrilled." So he could see that she was Beth, though she looked like Mercutio.

This was the first time Beth had seen Richard since he had ordered Tybalt to kill Mercutio again. Hatred flashed through her body as it never had before. She shook with rage. She steeled herself not to rush at him and strike him. She knew she could not do him physical damage, because he was a different kind of being, a character. It was against her principles anyway, but she wasn't sure she could have held on to her principles if she had been certain she could kill him. Could she kill him as Mercutio? No, Richard might just spring up again as he had this time. Could he kill her now that she was wearing Mercutio? She wasn't ready to die as Mercutio yet.

"Pardon me for not addressing you as Mercutio, but I know that he is far deader than I am. But if you are going to play his part, won't you drink some wine?" The king picked up a golden goblet and offered it to her.

"Mercutio wouldn't drink with you if he came back knowing that you killed him," Beth said, her voice almost a snarl.

"If you were truly Mercutio, you would lunge at me with your sword." Richard laughed. His laughter reminded her of a hyena's. "But you are wiser than he was. You have a greater instinct for self-preservation. And because you aren't really a character, you probably cannot kill me either."

"That's too bad," Beth said. Why pretend to be polite?

"Nonsense. You don't have the stomach for killing. We both know that. Here's to your petty morality!" Richard raised a goblet to her and drank.

"I guess you're alive because Lady Macbeth just killed Richard, not Mordred," Beth said. The heat in Richard's sauna-like hall made her sweat.

"Congratulations. You have deduced the correct answer." Richard smiled his worse-than-wolfish smile. "I am two characters combined, one more ancient and powerful than the other. That is why I am stronger than any other character."

"And more evil," she said.

"If you wish to call my strength evil, I give you permission to do so," he said with a magnanimous gesture. "You must know that I am still seeking to persuade friend Shakespeare to write a play about King Arthur in which Mordred kills Arthur but survives and becomes king. Mordred Rex." He spoke those words as if they were the sweetest in the world. "Unfortunately, you are the only person I know who can help me by summoning Shakespeare. So I must be polite to you and offer you another opportunity to work with me. A strange alliance, true, but alliances often are."

All Beth's muscles tightened with anger. "You know I'll never work for you. Don't pretend that your henchmen are allies. You are always in control and kill them on a whim."

"If you won't help me, others will. But you might be less than pleased with that result," Richard chortled.

"I can't imagine who would be fool enough to help you," she said.

"That's exactly it. You can't imagine. But it is some person or persons known to you." Richard rose from his throne and walked towards the gilded door.

Beth gasped. She almost called after him, "Tell me who?" But who could believe Richard? Would any of her friends help him? She must not have such thoughts. He wanted to disconcert her. Her life was difficult enough without him. She must concentrate on trying to bring back Mercutio, not on other matters. She saw herself in the many mirrors. It was like seeing a hundred Mercutios, but knowing they were all false. She tried to stop looking at the reflections.

She hadn't expected to miss the real Mercutio so much. What was he but a jester, a delightful fool? Yes, Mercutio should have been a fool, should have renounced violence, Beth thought. He had failed to see his true vocation. He had wanted to be a warrior in a history play, but he was born, or created, or whatever he had been, for a mixture of comedy and tragedy, with the emphasis on the comedy.

Richard turned back to her and paused. "You refuse to take my hint? You won't help me, but I will help you. And as you help Mercutio, who helped me in the past, you may find that you must help the one who is helping me now." Richard paused to laugh at her confusion. "Beth, the always cheerful helper. You're such a helper that you can't help yourself." His eerie laughter resounded as he sauntered away.

Beth wished herself to be anywhere else in Shakespeare's world. She spun away from the moist, incense-filled air through a bracing wind.

Beth stood in the world's bleakest garden, which she recognized as the Macbeths'. A raven perching in one of the bare trees croaked at her.

The air chilled her and the gray sky depressed her, but not as much as Richard's ostentatious hall. No flowers bloomed. Beth shivered. She wondered if it ever was summer in this garden. Did flowers ever bloom here?

But what she noticed above all was that she was Mercutio, judging the garden because it was nothing like Verona.

"Greetings, Mercutio," said Lady Macbeth, stepping along the garden's flagstones. She was as beautiful as ever, with gleaming red hair, dark eyes that looked right through you, and dainty hands. Dainty everything. She wore a black velvet gown and a dark brown fur cloak. Maybe the fur was marten. She looked much calmer than the last time

Beth had seen her, when the queen had just stabbed Richard III in the back and then had been deeply affected by the sight of his blood on her dagger and on her hand.

Beth bowed, trying to copy Mercutio's bow. "Greetings, your grace." She moved to kiss Lady Macbeth's hand, because Mercutio had done that. It was unnerving kissing a hand that she had seen stabbing a man to death, then covered with blood, but at the moment it was clean. It smelled of lavender soap, not blood.

When Beth raised her eyes, Lady Macbeth laughed briefly. "I know that you are Beth acting as Mercutio. I am on your side."

Beth gasped.

"Truly, I am," the queen continued. "I hate Richard. And now he will hate me. If he succeeds in his plots, he will no doubt kill me. Far worse, he will do anything he can to destroy the plays. He could even eliminate characters he does not like. Extinguish them. Can you imagine *Macbeth* without me?"

Beth closed her eyes, then opened them. "I'm sure he'd do horrible things. Does Merlin know that you want to be on our side?"

"Of course. That is why he sent you to me, so you can practice as Mercutio with someone who will help you."

"Thank you." Mercutio hadn't been frightened of Lady Macbeth, but Beth was, and she was sure it showed.

"One of the first things you must do is learn how to draw Mercutio's sword. You can begin now."

"But how can I draw a sword on a queen? Won't your guards rush to stop me?"

"An intelligent response." The queen nodded her approval. "I am glad that you are thinking. But I have already told the guards that you will be practicing and to disregard it."

"But what about King Macbeth?" Beth shivered at the thought of him. He would annihilate anyone whom he believed was trying to hurt his beloved wife.

"Never fear. I can handle everything."

Beth had no doubt that Lady Macbeth could manage many things, if not everything.

Beth drew Mercutio's sword. She found that she had only a little difficulty flourishing it, though it was heavy. She must have some of his muscle memories, she thought. But she doubted that she could fight as well as he could have. She hoped she wouldn't have to.

"I suppose that is all you can do for today," the queen said. Her face showed that she was underwhelmed by Beth's fighting ability. "You might as well travel to another time and place. But do not engage in fighting unless necessary."

Beth bowed and said, "Farewell."

She spun to warmer air.

Beth landed on the shore of a blue sea. She drank in the smell of saltwater, which reminded her of trips to Rehoboth Beach, Delaware. Ships sailed in the distance. Small fishing boats worked the coast closer to shore, and shrieking gulls followed them. A large rock formation stood near the water, and cliffs loomed in the distance. The beach was rocky, not sandy. The tide was low, so tidal pools and seaweed stood between her and the waves.

She saw a thin man in draped clothes standing on the rocky beach. Perhaps he was Roman or Greek. He had a quiet, pleasant face, bland as an insurance agent's.

"This is the place where Aphrodite rose from the sea," he said in a mellifluous tone. "If one believes the legends." He inclined his head. "And now you have come to this shore, though not in your own lovely form. Beth Owens?" he asked.

She stared at him, then looked at her hand. Yes, she still wore Mercutio's body, but this man could see through it.

The man smiled like a crocodile.

At his smile, Beth felt the hair on the back of her neck stand up. He smelled of blood. Most characters had no scent.

"Are you Cassius?" she asked.

"I am not that noble Roman." His voice sounded so plausible, as if he were about to try to sell her some stocks that were a sure thing. "I am Venetian. I am honest Iago. This is Cyprus, not Italy."

Beth shivered. Iago had persuaded Othello that his wife, Desdemona, was unfaithful because another man had her handkerchief. Othello then killed his innocent wife. "Then you need no introduction," she said with little enthusiasm.

"Nor do you, Girl Who Speaks with Shakespeare." He bowed again. "You have many admirers. But that puts you in a difficult position. You don't know whom you can trust."

"I do know who I can't trust."

Iago raised his eyebrows. "You put your faith in Mercutio, and he betrayed you."

She choked. "Don't say anything bad about Mercutio."

"I understand that the subject is painful. You obviously identify with him. But he did betray you. And now you trust Lady Macbeth, of all people."

Beth pulled away. "Who I speak to is my own business."

"Yes, of course." His voice was still bland, horribly sincere. Even his brown eyes smiled with his lips. "I won't lie to you. It's always best to tell the truth. I am allied with King Richard III."

She gagged. "Good for you." That made sense. Iago and Richard were both villains. But the thought of Richard having Iago on his side struck her like a blow. How many other villains would work with Richard? How powerful would they be together?

Iago nodded to show he understood her. "I know that my news disconcerts you. Would you like a peppermint? Or perhaps a chocolate?" He reached into a pouch.

"No, thank you." That would make a great band name, she thought. Iago's Poisoned Peppermints. She could imagine an ad for Iago's chocolates: You can't believe how good they taste.

"Please relax. I know that you're under a strain." He sounded like a dentist getting ready to fill a cavity. "There are two sides to every story, and William Shakespeare was not fair to everyone. Perhaps I did try to make a foolish general jealous, but how could I know that he would brutally murder his wife? Why should you believe the inference that it was my fault? And does Shakespeare say it was, or is that merely directors' interpretations?"

A gull landing near them made Beth jump. Speaking with Iago strained her nerves.

"What do you want?" Beth asked. "Why are you working with Richard? Why should you care if he can find a play about King Arthur?"

Iago shook his head. "Unlike King Richard, I do not enjoy baring my soul. I do not tell my reasons for anything I do. I just want you to consider carefully what you are doing. What makes you think that Lady Macbeth is trustworthy? The fact that she stabbed King Richard in the back? That's hardly a recommendation."

Iago had a point, but Beth believed that listening to him was dangerous. "You aren't any more credible than she is."

"I understand," Iago said, as if he weren't offended. "Many of Shakespeare's characters are dangerous. Why would you want to take sides? Wouldn't it be safer for you to at least be neutral?"

Beth's muscles tensed. "How can I be neutral about a man who had my friend Mercutio killed? That's impossible."

"True. How can you be neutral about William Shakespeare?"

She choked. She had meant Richard III, but of course Shakespeare was the first one who had killed off Mercutio. "I know how you twist everything. It's foolish to listen to you."

"Can it possibly be wrong to listen to opinions you disagree with?" Iago sounded as if he spoke more in sorrow than in anger.

"You could persuade a robin to break its own eggs," Beth said. "I won't listen to you." She turned away.

"I understand your prejudice." Iago's shoulders slumped. "I must curb my pride so I do not shut you out. I will always be willing to listen to you. Think about whether I might know things that would be useful for you to hear. Have a good day."

After talking with him, Beth wanted to wash her hands. That thought reminded her of Lady Macbeth. Beth wished herself back to the castle in Scotland.

The drastic change in temperatures made her sneeze. She hoped she wouldn't catch a cold.

Lady Macbeth inclined her head in welcome.

"Iago is working for Richard!" Beth exclaimed. "I just met pure evil."

"Iago impressed you with his purity?" the queen asked, raising her eyebrows.

"His evil is pure because he doesn't even have a specific goal in mind," Beth said. "Or that's what some Shakespearean critics say."

"I am glad to hear that lust for a crown is less evil than revenge," the lady retorted. "If Richard has such a clever ally, we need soldiers on our side. Great warriors."

Beth shivered. "Real fighting over a play?" she asked.

"There can be battles over objects. Consider the relics in the Holy Land."

Beth didn't think the Holy Land was a major concern of Lady Macbeth's. But yes, Beth guessed where she should begin looking for a warrior.

She spun south again. So much traveling was making her dizzy.

Beth saw a black man in armor who was so muscular and majestic that she wondered who would ever dare to fight him. He sat under an olive tree. But the sparkling sunlight did not make him smile. He held his head in his hands.

It wasn't difficult to guess who he was.

Beth sat down beside him and bowed her head in the best Mercutio style. "Greetings, noble general. Would you honor me by drinking wine with me and telling me of your battles?"

Othello's somber face lightened. "That is kind of you, signor. You are a Venetian?"

"A neighbor. I am Mercutio of Verona, cousin to the prince."

"I am honored to meet you. Thank you for your gracious offer. I would be only too glad to tell you of my battles. If only I had died in one of them." Othello heaved a sigh.

Beth offered him Mercutio's wine flask. Doubtless Merlin had arranged for it to be filled with the finest wine.

Othello pulled from his pouch a battered pewter cup and let her fill it. "This cup saved my life when I battled a dragon. I kept the cup over my heart because my mother gave it to me. My sword pierced the dragon's heart, but he sent forth a final blast of fire that would have incinerated my heart, but it damaged only the winecup."

"Wonderful," Beth said. "What an adventure." She poured herself a few drops and pretended to drink.

Othello drank a healthy portion. "But the dragon was not nearly as powerful as a basilisk. I slew not just one basilisk but a dozen, all hissing together and trying to kill me. After that, I was tired, I can tell you."

"You are very brave."

Othello downed the rest of his wine, and she poured him more. Tears formed in his eyes. "But do you know who was the worst monster I ever slew? Myself. Never, never can I forgive myself."

His self-hatred was contagious. Beth began to hate herself for using Othello's tragedy as a way to get his support. But, remembering that she had to protect Shakespeare, she proceeded. "Iago deceived you."

"I should not have let myself be deceived."

Beth nodded. "True." She paused. "Iago is now working with Richard III in a plot against Shakespeare."

"Iago." Othello's face contorted with rage. He crushed the pewter cup in his hand, making another dent in it.

"Some other characters are joining together to oppose Richard."

"I am with you. Against Iago." Othello's hand stroked the hilt of his sword.

"Very good. Thank you." She tried to keep her voice calm though his anger made her tremble. She wouldn't want it to be directed against her.

Beth spun over the Mediterranean and marveled at its blue color. She wandered into another olive grove. Maybe she was in Verona. The warm sunlight reminded her of Italy. She soaked in the warmth, which was a welcome change from the chilly weather in Maryland. She was glad that olives on the trees didn't smell like olives on a plate, because that smell nauseated her and she refused to eat them.

Magpies scolded her for intruding in their world.

She turned down a path and saw a thin man in a gleaming white toga approaching her. His military bearing was as conspicuous as Othello's, though he was built like a reed, whereas Othello was built like a tree. The man's face was lined with wrinkles, accentuated by a frown. The chief plotter of Caesar's assassination probably never smiled.

"Hail, Cassius," Beth said, bowing her head to him. "I hope I have the honor of addressing the praetor Gaius Cassius Longinus. I am Mercutio, cousin to the Prince of Verona."

"Prince is a title deriving from birth, not won through merit." Cassius remained unsmiling. "I am *praetor peregrinus* only. I was supposed to be honored by being sent to govern the province of Syria. Scarcely the honor I deserved."

"Of course you deserved more honors, noble Cassius," Beth said. Cassius smelled far more like blood than Iago did. She realized that as a character she could smell other characters, though as a human she had not been able to smell most of them.

"Assassinating so vile a thing as Caesar should have brought me more honor." Cassius sounded aggrieved, as if he deserved a medal for killing his leader. "I was no bondsman, no sheep submitting to a dictator."

"True, Cassius," Beth said, keeping her disgust at the assassination out of her voice. "You were never meant to be a bondsman. But you died with honor, after valiant battle. When you died by your own sword, the sun of Rome set."

"That sun could rise again." Cassius looked into the distance, as if the olive grove had become the Capitol. "Our plan must not fail this time. If you are an honorable man, Mercutio, join with us in our plan to overthrow the tyrant Shakespeare."

Beth managed not to gasp. "Shakespeare was no tyrant, but a scribe who used Plutarch's history in telling your story."

"Shakespeare was a mere scribe." Cassius nodded. "And he has secured undeserved fame. But his words have shaped minds, and if they were undone, history might change."

"That can't be true!" Beth exclaimed. "Has Richard III told you that? Perhaps the lives of invented characters like me can be changed, but surely not history. Richard, not Shakespeare, is the tyrant."

"If Richard is a tyrant, he will be overthrown by and by, but Shakespeare is a far viler thing than Caesar. The tyranny of words is greater than the tyranny of dictators." Cassius's frown deepened. "You are a noble-minded man. If you wish to die a more honorable death than you died in *Romeo and Juliet*, you should join us."

"You are indeed noble, Cassius, but even you cannot defeat history itself," Beth told him.

"I am armed, and indifferent to danger." Cassius touched his breast, where he must have hidden a dagger. "And you? I have heard of your courage. Join with us, in a nobler cause than family feuds."

"Richard is the one I fear," Beth said. "I joined with him, and he betrayed me and had me killed. He kills even those who work for him. Do not align yourself with that ignoble monarch, for you are a champion of republicanism."

"I am firm in my resolution. I can make alliances, and I can break them. I have changed the course of history once, in killing Caesar, and

I can change it again." Cassius strode away, marching as if the olive groves were legions bowing to him.

Beth shook her head. The word "hubris" came to mind. She willed herself away from Rome, and back in Maryland.

Her room was colder than Rome, but she felt safer. She huddled under a blanket.

DID SHE STILL HAVE strength enough to travel? She closed her eyes. This time she felt a blast of wind and landed in a colder place. Yew trees sheltered her from the frigid gusts.

Beth saw a white-haired man who was gaunt but far from frail. Even though he stooped, he towered over her. The man's eyes were as wild as a tiger's. His fine but tattered robes were scant protection from the wind. He smelled as if he had been out all night in the rain. Actually, many nights.

She tried not to breathe too deeply. She bowed. "Good day, your grace."

He glared at her. "Who are you to 'good day' me, boy?" Age had not diminished the power of his voice.

A shiver went up her spine. "Sir, I am Mercutio, cousin to the prince of Verona."

"What is a prince of a hill town in a fragmented land? I am king of all Britain."

You were, but you no longer are, Beth thought. She had no trouble guessing who he was. "King Lear," she said. She bowed even lower.

"I am he. King of the wind and rain. Dare you speak to me, prattling fool who was killed in a brawl?"

"I do know pain, my lord."

"No!" he yelled. "You know nothing of pain. Your pain at its greatest was not a nutshell's worth compared with mine."

"Evil was done to you," Beth ventured.

"By vipers." His voice echoed. "Vipers."

"As one so injured, would you condescend to work with other characters against villains? Who knows what evil they might do next."

Lear bellowed at her. "You garlic-eating coxcomb! I know of Richard's plan. I have joined him. Do you think I would hesitate to give my soul to change the end of my play and save my precious Cordelia, my only loving daughter?"

Beth choked. Oh no, there were characters who would give anything to change the endings of their plays, no matter how much that hurt Shakespeare. Of course, King Lear would be one of them.

Nevertheless, she said, "But to ally with . . . ."

"Silence!" he screamed. "You offer nothing." He shook with rage. His scanty white beard shook also. "Nothing. All I want is to save my beloved daughter and see that my other two daughters, who betrayed me, suffer even more painful deaths than they did in the play. Get out of my sight, or I might kill you."

Beth spun away from his time.

She landed in Lady Macbeth's garden, which now seemed pleasant compared with Lear's landscape. The raven croaked, perhaps in greeting.

Lady Macbeth smiled at Beth. "You are traveling much," she said. "Well done."

"Well done?" Beth raised her eyebrows. "Are you kidding? Lear's totally against us."

"I know. And that ensures that his daughters Regan and Goneril will be with us. I shall ask them."

"Aren't they villains?" Beth stared at her. "They betrayed their father. Would you trust them?"

"Within limits. Why not? They know that if Richard's side wins, their father will slowly torture them to death."

"Oh." Maybe if you were Lady Macbeth, it made sense to work with Regan and Goneril, but Beth wasn't happy about it. How did she know she was on the right side?

Chapter 4

THE FIRST PLAY REHEARSAL was a welcome relief from Beth's travels. As she entered the drama classroom, she heard rude noises.

"You're Sir Toby Belch, not Sir Toby Fart," Arnie complained, holding his nose.

Beth giggled.

"Don't be such a wuss, Sir Andrew," Kevin said. "But that's what you're supposed to be. Type casting."

If Beth hadn't known they had been friends since first grade, she would have thought they didn't like each other. Boys were so weird, she thought for the ten thousandth time.

Lupe shook her fist at them. "If I have to be close to you, you'd better keep your stinks to yourself." She turned to the teacher, who had just entered the room. "Do I say the buttery bar line inviting Sir Andrew to touch my breasts?"

"Certainly not." Ms. Capulet frowned. "This is a high school production. Haven't you read my revised script?"

"How could she?" Kevin asked. "The wench is illiterate."

"What do you mean?" Lupe pretended to box his ears. "I write the letter to Malvolio."

"I can't believe that some of you haven't memorized the script yet." Frank shook his head. "That's so lame."

"Please don't use language that could insult persons with disabilities," the teacher said. "It's early to be angry that not everyone knows his or her lines. Stand in the front of the classroom and read the script."

They moved to the front of the classroom, near the theater curtains.

The poster of Shakespeare looked down on them. Beth wished the playwright really were there. No, that he would be there after they had learned their parts.

Beth felt at home. This play was going to be so much fun.

In an early scene, she met Duke Orsino and had to show, just a little bit, that she was falling in love with him. Though as Viola she was pretending to be the young man Cesario, she had to look at Orsino as if he were an unattainable but desirable man.

"O then unfold the passion of my love," Arnie said. He was in character as Orsino talking about his love for Olivia and how he hoped that Cesario would woo her for him, but he smiled too warmly at Beth. He was such a nice guy, but she didn't want to date him and hoped he wouldn't ask.

AFTER REHEARSAL, BETH STAYED alone in the classroom and decided to try time traveling. Life couldn't be all fun and rehearsals. She felt warm air and landed on a Mediterranean coast. Othello sat on a rock overlooking the waves lapping on the shore.

She approached him and inclined her head.

The general frowned at her. "I never should have listened to you," Othello said. "What a fool I was."

Beth's head jerked up. "What do you mean?"

"I am on King Richard's side now."

She gasped. "On the same side as Iago? How could you be?"

Othello sighed. "King Lear told me that Richard stands for changing the endings of the plays. He wants to save Cordelia's life." He shook his fist at the waves. "Can you imagine that I would do any less to change the ending of my play? To save my sweet Desdemona? To keep myself from slaughtering my innocent wife? There never was anyone who repented as much as I do."

"Oh." Beth hadn't thought of that. "But . . . ."

He rose from his rock. "But me no buts. Nothing matters but undoing what I have done."

"The consequences for other plays . . . ."

"No! I will not listen! I know what I must do." He turned and stalked away.

Beth shuddered. Too many characters longed to change the endings of their plays. Why didn't Shakespeare write more happy endings?

That gave her a thought.

Why not ask characters from the comedies for help? She wasn't sure they would be able to defeat the warriors, but it was worth a try. They at least wouldn't want to change their plays' endings.

She attempted to think comic thoughts. The scent of pines filled the air around her. She found herself walking through a forest. She heard splashing water and found her way to a stream where water rushed over mossy rocks. A man sat weeping by the bank.

"Are you Jaques?" she asked.

"A deer died today," he replied, weeping over it as he had in the play.

"I'm sorry," she said. Visiting *As You Like It* delighted her. Then remembering she was Mercutio, she added, "Venison is but a poor substitute for venery."

Jaques shook his head. "Your humor does not move me, Mercutio. But I could weep for you, a poor creature who cannot live to experience all the seven ages of man."

Beth gulped at the thought of Mercutio's short life, and of dying for him, but forced herself to smile. She picked up a small stone and skimmed it across the stream. "Why should I want to become so old that I must crawl? Or to let lines spread over my handsome face? And to be so old that I could no longer do as I wished with women would be misery indeed."

Jaques shook his head. "Perhaps it is just as well that your wit exceeds your wits. There is more than one fool in the forest."

"You are clever indeed, friend Jaques," Beth told him. "Surely too clever to want to change the endings of plays." She tried to balance on a mossy rock and almost slipped. Bad move. Mercutio was nimble. "Richard III is gathering a band of characters to try to force changes in the endings of our author's plays. But other characters oppose him. Will you join our band?"

Jaques shook his head. "The endings will be as they will be, but if you think I am a man of action, you mistake me. You must look elsewhere. If the endings are overthrown, I will weep over it, but that is all." Tears for the deer still dripped down his cheeks.

Beth realized that she shouldn't have expected more of him. "You are a poor fool, after all. Come looking for me if you change your mind."

She walked further into the woods. Sunlight streamed through the trees, but the path was narrow and she wasn't used to hiking alone. What if someone or something dangerous burst out at her? Touching her sword, she wished she knew how to wield it better. But if she must be alone in the woods, even the Forest of Arden, she was glad that she appeared to be a man.

"Ho!" A man who was clearly no man appeared from behind a tree. "Who are you, stranger?"

"I am Mercutio, O Ganymede," she said, using the name the lady Rosalind had chosen for herself when she pretended to be a man.

"Mercutio!" Rosalind smiled. "I am glad to meet a man who is not foolish enough to write his lover's name on trees, as Orlando does, but sorry to meet a man who is too foolish to fall in love."

"You mistake me, good Ganymede, for I have fallen many times but never broken a limb, nor even sprained one in the fall." Beth laughed inwardly because not even Rosalind could detect that she was a girl hidden in Mercutio's body.

Rosalind shook her head. "You have not loved, and pity the woman who ever loves you."

"Nay, pity all those who have not, for I catch women when they fall," Beth said. She wondered whether she was a fool to care so much about Mercutio.

"I am so glad not to be a woman," Rosalind said.

"What a pity. I thought you were the fairest and cleverest of them all." Beth bowed to her. "Dearest, woman or not, I have come on a mission. Richard III is gathering together a band of characters to try to force a change in the endings of Shakespeare's plays. I hope you will join me in ardently opposing him."

Rosalind's smile evaporated. "Richard III? A villain worse than my uncle who exiled my father and me, far worse. Some characters might want to change the end of their tragedies, but who could want to change the happy endings of comedies?"

"If he can change the endings of tragedies, he can change the endings of comedies as well. No one is safe," Beth warned.

"But why should you not join Richard?" Rosalind asked. "Your own end was sad."

Beth sighed. "Alas, I did join him. I hoped that I would become a warrior and die a noble death in war. I died indeed, but not nobly. Richard slew me as he does all those who support him after they have served his purpose. I do repent that I believed him." She struck her forehead in a gesture of repentance. "My own purpose now is to oppose all his deeds. My death in *Romeo and Juliet* was tragic, but my death when I served Richard was ignominious." Beth hoped that Mercutio would repent if she could bring him back to life, but she couldn't be certain that he would.

"It is good that you now see more clearly," Rosalind said, patting Beth's hand. "Of course I will try to help you, and I will ask all my play's other characters to help you also. But I do not know how to fight, and I don't know what I can do."

"We may need your cleverness, lovely Rosalind, and the wrestling skill of your Orlando. He has killed a lion, so perhaps he can kill a boar." Beth thought of Richard's boar standard and shuddered.

"No need to call me 'lovely Rosalind,'" Rosalind reproached Beth. "Those of us who dwell in the Forest of Arden will do all we can to help our native playwright."

Wondering whether she would ever have a chance to play Rosalind's part when she returned to being Beth Owens, Beth bowed to Rosalind and went her way.

Beth passed a clearing where red squirrels chased each other. She enjoyed seeing their pointed ears, so different from those of the squirrels at home. She walked further down the woodland path and came to a meadow. There she encountered two women, both blowsy as to hair and dress and bosomy as to body.

"Who are you, noble sir?" asked one. "I love you at first sight."

"No, I saw him first," said the other, elbowing the first woman and pushing herself forward.

Oh no. Phebe, who had thrown herself at Rosalind while Rosalind was posing as a man, and Audrey, a woman of somewhat easy virtue. Beth decided she had better not say she was Mercutio.

"Away from me, lovely ladies! Do not tempt me!" she cried. "Fear me, for I suffer from a dreadful pox that would mar your looks forever if I so much as touched you."

The two women backed up so fast they almost tripped.

"What a pity that such a handsome face should cover such a deadly sickness!" Phebe exclaimed. "I cannot love you, though I do."

"No more can I," Audrey said, turning away.

"Find sounder lovers than I am," Beth told them. She suspected that Mercutio would be angry at her for so maligning him. If only she could bring him back to life, let him be angry!

Beth rushed away. She could feel some part of Mercutio's brain stripping Audrey and Phebe naked and liking the size of Audrey's breasts. No, I don't want to be that part of Mercutio, she thought. She tried to think of a joke instead, but all she could devise was a jest that Mercutio would tell about Audrey's breasts.

Darn you, Mercutio, she chided him. Are you worth all the trouble I'm taking to save you? She was pretty sure that he wouldn't have hurried away from the women. She could enact Mercutio only so far. She wondered whether his quick temper and urge to fight would spring up in her when she least expected it. But she had enough of Beth in her to moderate the Mercutio part. She cared about being a good actor, but she didn't want quite that much of her character's perspective.

Had Mercutio mentally stripped her clothes off? Did the boys she knew do that? She tried not to worry about it. The thought made her too miserable.

It was time to leave the Forest of Arden. She took a last look at the running brook and saw several books floating down it, miraculously dry. She remembered Rosalind's father's line that it was good to be exiled to the forest because there are books in the flowing brooks and sermons in stones. She saw that one book was the script of *Twelfth Night*. She hoped she wouldn't have to get drunk to join those characters.

She wanted to meet Viola, but instead she found herself in a dark hall, lit only by tapers, where several men sat at a table holding large tankards. The smells of ale, wine, and whiskey permeated the room so much they almost stunned her. But she supposed that Mercutio wouldn't mind them.

She addressed the heaviest man there. Drink dripped from his beard.

"Hail, Sir Toby! I am Mercutio, cousin to the Prince of Verona. I salute your service to the god Bacchus!" She flourished a bow.

"What? Mercutio, join us! Maria, serve him the best of our wine. I know Eye-talians like wine. But don't serve him too much from your buttery bar, my girl."

Maria let her blouse slip further down than it already was.

Beth winked at her and hoped that would be a sufficient response.

"Mercutio." A thin, pock-marked man frowned. "I hope you are not a suitor to Lady Olivia."

"Far be it from me to try to compete with one as handsome and articulate as you, Sir Andrew," Beth said, nodding to him. "I greatly dislike losing, and so I shall hold back from trying, however fair the lady may be."

Sir Toby belched. "Don't be too hasty. An Eye-talian noble might be a very suitable match for my niece. A prince's cousin might outrank that Duke Orsino. Drink up, Mercutio!"

Beth smelled the wine that Maria had served her. "French wine! I do not wish to be discourteous, but my palate is sensitive. I drink only wine from Italian grapes, my good host. I have a flask of it, and I pray that you drink from it first." She pulled out her wine flask and poured drinks for Sir Toby and Sir Andrew.

"Damned good manners," Sir Toby said, tasting it. "And good wine, too."

"When that I was and a little tiny boy, with hey, ho, the wind and the rain," sang Feste, who was by far the best-looking man in the room, and the youngest.

"Ah, Feste, how glad I am to meet you," Beth clasped his hand. "But you should have lived in Verona, where we do not have so much wind and rain. I cannot hope to match you, either in song or in an exchange of wits."

"Or, it seems, in drinking," Feste said, being the only one of the company sober enough to see that Beth had drunk nothing.

"Wine is the drink of love," Beth said, "but I fear that wooing is not my errand tonight. Richard III is gathering together a band of characters to try to force changes in the ends of all Shakespeare's plays, and I am trying to form a band of characters to oppose him. Surely you do not want the end of your play changed."

"Who can change the wind and the rain?" Feste asked.

"Change the end?" Sir Toby shouted. "And have Malvolio triumph? The stout, true men from this play will join you. We are great heroes with our swords."

"Indeed," said Maria.

"I have no doubt," Beth said. "Thank you."

"Oh, no, we can't change your precious ending," Malvolio sneered. He sauntered into the hall as if he owned it. He wore his lemon-colored stockings. "Destroying me was so amusing."

Malvolio spat in the direction of the other men. He turned to Beth. "Your cause is doomed if you depend on these rum-soaked blowhards. You may be sure I will join Richard. I do not care whether he will destroy me. At least he won't break my heart in doing so, because I won't love him."

Malvolio strode out.

Beth couldn't find it in her heart to blame him.

"The rain it raineth every day," Feste sang.

"It rains every day wherever that nasty steward takes himself," Maria said.

"Do not invest him with the power of causing rain," Beth told her. "For gloom is a corrosion that seeps into men's souls, and women's too. I hope that Queen Mab sends Malvolio gentle dreams, for you drove him to despair."

"You would have mocked him, too, Mercutio," Sir Toby said. "He was a perfect target."

"Mocked him, yes, a thousand times, but I would not have cast him into a dark pit," Beth replied.

"So you would change Shakespeare's words after all, pretty Veronese?" Maria asked.

"I would not dare." Beth shivered. "The attempt cost me my life."

The sound of rain pounding on the roof of the hall made her shiver still more. "Stop singing that damp song," she said to Feste. "You could cause a flood."

"Rain does not drown so much as drink does," Feste argued. "Rain soaks the body, but drink soaks the spirit. Get King Richard drunk," he said. "That's the solution. Then he will turn into a fool, and if he is a fool, and a fool from Shakespeare, he will be a wiser man."

Beth smiled. "Your wit shows me why I seek help from fools. Perhaps you should offer yourself to that detestable monarch as a fool. Perhaps your rain would impede him and your wit would make him sounder."

Feste snorted. "I am not such a fool as that. A fool who jests with him would be a dead fool. The fools in this play may bore me, but the boar would stab me."

"True, comedy does not thrive when tyrants hold sway," Beth agreed. That was true in her day, too. She remembered reading about regimes that banned comedians. "But perhaps your mockery could move those who follow him to understand that his overpowering ambition is only folly and will lead them down the path to destruction."

"It seems to me that you have wit enough yourself to pursue that course if you choose," Feste said. "Perhaps greatness has been thrust upon you."

"I hope not." Beth shuddered. Was she crazy to try to challenge Richard? What difference did all these characters make? They weren't real people after all. So what if their endings were changed?

In the sound of the rain, she heard weeping, coming from a distant land.

"I must go where the wind blows," she said, though she had no idea why she said it.

She flew through the rain. It drenched her and the wind blew her off course. She wondered whether Peter Pan flew only when the weather was clear.

Beth landed in the Midsummer World. Even there, rain poured down from a gray sky and turned the earth to mud. It beat down flowers and silenced birds. Despite the wet reception, she was glad to be there. She hoped to see Bottom the player and wondered what lines he was mangling now. After Richard III had killed Mercutio, he had threatened Bottom in order to persuade Beth to summon Shakespeare. Sita had imitated Queen Titania's delicate voice perfectly and ordered Bottom away from Richard's world and back to his own.

Beth's green velvet Mercutio attire was soaked through and clung to her. She pulled out her sword and tried to wipe it so it would not rust, but she lacked a dry cloth for the task.

The weeping increased. She saw Moth, Peaseblossom, Cobweb, and Mustardseed sobbing. Their hair and fairy garb oozed water. Their wings sagged.

A young creature of indeterminate sex sat in a tree and pouted. Beth guessed that he must be Puck. "Up and down," he grumbled. "Why should I want to lead anyone up and down in this nasty storm?"

"Welcome, Beth! You have come at last!" Titania's sweet voice chimed. Even though she was as damp as the others, the fairy queen retained her dignity.

"You can see who I am?" Beth asked.

"Merlin's magic is powerful, but I would know you in any guise, dear Beth." Titania touched Beth's hand, and the touch was like magic. Beth was still just as wet, but she didn't feel drenched anymore.

Rivulets of water covered the path on which they stood, and a nearby lake flooded over its banks.

"Can't you stop this flood?" Beth asked. The sight of this beloved world in such disarray broke Beth's heart.

"If it grieves you, I can stop it for a moment." Titania waved her hand. The rain ceased. The rivulets ran into the lake and the lake retreated to its boundaries. Beth's clothes dried. The fairies were no longer wet and looked as if they were ready to attend some magical dance.

"The rain is this world's expression of grief," Titania told Beth. "We are sad because one of our own has disappeared. Bottom is gone." Her voice echoed, "Gone, gone, gone."

Beth gasped. Bottom was one of her favorite characters. "But how do you know? You and he weren't able to see each other after the play ended."

Titania bowed her head. "I can feel that he is gone. He is not dead, but I don't know where he has strayed or what world has taken him. The Midsummer World is Bottomless. And so our grief is bottomless."

"Bottom is gone," the fairies sobbed.

"Without him, our play is ruined," Titania said. "There would be nothing but the two sets of lovers lost in the woods. Or would I awaken and fall in love with someone or something worse than Nick Bottom?"

"No!" Beth exclaimed. "The world needs Bottom. My world as well as yours."

There is no laughter in such a world, she thought. No mistakes. Everyone's speech is precise. Everyone does the right thing at the right moment.

The fairies' glade is dull without Bottom, Beth thought. Yes, there's still a Puck, but there's no one for him to ridicule. There is only uniform prettiness with no ass for contrast. Just an endless world of nectar. Dancing under the moon with no dancers stumbling.

Was Bottom's disappearance a punishment for her from Richard? Was it her fault? What could she do about it? Beth's heart raced.

Chapter 5

BETH CAME BACK TO her old self. She wore her flowered tunic over tights and sat in the classroom. But Kevin had entered the room and was staring at her. He was not the person she most wanted to see at the moment, but she was so distressed that she couldn't pretend to be calm.

"You weren't here, and then you were," Kevin said, sounding as if he were accusing her of a crime. "Am I crazy, or are you?"

"Bottom is gone," Beth wailed. "I must find Bottom."

"What are you talking about?" Kevin asked.

"The character Bottom is missing from *A Midsummer Night's Dream*. The play needs him. I need him, and I will find him." She struck her fist on her other hand for emphasis. "There is no *Midsummer Night's Dream* without Bottom. Without Bottom, there is no dream."

"You're crazy." Kevin stepped away from her. "How could Bottom disappear from the play? And he's just one character."

"He's a vital character. He's the central character. He's the one who puts us in the dream. I must find him."

Disregarding whether her disappearance would shock Kevin, Beth vanished.

Where should she go first to find Bottom?

She let her mind leap, and her body thudded into Macbeth's castle. Hitting the flagstones hurt her feet. She stood in a dark room lit by only one candle on a table.

"Dear Beth, what an unexpected pleasure to see you," said Lady Macbeth, drying her hands. "It is the middle of the night. The owl calls. I do not remember what I was doing."

Beth thought it was best not to remind the queen why she had been scrubbing her hands.

The owl's mournful sound filled the night air.

"Bottom is gone," Beth shrieked.

"What do you mean, dear? The clown from the midsummer play?" Lady Macbeth listened like a therapist, as if the disappearance was a product of Beth's imagination. "Is that a problem for you?"

"Don't you understand?" Beth gasped, though it was evident that the queen did not. "Bottom's disappearance is serious. Richard must be responsible."

The queen winced at Richard's name. "I should think there are enough asses as it is, dear. Why should you wish for more?"

"I need to laugh." Beth suppressed tears. "I can't survive without laughter. Most people can't."

"Aren't there enough clowns and fools in the other plays?" the lady asked. "Bottom isn't strictly speaking a fool. That is, he is not a discerning fool, but is merely foolish."

"Of course there are fools in the plays, but most of them are too clever." Beth strained to explain. "Bottom is different. He reminds me of myself. I love how he wants to play every part."

"Do you wish to laugh at yourself?" Lady Macbeth asked, uncomprehending.

"Yes." Of course Lady Macbeth wouldn't see herself as funny. Not ever. "I knew you wouldn't understand. But I thought you might have some idea where I could find him."

"I do not suppose you would want me to torture his fellow players to learn whether they know anything?"

"No!" Beth shouted, then remembered her manners, and said more quietly, "No."

"I thought not. There's no need to shout, my dear." The lady's voice was soft, unlike her character. "If you want to find a person, I suppose you should look in his favorite haunts, and I doubt that my husband's castle is among them."

"A stage!" Beth exclaimed. "Stages are his favorite haunts. Thank you."

She wished herself at the Globe. Unfortunately, she landed in surging, muddy water and struggled to keep her head above it.

The water smelled so rank that it must be the Thames. Beth tried to yell for help, but she swallowed some vile water, tried to spit it out, and choked. The current pulled her under.

She held her mouth closed, kicked her legs, and tried to swim to the surface. When her head was clear, she called "help," but then she was pulled under again.

She swam away from the bloated body of a rat.

She kicked harder. When her head next managed to get above the surface, she saw that the current was carrying her to London Bridge, where she was likely to drown or be smashed against the pillars. In Renaissance London, she could be hurt. Maybe she could even die.

She tried another call for help, and spat out more stinking water. She couldn't speak, but she tried a silent call. "Merlin! Merlin!"

If Merlin heard her, he probably would help her escape.

She surfaced again and saw that a barge was just about to collide with her and knock her unconscious.

She tried to swim away from it. But a pair of arms reached out of the barge and grabbed for her.

Whoever it was, being with him on the barge must be better than drowning in the Thames. She kicked closer, reached the arms, and was pulled aboard.

She vomited so copiously that she was conscious of nothing but her own barfing.

"That is disgusting, and you smell like a sewer, but I'm glad that I came in time." Adam Greenwood, a twentyish actor she knew in both worlds, handed her a cloth to wipe her mouth.

Beth wiped her mouth, then was sick again.

She lay down, unable to move. She was too sick to be properly glad to see Adam. Memories of him drifted through her mind. Meeting him when they had acted in *A Midsummer Night's Dream*. He had been nice about her inadvertently turning his ears to donkey's ears. Seeing Adam playing Bottom on the Globe in Shakespeare's time. Merlin had sent him to London to help protect her. When Mercutio met Adam, he had become jealous and claimed that he was her only protector. Maybe that was why Adam hadn't grieved over Mercutio's death, at least not enough to satisfy Beth. Adam cared more about acting than about anything else, she thought.

Beth felt the boat lurch into the rapids under London Bridge. Fear wiped every thought out of her mind.

The boat shot through the arches of the bridge. Water rushed over the sides, but the boat did not capsize. Whoever was steering was competent, Beth thought with relief.

Someone splashed a bucket of water over her. She spluttered.

"I think you need to clean up, I don't want to get anywhere near you." Adam moved as away from her as he could. "Perhaps you could go back home and reappear some other time."

Going home and landing in her bathtub was her fondest wish, but the wish wasn't granted. She still lay in the boat. She opened her eyes, and saw Adam standing as far away from her as was possible, at the other end of the barge.

"Thank you." She shook herself off like a dog.

"What are you doing here?" he asked, moving a little closer. He was drying his arms with a cloth that looked too fine for the purpose.

"I'm looking for Bottom."

"You almost found the bottom of the river. Did you want me to let you drown?"

"Not that bottom. Bottom, the mechanical. The player from *A Midsummer Night's Dream*." Her sides ached. She didn't feel like talking.

"After playing him more than once, I feel a certain kinship to him. I hope he isn't in this river."

Without coming too close, Adam extended a wine flask to her. "I got the idea of carrying a wine flask from Mercutio. A great idea."

Beth took the flask and swallowed some wine. It wasn't too bad. She could get used to that. Especially compared with the Thames water. But she knew she wouldn't drink it at home, where she could have soft drinks with caffeine instead.

"I wished to be at the Globe, but I fell short."

"Very short. Even in the odiferous company of its patrons, you would probably be unwelcome."

"Who am I?" Beth asked, looking at her clothes. She was wearing the clothing of Ben, the rich merchant's son, the disguise Merlin had given her for time traveling before he had turned her into Mercutio. She sighed with relief. Being Mercutio was a strain. She was glad to be Ben in Renaissance London. And with a disguised female body, not a mostly male body.

"Do you really want to ask existential questions now?" Adam shook his head. Now Beth could detect his Old Spice shaving lotion, but it was much fainter than her own odor.

"They are very real questions to me." Beth grumbled. She wished that Queen Titania's power to dry her off extended to the Thames. "As you ought to know. I can see that I am now Ben. But did you know that Merlin changed me into Mercutio in the worlds of Shakespeare's characters to try to bring him back to life?"

"How would your masquerading as Mercutio accomplish that?"

"I'll have to die as Mercutio to bring him back," she told Adam as calmly as she could, but her voice quavered.

"You want to die for him? You're crazy." Adam put his hand to his head.

"But he died trying to save me."

"That's different." His voice was harsher than it had ever been in her hearing. "He's a character. You're a person."

"So I guess I'd die as a character, not as a person."

"Are you sure?" Adam shook his head.

"Not entirely." Beth tried to make her voice calm.

"That's completely insane. Liking someone, having a crush on him, even loving him, doesn't mean you have to risk your life for him." Adam offered her the flask again.

"It does for me. I guess. No more wine. I've had enough." She wished for a well-caffeinated soda.

"You sure have had enough Thames water."

"But now I'm looking for Bottom. He's gone missing. I suppose you'll think that's crazy, too."

"Not at all. I like Bottom. I enjoy playing him. But how can we find him if he's missing? Has he just wandered off somewhere? Maybe Puck has changed him into some other creature."

"No, for once Puck is innocent."

"Wrong word."

"OK." Beth almost smiled. "Didn't do it. I hate to admit it, but I'm afraid that Richard III's to blame."

"But he's dead. We saw Lady Macbeth kill him. If Mercutio's dead, so's he."

Beth shook her head. "If only you were right. But no, Richard's back again. I've seen him. He's worse than ever."

"Maybe he's not so bad if you don't get in his way," Adam said, looking over his shoulder. "I hope the man who's piloting this boat doesn't hear this crazy conversation. I worked for Richard once and he was a good employer. Fair pay, all the time off I wanted."

"You were just a lowly guard. You've seen how many people he kills."

"Not people," Adam corrected her. "Just characters. We don't qualify, and I'm glad of that. Remember that Richard saved us from Marlowe's Tamburlaine."

"After watching him kill Mercutio, you can still think of that?" Beth gave him a disgusted look. "Can't you think of anything but your own skin?"

"Wrong. I also think about my acting."

Beth shook her head. "Even if you don't care about the characters, don't you care about Shakespeare's plays? Richard is gathering together a group of the fiercest characters to try to change the endings of all the plays."

"He couldn't do that."

"How do you know?"

"I don't," Adam admitted. "But I do know that you're going to try to stop him. And you think Bottom's disappearance is connected to Richard's plot."

"Right."

"But how do you know that it's not a setup? Richard knows you're fond of Bottom. So he might be fooling you into looking for Bottom instead of trying to fight against his plot to change the plays."

"You may be right." Her job felt impossible.

The boat landed at a dock. The boatman approached them, and Adam paid him.

"That'll be extra for cleaning," the man said, looking with disgust at the pool of vomit.

Adam gave him an extra penny. Then he climbed out of the boat and helped Beth out. She would have preferred to climb out on her own, but her legs were still wobbly. She saw that the boat had landed far from the Globe and wished they were nearer.

"You're trying to save Shakespeare's characters one by one, but that might not be the best strategy."

Beth paused and thought. "Thank you. You're making a good point. But what is the best strategy? Should I just keep on doing what I've been doing, going to all the plays as Mercutio and trying to enlist the characters, or at least to persuade them not to work with Richard?"

"If your efforts are threatening him so much that he'd disappear Bottom, then yes, I think you need to continue."

"And is Bottom expendable?"

"Come on, Beth. I'm not saying that. I think the way to help Bottom is to defeat King Richard." Adam hit his head. "What am I saying? Do I have any ambition to try to defeat one of the greatest villains in literature? I'm just an actor, not a fighter."

"But you will help me?"

"Sure. I'm working at the Globe now. I'm the soothsayer who tries to warn Julius Caesar about the plot to kill him. Do you want me to warn Shakespeare?"

"Maybe not yet. I'll think about it."

Adam sighed with relief. "Good. I'd rather not. I don't want to alienate him. I have to live in this world, after all, and you don't. I still don't know whether this is the world I was born in."

"I know that's hard. It's crazy that Merlin doesn't remember whether you're from the twenty-first century or this one." That was the thing about Merlin that bothered her most. If he could forget where Adam came from, could Beth also be forgotten and stranded in the old world? Did she have enough magical powers to get herself back home?

Home. Beth remembered what she had said to Kevin before she had plummeted into London and the Thames. What would Kevin think—especially if he saw her disappear? "I'd better go home for a little while."

Beth closed her eyes, and opened them in the classroom. Kevin stood beside her, but so did Sita and Arnie. Oh no.

Beth plopped down onto a chair. At least she was dry, but she had a few other problems.

"What's happening?" Kevin asked. He stared at her. "You've been weird for a long time, but now you've got to open up," he demanded. "You disappeared. That freaked me out. I texted Sita and Arnie, and they got here right away. Now you appear again. What are you up to? I'll bet Sita knows about it, but you have to tell us all."

"Be easy on her, Kevin," Arnie said. "She's probably unsettled from time travel."

"Time travel!" Kevin shouted.

"Will you quiet down?" Sita frowned. "You can't shout about something like that. Too many people know already." She touched Beth's shoulder. "OK, Beth, what's happening now? I thought you told Merlin you were over it."

"Merlin!" Kevin exclaimed.

"Listen and be quiet." Arnie nudged him.

"There isn't time to explain everything." Beth wished she didn't have to. "Maybe Sita can fill you in on the background later. Last semester, Merlin sent me to Shakespeare's time and to his plays. I met many of the characters. I liked Mercutio a lot, but Richard III killed him. Then Lady Macbeth killed Richard. Now Richard is back, but Mercutio isn't. Merlin persuaded me to go back as Mercutio. So I'm traveling to the plays, looking and sounding like Mercutio. And I discovered that Richard is trying to enlist characters from all the plays to help him push Shakespeare to change all the endings. So I have to stop Richard. Is that clear?"

"If I hadn't seen you disappear, I'd call a cab and take you to the emergency room," Kevin said, shaking his head. "But I envy you. I wonder why Merlin picked you instead of any of the rest of us?"

"For one thing, she's discreet, which you had better learn to be. Starting right now," Sita told him.

"Like Horatio and Marcellus in *Hamlet*," Arnie said. "They never tell anyone except Hamlet that they've seen the ghost."

"But they leave Hamlet to duke it out alone with Claudius," Kevin objected. "No way are we going to let you fight all this alone, Beth."

"Thanks," Beth choked. "I don't know what you can do, or whether you can travel to Shakespeare's worlds, but it's good to know I have your support. It's been lonely."

"Please be careful," Arnie said, looking at Beth as if she were about to step off a cliff. "We don't want you to get hurt."

"Mercutio's a great character, but he's still in the plays no matter what happens in this magical world," Kevin said.

"I'm not sure about that anymore. That's why I have to defeat Richard. To protect all the characters." Beth was near tears. "Now Bottom has disappeared."

"It's time for you to get some food and caffeine in you," Sita said, taking her by the arm. "Then you can worry about saving Shakespeare's world. We'll see you later, guys."

"All right." Beth went with her, just saying "good-bye" to the boys. But she knew that they were still staring at her.

Beth had a feeling, like a pricking in her thumbs, that Sita had known about what she was doing and was just pretending not to know.

A pricking in her thumbs. Beth hoped to see the witches the next time she traveled. Perhaps they could help her find Bottom.

As she walked down the street, avoiding mud from snow melt, Beth said, "I'm getting tired of seeing bare trees. I can't wait until spring." The street was lined with small, bare trees, which were more pathetic than large, bare trees, Beth thought.

"The winter of our discontent," Sita said. Beth winced. "There's something you aren't telling us." Sita's voice was less than sweet. "Something big. Out with it. Just how are you going to save Mercutio by pretending to be him?"

Beth groaned. "You would ask. I didn't want to tell that part. I have to die as Mercutio to bring him back to life."

"No, absolutely not." Sita grabbed Beth's arm. "You're in love with Mercutio, but this is going too far."

"Not exactly in love," Beth said. "I just like him a lot."

"Come on, Beth. It's love." Sita's glared at her. "You've been infected by *Romeo and Juliet*. You want to die for the guy you love. Don't do it."

"But I wouldn't die as Beth. Just as Mercutio."

"Like it's so easy to control what happens in magical worlds," Sita said with sarcasm.

After they had gone to a diner and had grilled cheese sandwiches, fries and Cokes (in Beth's case, more than one), Beth was ready to go home. That is, after she'd had a chocolate shake to make sure the taste of the Thames mud was out of her mouth.

They walked down the muddy streets. Sita turned down her street, which had larger houses and lawns than Beth's. But Beth was glad enough to go to her own red brick townhouse. She knew that her mother worked hard to pay the mortgage.

As soon as she was home, Beth contemplated her homework. Geometry, or trying to find Bottom. Biology, or trying to find Bottom. French, or trying to find Bottom.

She changed her screen saver to Kevin Kline as Bottom. Too bad Kevin Connelly wasn't as cute as Kevin Kline, though he was kind of nice looking. She stared at the screen, then closed her eyes.

The smell of the heath wafted in the air. Fog shrouded her. She was getting tired of dampness, though at least the fog wasn't as bad as the water of the Thames. Then the odors of the witches' cauldron drowned the heath scent.

"Mercutio comes," chanted the witches.

Beth surveyed her clothes. Green velvet, looking as fresh as if it had gone to the dry cleaners. She extended her hands. Yes, large man-fingers with heavy rings. When this masquerade was over, would she miss wearing jewels, or would she never want to wear them again?

"Bottom the weaver is missing," she said. "Can you help me find him?

"Bottom," the witches chanted. "Weaver, weaver, weaver."

"How can I find him?" she asked.

"You sound like Beth, not Mercutio," the first witch said.

"You must be Mercutio," the second witch said.

"Mercutio first. Then ask about Bottom," the third witch said.

"But is Bottom in danger?" Beth asked.

"Mercutio, speak!" the witches chanted.

"You witches are fair," Beth said, bowing to them. "Fair as cats that have howled and prowled all night. I swear that I am in love with all of you."

"Mercutio!" they chanted. "All hail Mercutio."

"Queen Mab herself has sent you to dream me a way to oppose the boar-king. For you are more powerful than he."

"You will find a way, but will you take the way?" they chanted.

"I will take the way."

"Mercutio will take the way. Take the way. Take the way?" they chanted.

"I am more than Mercutio," she objected.

"More than Mercutio and less," the witches chanted.

"That's true," Beth agreed.

"Beware of your friends," the first witch said.

Those words hit Beth harder than the cauldron's stink.

"My friends, or Mercutio's?"

"Watch out for your friends," the second witch said.

"Do you mean that I should take care of them, or be afraid of them?" Beth asked.

"Fear them and fear for them," the third witch said.

"Do you mean my character friends, or my human friends? It would make sense to be wary of Lady Macbeth," Beth said. She didn't want to believe that she needed to fear any of her human friends.

The witches laughed. Their laugh was more like a warning bell than a cackle.

"Beware," they chanted.

Great, Beth thought. Beware of everyone. Perhaps she should beware of the witches.

"Will you help preserve Shakespeare's work as he wrote it?" she asked.

Their laughter hurt her ears.

"If Shakespeare is not great, are we great?" they chanted.

"If Shakespeare's words do not stand, then neither do our prophecies."

"Great. You're on our side. Thanks." Beth smiled at them, but she had to cover her ears at the hail of eerie laughter that sounded as they disappeared.

Chapter 6

"THIS PRODUCTION IS MORE like Eleventh Night," Sita grumbled at *Twelfth Night* practice. The drama classroom was stuffy because it had no windows. "It hasn't come together yet."

"Maybe it will at the Eleventh Hour," Amelia said, smiling at Sita. Amelia's blonde hair flowed over her shoulders like a storybook princess's. "As Feste, you have to be moody. But I'll get what I want at the end, so I don't have to worry."

"And I'll be stuck with the wind and the rain, hey nonny," Sita said.

"You asked for the part," Beth reminded her. She noticed that Sita was wearing a new yellow silk blouse. "I'm glad I have mine." Not so much my Mercutio part, Beth thought. If she could just be Viola/Cesario, and not Mercutio too, life wouldn't be so complicated.

She felt that her identity was splitting the way her mother shredded old credit cards.

"Viola, Olivia, your first scene," Ms. Capulet ordered.

Beth stuck out her uncomfortably bound chest. She tried to act the way she did as Mercutio, but softer, because she was supposed to be a girl playing a guy, and a guy who was better mannered than Mercutio.

"Most radiant, exquisite and unmatchable beauty," Beth addressed Amelia.

The words were rather silly, because Viola/Cesario had not yet seen Olivia's face. After quite a few exchanges, Viola said, "Good madam, let me see your face."

A few more lines, and Amelia pretended to lift a veil.

"Excellently done, if God did it all," Viola said.

Beth knew there were productions of *Twelfth Night* where Viola really is smitten when she sees Olivia's face. Beth wasn't sure that James Dean High School was ready for a lesbian Viola, but she thought there probably should be undertones of attraction. She tried to hint at real feeling behind Viola's words.

Amelia responded well. She almost swooned over Viola.

When Beth said, "Make me a willow cabin at your gate and call upon my soul within the house," she tried her best to sound romantic. She had seldom played a woman in love, and she decided to make Cesario convincing, though of course she would have to show subdued love for Duke Orsino, who also believed that Viola was a boy. Yes, being Mercutio helped her with Viola, and Viola helped her with Mercutio.

Amelia's Olivia plunged further and further into passion.

"Good work!" Ms. Capulet said when the scene ended.

"This is wonderful," Amelia whispered to Beth, and it occurred to Beth that Amelia might be attracted to her.

"It's a great play," Beth said noncommittally. She was only acting, but if Amelia wasn't, Beth didn't want to hurt Amelia's feelings.

Sita came over to Beth and gave her a wicked grin. "Don't lead her on," Sita said. "She's a good kid."

"I won't." Beth blushed. "What am I supposed to do? Rush over and kiss one of the guys to show that I'm heterosexual? Tell her, 'by the way, I have a boyfriend,' even though I don't?"

"Don't be dumb," Sita chided her. "You can be subtler than that."

BETH SLUNK INTO HER history class the next day. Arnie beckoned her to sit beside him, and she did. Sita swooped in wearing a fashionable new scarf and sat behind Beth. Kevin clumped in, wearing boots that looked as if they belonged to a lumberjack.

Today was the day they would start reading *Richard III*. Beth brought a bottle of water to keep her going, and had some aspirin handy. She had taken Dramamine and wished she could bring a barf bag.

Mr. Clarke brandished a copy of the play. "We shall read the play aloud instead of watching the movie," he said. "Remember that Shakespeare's Richard is not the same as the real Richard, the one whose bones were discovered recently. The real Richard might not have been treacherous. There is no conclusive evidence that he killed the princes in the Tower. Shakespeare's play is a clever piece of propaganda to show that the Tudors had the right to the throne. Nevertheless, we can revel in the cunning of Shakespeare's Richard."

You revel in it, Beth wanted to say. And let me go to the girls' room and be sick.

"Kevin, you read Richard's part," the teacher said. "Start with the opening speech."

Kevin rose from his desk. He grinned at his classmates. It was a malevolent grin. "Now is the winter of our discontent," he said, "Made glorious summer by this sun of York. . . ."

Beth gripped her desk.

"Now are our brows bound with victorious wreaths . . . ."

The voice was Richard's. The king stood in the classroom, a laurel wreath on his head.

Beth fainted.

She woke with the feeling of hands massaging her forehead. She opened her eyes and saw that the hands were Sita's. Beth lay on the floor. Arnie pressed smelling salts to her nose. Nice that he had thought to bring them.

"What's going on here?" Mr. Clarke demanded. "Are you sick, Beth, or are you playacting?"

"I ... ." she stammered.

"She didn't eat breakfast this morning," Sita chimed in. "Beth has been dieting too much lately. I've told her that she looks fine as she is."

"Yes, you're right," Beth managed to say. She never dieted because not eating meat was restrictive enough.

Sita and Arnie pulled her up.

Kevin hovered nearby. His face paled.

"Are you okay?" he asked.

"Yes." She nodded.

Mr. Clarke frowned at Beth. "You're supposed to be the Shakespearean scholar here. I expect you to arrive in class in shape to participate. Go to the nurse's office now, but you must never let anything like this happen again."

"Yes, sir."

Beth leaned on Sita, who led her away. Arnie's gaze followed them as if he wished he could come along.

"You see, it's good that we know what you're going through," Sita told her. "We can help you."

Beth nodded, but she still didn't feel like speaking.

Instead of taking her to the nurse's office, Sita led her outdoors and they sat on a bench under a tree near the tennis courts. The ground there wasn't muddy. It was a warm day for January, almost sixty degrees. Beth took off her sweater. Sita brought a thermos of chamomile tea out of her bag and gave Beth some to drink.

The taste made Beth want to spit, but she accepted the drink.

They stayed there for lunch instead of going to the cafeteria. Arnie and Kevin joined them and brought sandwiches.

"I'm sorry my reading was so hard for you," Kevin told her, handing her a hummus sandwich on pita.

"It's not your fault," Beth said. "Thanks." The hummus wasn't as good as the kind her mother bought, but it tasted all right.

"Maybe it is his fault," Sita said, staring into Kevin's eyes.

Kevin laughed. "Don't be dumb. Did you see how many girls came up to me afterwards and told me I was great?"

Arnie put down his chicken salad sandwich. "Meanwhile, our friend Beth became too sick to stay in the classroom. You shouldn't play Richard again. I'm going to play him tomorrow."

"If you think I'm giving up a role like that, you're crazy." Kevin crunched his potato chips.

"You could be sick tomorrow," Sita said sweetly.

"I don't like the way you said that." Kevin glared at her.

"Beth, tell him to be sick," Sita said.

"Of course I won't say that." Beth gave Sita a dirty look. "You know that might make him really sick."

"OK." Sita's smile was so saccharine that it gave Beth goosebumps. It reminded her of Sita's acting the part of Lady Macbeth the previous autumn.

Chapter 7

WHEN BETH WENT HOME that afternoon, she cleaned up the sink, which her mother had left messy after breakfast, and put the dishes into the dishwasher. Their kitchen was thirty years old, but Beth wondered why some women made a big deal about fancy kitchens and granite countertops. All that mattered was having a working stove and refrigerator. The linoleum on the floor didn't look too bad.

Then Beth went to her room and pushed her dirty clothes under the bed because the clothes hamper was full and she didn't feel like doing a wash. Then she did some geometry. Some people thought geometry was mystical, but she didn't have any love affair with quadrangles. After she had finished her homework, she decided it was time to visit Lady Macbeth. Beth closed her eyes and thought of Macbeth's castle.

She moved through Maryland's air to chilling winds. Ravens gronked and dove around her. She landed in the bleak garden. Its bare trees had a more melancholy look than bare trees did in Maryland.

Beth had grown taller and thicker, and Mercutio's rings were on her hands. She had worn green nail polish at home, but now her nails were bare. They looked so good that she guessed Mercutio sometimes had manicures.

"Welcome to your double selves, my dear," said Lady Macbeth. She wore her fur robe. "Would you prefer to come indoors? I could serve you some mulled wine."

Beth didn't want to enter the moldy castle, whose walls emitted a deeper chill than the cold garden. But she had to think what Mercutio would say. "Whatever is your pleasure, lovely lady."

Lady Macbeth smiled, which was a close as she ever came to a laugh. "I can bid one of our servants to bring mulled wine to the garden. If you are Mercutio, you must learn to drink without being much affected." She pulled a small bell out of her sleeve and rang it. "But you do not have to address me with as many compliments as he would."

Beth felt the urge to kiss Lady Macbeth's hand, and did so. "If you wish, my lady."

What was she doing? She had been repulsed when Mercutio kissed the blood-stained hand, though the blood was not visible. She noticed that the queen now smelled like faded rose petals. Fortunately, no scent of blood clung to her hand. How would she react if the lady ever smelled of blood?

Lady Macbeth shuddered and withdrew her hand into her sleeve. "Merlin's transformation is working well, I see. I am grateful that he did not change you into Romeo, or you would be showering me with profusions of love."

During Beth's earlier journeys, Romeo had imagined he was in love with the Scottish queen.

"I have started visiting characters from the comedies. They seem more willing to oppose King Richard"—Beth winced as always at saying his name—"than those in tragedies are."

"I wonder that you have not yet asked Henry V. He might be willing."

Beth shivered. She had seen Henry killing in battle, and she had no great affection for that young king. "I suppose he would. He must like the ending of his play. He won."

"I see that you are reluctant. I would ask him myself, but he probably dislikes me for killing a king." Lady Macbeth shook her head as if that were a trivial objection.

A gangly servant appeared with huge silver tankards of mulled wine.

The scent filled Beth's mind with dreams. She was grateful that spices from the East had come to England—and apparently, Scotland—by Shakespeare's time.

She drank. The wine moved through her, warming her and cheering her so that even the thought of meeting Henry V no longer troubled her.

"My lady, your mulled wine is the finest I have ever drunk." Beth inclined her head.

"Also the only mulled wine, I'll wager," the queen said, sipping from her own tankard. "And after Henry V, there's always Hamlet."

"But wouldn't he want to change the end of his play?" Beth asked. "He was killed."

"Hamlet cares more about justice and honor than life," Lady Macbeth replied. "Hadn't you noticed?"

"Perhaps." Beth's tone was dubious. She drained her tankard, yet did not feel the wine go to her head. "I shall take my leave, my lady." She bowed.

"Farewell, dear friend, double but true," the lady said.

What a pity that the lady was a villain, Beth thought. She couldn't help liking some aspects of Lady Macbeth.

Beth closed her eyes and found herself in a tent of sumptuous silks. Golden goblets were perched on a gilded table. Henry V sat on a throne studying a large map, doubtless a battle plan.

Beth had hoped to meet him in his castle rather than near a battle-field. She had seen more than enough of his fighting.

Fortunately, he was alone. She took off her velvet cap and bowed low to the ground as he raised his eyebrows in surprise.

"Your majesty, I am honored to see you. I am Mercutio, cousin to the prince of Verona."

"I've always liked brawlers and bawdy jesters. Welcome, Mercutio," Henry put down his map and smiled. "Pour yourself some wine."

"I am grateful for your condescension, your majesty." Beth poured wine from a golden pitcher into the golden goblets and prayed that she did indeed have Mercutio's capacity for drink. She took a sip. The wine was much sharper than the mulled wine she had drunk in Scotland. It must be what people called a dry wine.

She managed to swallow it without choking. "Excellent wine, your majesty."

"What capers have you been engaging in? I have not had much amusement lately," the king said. He smelled horsey. He must have been riding earlier.

Beth frowned. Mercutio would not like a king to treat him as if he were a jester. "Your majesty, I am not one of your tavern fellows. True, I have met in recent days some fair ladies and fair women who were not ladies, and, as you can imagine, I greeted them warmly." She winked. "But I have come to see you on more serious business."

Henry drank. "Will you help me against the French in case they rise up against me?"

Beth cleared her throat. "Your majesty, we face an enemy far more dangerous than the French. Richard III."

Henry raised his eyebrows. "Him? I could make mincemeat of him."

"Allow me the liberty to say that won't be so easy, your majesty. He had strange powers way beyond those of Richard in his play. Mordred is in his blood."

Henry turned purple. "Mordred who slew King Arthur?"

Beth nodded. "The same, your majesty. Richard and Mordred are one. They are determined to force the endings of Shakespeare's plays to change. They have enlisted many characters who want a change—Othello, Iago, Lear, Cassius, and who knows how many others."

"Othello!" Henry exclaimed. "Surely he is too noble to join with such wretches."

"I had thought so, too, your majesty. But he so repents of killing Desdemona that he would do anything to undo that."

"He must stand by his own deeds, as everyone must." Henry pounded the small table, and it shook. "Richard will not undo my victories, or unjoin me from my French bride. But he and his band cannot change history."

"Beg pardon, your majesty, but I fear he is so ambitious that he may want even that."

Henry leapt up. "I will oppose him, and so will every man in my army. No one can take our glory from us. Every Crispin Crispian's, the world will remember us."

"Of course it will, your majesty." Beth didn't bother to tell him that no one even knew what Crispin Crispian's day was anymore, though many had heard his speech urging his men to battle. Remembering that she was Mercutio, she said, "If only I had fought for you on that noble day. But I must take my fate, and so must every character."

"So be it. Let me know what I can do to oppose the villain."

"In time. We must be patient. Thank you, your majesty." Beth bowed and backed out of the tent.

That hadn't been so bad after all. She just hoped Henry wouldn't start a bloodbath.

Perhaps she should visit Hamlet, but she was too tired, and there was homework to be done.

She returned home and began her homework. French. She thought Henry should be taking the lesson with her since he claimed to be the rightful king of France as well as England.

Chapter 8

WHEN BETH ARRIVED AT the next history class, Kevin wasn't there. The room filled with students, but he never appeared.

Mr. Clarke frowned. "Kevin would be the best one to read Richard's part, but he called in sick. He must be very sick, because he wouldn't miss this chance otherwise. I wonder what virus is in the air? I'm tired of my students getting sick. Be careful. Cover your mouths when you cough and use tissue if you have to sneeze."

Arnie's hand shot up. "May I read Richard's part today?"

"Yes," the teacher said without much enthusiasm.

Beth heard a boy with thick blond hair whisper, "The teachers always pick kids from the same drama class clique." Beth hadn't thought of her friends as a clique, but she was too worried about Richard to care.

Ms. Capulet entered the room. "May I watch your class today, Mr. Clarke? I do want to see how my students handle the reading. That will help me in casting future plays. I was unable to come yesterday because the principal asked me to take over another class."

"Of course you may watch." Mr. Clarke inclined his head. "You may sit in the front. Sita, let Ms. Capulet have your seat."

Sita smiled one of her strange smiles and rose from her chair. Ms. Capulet sat in it.

"We shall do the scene with Lady Anne," Mr. Clarke said. He looked at Beth.

She caught her breath at the thought of pretending to fall in love with Richard, but Sita exclaimed, "Please, Mr. Clarke, let me read Lady Anne."

"All right," the teacher said.

Surely if Arnie and Sita were playing the scene, nothing terrible would happen, Beth hoped.

Sita began Anne's speech lamenting her father-in-law's death and her husband's. She read so well that Beth almost enjoyed hearing her despite it being Richard's play.

Then it was time for Arnie to speak.

"Stay, you that bear the corpse, and set it down," he commanded.

Beth shivered, but not as much as she had when Kevin read.

They continued the reading. Arnie's delivery was just as good as Kevin's though subtler. Beth's head spun only a little. She had taken both aspirin and Dramamine.

Arnie began to woo Anne, whose father-in-law he had killed. He had probably been responsible for the death of her husband too. He was properly insidious. But when he began to say "Fairer than tongue can name." He paled.

Sita's sharp response, "Fouler than heart can think thee," roused him.

All proceeded well, but when Arnie said, "To undertake the death of all the world, so I might live one hour in your sweet bosom," implying that he had killed her husband so he could have her, he trembled.

Beth remembered that Arnie had once dated Sita, but she didn't think that was the reason Arnie trembled.

When he held out an imaginary dagger and offered it to Sita, he closed his eyes for a moment. She pushed the imaginary dagger against his chest. He opened his eyes and, after staring around the room, looked at her as if he were relieved.

When he offered her his ring, he shook like a leaf. Was that acting?

Sita looked into his eyes, and he revived.

Beth gagged. She could almost feel Richard.

When Sita moved away and Arnie began saying, "Was ever woman in this humor wooed?" he appeared to be pulling himself together. He stared at the page and did not let his eyes leave it.

Beth shook. Something was wrong. Arnie should not find the reading this difficult. Arnie never had the fear of Richard she had. Arnie had never met Richard.

She saw that Sita was mouthing the words along with him, and so was Ms. Capulet. In fact, Ms. Capulet had been moving her lips during Arnie's entire performance.

When he finally read, "Shine out, fair sun, till I have brought a glass, that I may see my shadow as I pass," Ms. Capulet and Sita burst out clapping. The whole class joined them.

Beth pressed her hands together, but no sound came out.

Ms. Capulet jumped up and put her arms around Arnie. "Good job," she exclaimed.

Beth had the feeling that the drama teacher was holding him up. His face was white.

She saw the blond boy roll his eyes and heard him whisper, "Arnie was okay, but what's all the fuss about?"

"Good work, Arnie, though Kevin might have made the part a little more devilish," Mr. Clarke said.

"Would you mind ending the class now?" Ms. Capulet asked him. "What could surpass that reading?"

Mr. Clarke raised his eyebrows. "If you wish, Ms. Capulet. We'll resume reading the play tomorrow."

"Sita, Arnie, and Beth, please come with me to my office," Ms. Capulet said in her firmest voice. She held Arnie's elbow.

Beth's legs felt like rubber, and she had the sense that Arnie's did also. Sita walked beside her and watched her in case Beth couldn't make it alone.

When they entered the teacher's office, Beth and Arnie collapsed into the two chairs available for students. Sita hovered over Beth's chair.

"What happened?" Beth asked. Her voice shook.

Arnie let his head sink to his lap.

"Richard was trying to enter," the teacher said, "but Arnie didn't let him. Sita helped him work to keep Richard out."

Beth gasped, but she had known it all along.

"You helped, too," Arnie said to Ms. Capulet. His voice faltered. "Thank you both."

"Richard managed to use Kevin yesterday," Ms. Capulet said. "I'm so sorry I wasn't there to stop it."

"Kevin let him do it," Sita snapped. "The idiot made a pact with Richard. He bragged about it to me. Kevin actually believes that he can be a double agent and oppose Richard that way."

"Oh no!" Beth groaned. "Poor Kevin. What will Richard do to him?"

"Poor Kevin, my ass!" Sita snapped. "I made him get sick. I have the power to do that. I only wish I had made him sicker."

"He doesn't understand the risk to you." Arnie looked at Beth. "But I do. I'd do anything in my power to keep Richard from you."

Tears sprung into Beth's eyes. "Thank you," she said.

"But Beth is right," Ms. Capulet said, handing a bottle of water to Arnie. "Now we have to worry about saving Kevin, too. You were very brave, Arnie, but I don't know whether you can stand to go through that every day until the play is finished."

"Please don't," Beth said. "You looked like you were in pain. Can't I just be sick every day and miss the play?"

"And not get promoted at the end of the school year?" Sita asked. "They don't allow that many sick days. You can't take that chance."

"We'll find a way," Ms. Capulet said. "We have to make sure that Richard doesn't make you sick. Perhaps Merlin could devise some magic to strengthen you. We haven't heard much from him lately. He's leaving you on your own too much. It's time for him to help."

"You're right," Beth said, mentally chastising the wizard for getting her into this situation in the first place. "I don't want Richard to make Arnie sick either." She looked at Arnie, who was still pale.

Arnie straightened up in his chair. "I'm all right," he insisted.

Beth glanced at Sita, who appeared unaffected by the experience. Sita smiled, but the smile disturbed Beth. It was Sita's Lady Macbeth smile. Was it necessary to have two Lady Macbeths?

WHEN BETH RETURNED HOME that afternoon, she ate some leftover guacamole and chips and cut herself a slice of bakery apple pie. Her mother had an evening class, so dinner would be late.

Fortified for an encounter with Merlin, Beth went upstairs, sat at her computer chair, and said, "Hello there, Merlin, it's time to appear."

The wizard appeared, dressed in purple robes like a king. He sat on her bed, the better to spread them out. "I dislike the over-familiar tone you are taking with me," he chided her.

"And I dislike going on missions without adequate protection," Beth replied, folding her arms.

"Do you want Mercutio to lug along a cannon?" Merlin scoffed.

"No, I mean protection as Beth. My history teacher is making us read *Richard III* aloud, and Richard keeps trying to break through into the classroom."

Merlin turned white with anger. "Richard must not be allowed into your century," he demanded. "That would be very dangerous."

"No kidding," Beth said. "He's knocking me out, literally. And he devastated my friend Arnie when Arnie tried to read the part and block him out."

"Tell your numbskull teacher not to let the play be read aloud in your presence," Merlin commanded. "I believe that students in your time are allowed considerable liberties."

"Not that many!" Merlin's lack of understanding of her world annoyed her. "I can't order people around the way you do. The worst thing is that Kevin let Richard channel through him."

"Little idiot!" Merlin hit his palm with his fist. "He'll be lucky if Richard doesn't strike him dead."

Beth flinched. "You have to do more to help us. This is too much for us." She worried that asking Merlin would be about as effective as praying to St. Jude, patron of lost causes.

"I can't appear to every teen at your high school," Merlin complained. "Can't Portia Desdemona Capulet do something?" he said.

"She is trying. She's mouthing all the words in the play along with the students, and that seems to help. And so is Sita."

"Hmpf. I think that Indian girl could cause considerable trouble."

"Why do you say that?"

"She has power in herself, but she hasn't asked to work for me. That in itself is suspicious."

"Sure, anyone would want to be your minion. Great pay, great benefits."

"Like seeing Shakespeare," the wizard reminded her.

Beth remembered her parting from Shakespeare. She didn't think he'd want to see her again. But he didn't know that she was trying to help him. "And have you planned any visits for me?"

"It's interesting that you haven't tried yourself. You had a little tiff with the illustrious playmaker, perhaps?"

Beth had no intention of telling him about her last meeting with Shakespeare, which was confidential.

"Don't change the subject. I'm asking for protection to keep Richard from using my class as a springboard to the twenty-first century. At least I need something to keep myself from collapsing whenever he tries to break through."

"Do you imagine that I could give you a potion that would help?"

Beth looked him in the eye. "Yes, I think you could. And I want some for my friends, too."

"Very well," Merlin conceded less than graciously. "I shall give you a potion that may keep you from fainting. But if one of your friends has decided to help Richard, that is another problem entirely."

"Can't you give me something for Arnie and Sita, too?"

"Sita can take care of herself, but I'll give you something for Arnie."

"Do you dislike her because she's Asian-American?" Beth demanded. "What's your problem with her? She's my best friend."

"Don't accuse me of harboring the absurd prejudices of your time." Merlin scowled. "If you can't see that Sita is playing some game of her own, you're unobservant."

"She's my friend and I trust her." Beth decided not to let herself doubt Sita.

"Good. You trust her. Now, as for the potion you requested, just drink orange juice for breakfast tomorrow. I'll cast a spell on it. You should also call Arnie and tell him to drink orange juice, too."

"I'll look stupid."

"Protect him or not. It's all the same to me."

Merlin stood, swirled his purple robes, and vanished.

Beth had never called Arnie before. She wondered what his parents would think. She dialed his cellphone and he answered. She had hoped to leave a message on his voicemail.

"Hi, Arnie." She rushed into her message, not even letting him finish saying "Hello." "You should drink orange juice for breakfast tomorrow. I know this is weird, but don't ask why."

"It's not so weird. Don't worry, I'll drink it."

"Thanks." She hung up. He certainly was cooperative.

Now for Hamlet. He was perhaps the greatest character in literature, so why did she feel so reluctant to talk to him? Maybe because he was the greatest, and she didn't want to look foolish by comparison. Besides, Hamlet was so suspicious that he might sense that Mercutio was not entirely who he should be.

She thought of Denmark. It was probably cold this time of year. She hoped Merlin would provide warmer clothes than usual for Mercutio.

Beth flew through a snowstorm with large, soft flakes, the kind whose shape you can see. Then she landed on a snowbank on a cliff overlooking the sea. Was it the Baltic? A castle formed of brown stones stood nearby. It had several turrets pointed as sharp as Hamlet's words. Elsinore.

She wore a fur-lined velvet coat with fur trim. As Beth, she would never wear fur, but she was glad that Mercutio would.

A pale young man, also clad in fur, stared out to the sea. He must know someone was near him, but he took his time about turning to Mercutio.

"Noble and most unlucky prince." Beth bowed to him. "I am Mercutio, cousin to the Prince of Verona. It is a great honor to meet you."

"I have no need of another foppishly dressed prattler," Hamlet said. His gaze went past Mercutio. "Go speak with Polonius. He might appreciate your jests."

"But you are the one I must see, noble prince." Beth kept her voice calm and showed no offense. "I hope that Queen Mab will bring you pleasanter dreams, for you dream of nothing but murder most foul."

"It's no dream. You cannot help me, so leave me be. Don't force me to banter with you. I am sick to death of bantering." Hamlet stared at the castle's ramparts as if he could see his father's ghost still walking there.

"You have good reason for your misery, Lord Hamlet, but I must trouble you a little longer. I suppose you would not want wine ... ." Beth pulled out her flask.

Hamlet pushed it away. "My mother was poisoned when she last drank wine. I no longer drink. My mind tosses enough without it." Hamlet heaved a sigh.

"I have come seeking your help."

"Then you have come on a fool's errand. Everything has turned to dust." He sighed again. "I have lost everything and can help no one."

Beth used her most serious voice—or rather, Mercutio's most serious voice. "Prince Hamlet, Richard III is gathering together a band of characters who seek to force a change in the endings of Shakespeare's plays. I am trying to gather a band to oppose him. I had hoped you would join us, because you are so clever and subtle. Would you want to see the ending of your play changed?"

"Change the ending of the world's greatest drama? Of course not." Hamlet shook his head. "It is my fate, or my destiny. No one can change fate."

"I am afraid they can. They might even want to alter your lines. That would indeed be tragic." Beth tried to look him in the eye, but Hamlet still stared beyond her.

"I am weary past enduring. Do you think I know how to prevent tragedy? Impossible."

"You killed one evil king. Surely you could help us devise a strategy to defeat another."

"Richard did not kill my father."

"No, but he killed other fathers. And who knows what havoc he could wreak in Denmark? He might already have won your uncle to his side."

Hamlet raised his hand to his brow and covered his eyes. "Tell me when you know more. I am not certain that I trust you. Why should you be the instigator of the opposition?"

"I was fooled by Richard and he had me killed. I seek revenge. That's a sentiment you should understand."

"I have lived and died for my own revenge. Why should I work for yours?"

"To protect Shakespeare."

"The author of my miserable life? The author of my glorious life? Perhaps. Come back another time."

Waving Beth away, Hamlet walked back to the castle.

Beth was not surprised, but neither was she pleased. She returned to her warm room and took out her French book. Whatever happened in the world of Shakespeare, she had to pass her next test.

Chapter 9

THE NEXT MORNING BETH's orange juice tasted no different than usual, even if Merlin had put a spell on it. She also took aspirin and Dramamine because she didn't want to take any chances.

She took a deep breath before she entered the history classroom.

The obnoxious blond boy walked up to her. "Why are you friends with that freaky cow-worshipper? Hindus pray to elephants," he scoffed.

Beth flushed and glared at him. "That would make more sense than killing them," she said. "Ganesha has an elephant head, but he isn't an elephant. If you ever say anything else nasty about Sita, I could change your he. . . ."

"That's not necessary," said Sita, who had come in behind Beth. "Don't even deign to speak to him."

The boy sneered. "What caste do you belong to?" he asked Sita.

"The cast of *Twelfth Night*," she said, taking her seat.

Arnie joined them. He wore an orange sweater. "We belong to the Order of the Orange," he whispered. Beth chuckled. She knew he wasn't talking about the anti-Catholic Northern Irish. Or about prisoners.

The other students filed in, Sita among them. And Ms. Capulet. Beth exhaled with relief at the sight of her.

"Is Kevin still sick?" Mr. Clarke shook his head. "What a pity. Arnie, you read Richard's part again. Beth, you will read Queen Margaret."

At least Queen Margaret hated Richard. It wouldn't be hard to get into that, Beth thought. "Out, devil!" she said with all her might. And soon she had a chance to say, "A murderous villain, so still thou art."

Arnie's face retained his normal color. Richard apparently was at bay.

But Beth nevertheless had the chance to say, "Hie thee to hell for shame, and leave this world." She had never in her life spoken with more sincerity.

Sita and Ms. Capulet mouthed all the lines, and Arnie proceeded from outrageous statement by Richard to outrageous statement without shaking.

But later in the dialogue, when Beth had to call out "Richard," she feared that she might summon the real Richard.

"Ha!" replied Arnie, but he was simply playing the part.

"I call thee not," Beth said. Was that ever the truth!

They got through the class without interference from any other world.

Arnie slumped back in his seat, but he smiled, and Beth smiled back.

They moved to the French classroom to take a test. No ordinary exam could be as worrisome as the test they had just taken, Beth thought.

At lunch, she met Sita and Arnie as usual.

Beth bought more orange juice, just in case, and she saw that Arnie did too. Orange juice didn't go too well with the hummus she ate or the tuna salad that Arnie ate, but that didn't matter.

"Tuna salad again," Sita groaned, and they all deplored the frequent appearance of that mediocre dish.

"Just call it salad Niçoise and it might taste better," Arnie said.

A shadow appeared over their table. Kevin stood over them and set down his tray with a loud clunk.

"Strangely, I got better just after the history class was over." He glared at them.

"I'm, ah, sorry you were sick," Beth said, though the words tested her acting abilities. "I'm glad you feel better."

Kevin's face reddened. "Sita's not sorry, are you? You're the one who cursed me."

"Silly Kevin. Can't you take a joke?" Sita said, smiling like a Cheshire cat.

"That was no joke." Kevin glowered.

"You're right. Everything is serious. You've been playing with fire," Arnie told him. "Let's go outdoors and discuss it after lunch."

"There's nothing to discuss, Silver," Kevin said. "What a weak Richard you must have been."

"Arnie is far from weak," Beth interjected, her voice rising. "He's right. We need to discuss this later. But not outdoors. In Ms. Capulet's office."

"Is she the new principal?" Kevin scoffed. "Oh, I'm terrified of her."

"If you had any sense, you'd be terrified, but not of her," Arnie said.

It didn't take long to finish lunch, and the journey to the drama teacher's office was short.

She opened the door. "I was expecting you," she said. "Welcome back, Kevin."

"Thank you, ma'am." His voice reeked of sarcasm. And he reeked himself that day, too, Beth thought. He must have been too irritated to take his shower this morning.

There weren't enough chairs. Arnie gestured that the girls should sit down, and they accepted it.

Kevin slouched against the wall. Arnie stood near Ms. Capulet's desk.

"Did you really try to make a deal with Richard III?" Ms. Capulet asked, staring at Kevin as if he had spray-painted the Lincoln Memorial.

"Some people talk too much." He glared at Sita.

"Some people brag about things that no one should brag about," she replied. She wouldn't look at him.

"It's true." Kevin beamed with pride. "King Richard appeared to me in a dream and I decided to help Beth. I told Richard I'd cooperate with him if he left her alone. I pretended that I thought he was a great guy."

Beth groaned.

"And of course he couldn't see through you," Arnie said. "Of course you're brainier than a vicious character with magical powers. Didn't you see how your cooperation hurt Beth? She fainted in class."

"I didn't want her to faint," Kevin objected. "I didn't think she would. You're all right now, Beth, aren't you?"

She nodded. "Yes."

"No thanks to you," Sita said, shaking her head.

"But now Richard believes I'm on his side, so he might let me in on his secrets," Kevin said, standing up straighter. "I can save the day."

"Kevin. Kevin. Kevin." Ms. Capulet let out a sigh each time she said his name. "You've just been recruited to a terrorist network. Your allowing Richard to almost enter this school put all of us in grave danger, and many other people besides. You cannot allow a villain to enter this world. There is quite enough evil here without him. Who knows what he could engage in? At a minimum, he is trying to inca-pacitate Beth. You absolutely cannot do anything else like this again. There is great danger that you will hurt your friends. And yourself, though you might not believe that."

As Kevin listened to her, he paled. "Damn!" He clenched his fists. "But how can I undo a relationship with Richard III, now that I've entered one? Will he let me go?"

Beth felt sorry for Kevin.

Ms. Capulet heaved another sigh. "I don't know. Just resist him instead of encouraging him. Try to shut your heart to him. Don't listen if he talks to you. Treat him as if he were a drug dealer trying to persuade you to sell his drugs."

"I don't believe Kevin is strong enough to resist Richard," Sita taunted him.

"Yes, I am," he snapped. Then he paused. "Cute trick, Sita. Nobody seems to have any confidence in me."

"That might balance the fact that you have an unbelievable amount of confidence in yourself," Arnie told him. "Don't you remember the time that Richard stuck us in the Tower? We were little boys, and he threatened to kill us. But Beth saved us."

"Richard did that?" Kevin choked. "That wasn't just a dream?" He drew a deep breath. "What is this? An AA meeting?" he asked. "Am I supposed to say that I'm weak and need a higher power to help me?"

"That might not be a bad start." Ms. Capulet looked him in the eye. "Merlin has entrusted Beth with the task of opposing Richard. That is a formidable enterprise, and if we're going to help, we need to work together, not strike out on our own. Now, how did you contact Richard in the first place?"

"He contacted me." Kevin's voice had lost its bravado. He slouched so much that he seemed to have shrunk. "I kept seeing a king in my dreams. I saw his boar emblem, and knew it must be Richard. He asked if I wanted to be powerful, and I said I did. I figured that I could spy on him and help Beth in whatever this quest is."

"Never believe a word that Richard says," Beth told him. "That's the first step. He kills the people who work for him." Her voice quavered. "He killed Mercutio."

"Kills?" Kevin's voice hit a higher note than it had since he had reached puberty. His foot knocked over a stack of books on the floor.

"I mean characters," Beth said to reassure him. "He can't kill human beings. But he can make you miserable, believe me. Try if you can to stop listening to him."

"I'll try." Kevin sounded chastened.

Or was he acting? Beth wondered. He was a good actor. She guessed that the others were wondering the same thing.

"I know this sounds strange," she said, "but you should also drink orange juice."

Kevin laughed. "Orange juice? Orange is the new magic?"

"No joke. It can't hurt you, can it, Connelly?" Arnie shook his head. "When will you ever learn?"

Chapter 10

BETH DRANK PLENTY OF orange juice before the next history class. She guessed that Mr. Clarke would ask Kevin to read Richard's part again, and that's just what happened.

Kevin acted well. Beth felt only her usual nausea, not any overpowering weakness, at hearing Richard's words.

"I pray you all, tell me what they deserve that do conspire my death with devilish plots of damned witchcraft, and that have prevailed upon my body with their hellish charms?" Kevin read, just before Richard begins ordering the deaths even of those who have served him.

But only Kevin's voice, not Richard's, came from Kevin's mouth, and Kevin resembled only himself.

Beth managed to get through the class. She hoped that Kevin had learned a lesson. But she wondered whether Richard had only become subtler.

"See, nothing to it," Kevin said to her afterwards.

"Thanks," Beth said, but she doubted that Richard had abandoned Kevin and she wasn't sure that Kevin had abandoned Richard.

Beth went home that evening and returned to her computer chair. So the witches had been right when they told her to beware of her friends. They had said "friends" plural, but she didn't want to think about that.

She longed to see Mercutio. Not to be him, but to see him and talk to him. Tears dripped down her cheeks. She was working hard, but how could anything she did bring Mercutio back?

The answer flashed in her mind like a light bulb in a comic strip. *While you're being Mercutio, you'll get killed, dummy. That's how you're supposed to bring him back.*

Her spirits sank lower. Would getting killed as Mercutio hurt? Was she really a character when she was Mercutio? How could getting killed again bring Mercutio back? Was it certain that she could still live as Beth? She didn't much want to die and come back to life. She could back out of this mission. Would her death as Mercutio save Shakespeare's plays? And who would kill her, anyway? She didn't think her predicted death would be an accident. Richard usually used some henchman to do his work, but who would it be? She hoped whoever it was would kill her quickly.

Beth jumped up, grabbed one of the pillows on her bed, and smashed it into the wall. Setting herself up to be killed was crazy.

I want to go somewhere where someone will comfort me, Beth thought.

She spun out of time. When she smelled the detested incense, she could barely open her eyes.

"Poor Beth," Richard said.

With great reluctance, Beth opened her eyes. She stood in Richard's opulent hall. She was Ben, dressed like Ben, the boy she had pretended to be in Shakespeare's London. She wondered why she wasn't Mercutio.

"I understand the challenge you have set yourself." The king smiled his hideous smile. "You are not appearing as Mercutio, because he would attack me on the spot, and you are not yet ready to die. You see, I do know what fate you face."

"Thanks for your compassion." Beth put as much sarcasm as possible into her tone. "That's one of your most notable traits."

"I am glad you have noticed that. I am not made of stone. Would you consider a libation?" He gestured to golden goblets on a table near his throne.

"No." She refrained from adding, "Thank you."

"Would you like to know who is going to kill you? I could tell you," he taunted her. "You see, I do want to help you."

"You would probably lie," Beth told him. "Or you might tell me who you ask to kill me, but that might not be the character who actually does it."

"Such a clever girl." Richard heaved a stage sigh. "What a pity you waste your talents on Merlin and Mercutio. What do you hope to gain from Mercutio? Do you believe that he would marry you? Would you want to be married to a character? If you did, you could find a nobler one."

"I don't want to marry him." Beth realized that was true. She let her face and voice show her anger. "Don't dare discuss him with me. And don't flirt with me. I'm not a fool like Lady Anne. I don't believe any woman would do what she did, marrying a man who had killed her husband. Shakespeare was a man, after all. He didn't completely understand women."

"But you would give your life for his words. What a romantic, girlish idea. You should not ruin your life for such a fantasy." Richard spoke in a fatherly voice that made her stomach sick.

"I'm leaving now," Beth said, hoping that she would be able to get away. "I won't say farewell because I don't want you to fare well in your plots."

She sat down in her computer chair. Her stomach growled.

"Honey, I'm home," her mother called from downstairs. "I've brought pizza for dinner. I hope you'll like it."

Beth jumped up. Was she ready for pizza? Yes. And she was sure that her mother had purchased her favorite kind, with mushrooms, extra cheese, and pineapple.

Chapter 11

BETH ENTERED THE AUDITORIUM. Today they would have a chance to practice there, where they would perform. She loved standing on the stage. Here at least she felt safe.

The rows of blue no-stain seats were empty, but in a few weeks they would be full with an audience of hundreds, she hoped. She had stood on that stage before and heard one of the sweetest sounds in the world—applause.

She sniffed the air, but the auditorium didn't have any overriding smell. That was just as well, she thought.

On the stage, Sita sang, "What is love? 'Tis not hereafter. Present mirth hath present laughter. What's to come is still unsure: In delay there lies no plenty; Then come and kiss me, sweet and twenty; Youth's a stuff will not endure." She sounded androgynously sexy.

"A mellifluous voice, as I am a true knight," said Arnie as Andrew Aguecheek. He managed to overplay it, so that one would doubt he was a true knight.

"A contagious breath," said Kevin as Sir Toby Belch.

"Very sweet and contagious in faith," Arnie replied.

Beth sat down to watch them. They were doing well.

A few minutes later, Frank stormed on stage. "My masters, are you mad?" He emphasized the word "masters" in a way that was truly creepy. "Or what are you? Have you no wit, manners, nor honesty, but to gabble like tinkers at this time of night?" His ranting had an unsettling quality of outraged servility. This Malvolio wanted people to hate him, relished their hatred and despised them for it at the same time. This Malvolio was so certain that he was above his "masters" that he let them see it.

Beth felt yucky, and knew that was how she was supposed to feel. Frank certainly could act.

When Malvolio stormed out, his departure left them gaping.

The others' conspiracy to humiliate him seemed to have a tinge of racism.

"This feels uncomfortable," Kevin complained as the practice ended. "Why do we have to make the characters seem racist?"

"Why?" Frank repeated. "Good Sir Toby and Sir Andrew and clever Feste could never be racist." His tone out-Malvolio'd his Malvolio tone.

"It's an interesting interpretation," Ms. Capulet said. "I think we should play it that way. The audience should both dislike Malvolio and sympathize with him."

"I don't need their sympathy," Frank said with a gesture of dismissal. "Let them just feel uncomfortable. When I want sympathy, I'll play Romeo."

Beth realized that she was gasping internally, thank goodness not externally. She guessed that some of the others also took a minute to be able to visualize Frank as Romeo. She had never seen a heavy Romeo, which seemed stranger than a black one. But Frank was probably a good enough actor to carry it off well.

"Hi, Viola." Amelia joined the group, but her gaze focused on Beth.

"Hi, Olivia." Beth tried to give a smile that was just friendly enough, and refrained from commenting on Olivia's matchless beauty as she would have if she had been sure Amelia was heterosexual. Beth felt remarkably like Viola.

Ms. Capulet clapped her hands. "It's snowing hard, and Montgomery County says we should go home early."

The students cheered.

"Snow day tomorrow!" Frank beamed.

"I hope so," Kevin said.

Beth didn't feel as eager as usual. If she was home, there would be more time for time traveling, which hadn't been much fun lately. She put on her coat and wool hat, and trudged out with Sita and Arnie, who both lived on the way to her house.

Snow covered the trees and the cars parked on the street. People drove their cars slowly. The street was filling with snow, and the snow plows hadn't come yet.

"Wrathful nipping cold," Arnie complained, brushing snow from his face.

"Showoff! I can't believe you're quoting from *Henry VI, Part II*," Sita said. "Who reads that?"

"You have." Arnie grinned.

"In winter with warm tears I'll melt the snow," Sita replied.

"*Titus Andronicus*," Arnie added.

Beth shivered. "I've avoided reading that one. I've heard that it's all blood. You're both hopeless geeks."

"As opposed to you, who live half the time in Shakespeare's world," Sita said, picking up snow and making a snowball. She held it up as if she were going to throw it at Beth. "You live Shakespeare."

"Just so I don't die Shakespeare." Beth rolled a snowball of her own and menaced Sita.

"What do you mean?" Arnie's eyes opened wide. "You can't die in Shakespeare's world."

"She can as Mercutio," Sita said, squishing her snowball on Beth's shoulder.

"You didn't have to tell him that," Beth objected, rubbing snow onto Sita's coat.

"What!" Arnie yelled.

Beth had never heard him yell before. "It's nothing, Arnie. Don't worry. I'll be fine as Beth."

"Did you mean that you're going to die as Mercutio?" Arnie planted himself in front of them, blocking the sidewalk. Snow began to accumulate on his shoulders.

"I'm not going to argue in a snowstorm." Beth walked off the curb and went around him, then climbed back onto the sidewalk.

"So invite us to your house and we'll argue there." Arnie spun around and walked in front of her again. "You'll come with us, won't you, Sita?"

"I can't wait to see this fight." Sita grinned. "It's more fun than snowballs."

"Thanks a lot for being so free with my secrets." Beth glared at her.

Sita shrugged. "You already knew I was indiscreet, at least compared to you."

Beth walked in front of Arnie again and led them to her house. They left their coats in the hall and went to the living room. Everyone knew Beth's mother was off teaching.

"How about some cider to warm us up?" Sita said. She was already on the way to Beth's kitchen, which she knew well.

"So I have to serve you as well as defend myself? I'll do it." Beth went into the kitchen, poured three mugs of cider, heated them in the microwave, and put in cinnamon sticks.

When she returned to the living room, she set the drinks on the coffee table and plopped down in her mother's armchair. Arnie was on the sofa and Sita sat in the armchair Beth usually used.

"Merlin turned me into Mercutio," Beth explained. "Above the waist," she added, blushing.

"Why?" Arnie demanded.

"To save Mercutio. He's dead, but if I die as Mercutio, I can bring him back. Anyway, Merlin says I can."

"Are you in love with Mercutio?" Arnie asked. He seemed to have shrunk on the sofa.

"Why does everyone ask me that?" Beth's face reddened again. What business was it of Arnie's? He wasn't her boyfriend. "A little bit, maybe. But I care a lot about him, and he died trying to save me from Richard."

Arnie put his hand to his forehead. "You have such a simple life, Beth. A typical girlhood. Why couldn't you visit Jane Austen's world instead of Shakespeare's?"

"I don't think Merlin's offering tickets to Jane Austen's books," Sita said. "And Austen didn't write plays. Beth wants to be the greatest actor in the world." She turned to Beth, "But you won't be, because that will be me."

"You mustn't risk your life," Arnie declared. He looked at Beth as if she were someone precious.

"I'm not just saving Mercutio. I think I'm also supposed to be saving Shakespeare's plays." It sounded crazy, but Beth's friends looked as if they believed her. Being able to tell the truth made her feel so much better. The cider didn't hurt, either. Even though she was talking about her own death, she felt warm and cozy.

"Look at the way she's smiling," Sita complained. "Beth has the starring role again, so she's happy, even if a violent death is thrown in."

"Well, it's just a role," Beth said.

"You hope," Sita retorted.

Arnie covered his face. "I could have joined the debate club. I could have been on the school newspaper. Instead, I joined a troupe of maniacal actors."

Beth tried to explain as much as she could, leaving out a few details, such as her recent conversations with Richard, because those would worry Arnie, and the witches' warning about her friends.

She started wondering about her mother. She hoped her mother's classes were canceled. Driving from the college where she taught was a long distance in the snow.

The phone rang. Beth picked it up and was glad to hear that her mother was on her way.

"OK, my mother will be here in half an hour, unless the highways haven't been cleared yet. So I can't tell you everything," Beth said.

"I've already texted my mother, but she keeps texting me back and telling me to come home," Sita said.

"Mine, too," Arnie admitted. "Be careful, Beth."

Beth hoped her face didn't show how relieved she was to see them go.

Chapter 12

AFTER AN EVENING OF hot chocolate and warmed-up pizza with her mother, Beth opened the front door to see how deep the snow was. It was poetic snow, not sloppy, but she decided to stay indoors. There was probably no school the next day, so no *Richard III* readings. She still feared that Kevin would let Richard slip into the classroom. Maybe if they had several snow days Mr. Clarke would move the class on to another subject and let them finish the play on their own.

"Wouldn't you like to do your homework downstairs?" her mother asked. "It's warmer here."

"No, I need to use my PC. I've been having problems with my laptop," Beth said.

"You can turn on the heat in your room if you'd like." Her mother's tone was less than enthusiastic.

Beth knew her mother fretted about the heating bills. Instead of turning on the heat, Beth wrapped herself in a blanket and rested on her bed.

She couldn't seem to keep out the cold. Perhaps that was because she had traveled to Lady Macbeth's castle.

At least there was no snow on the ground. Beth walked through the courtyard to the lady's chamber.

Two other ladies stood behind Lady Macbeth.

Beth had become Mercutio. She bowed and kissed Lady Macbeth's hand. "Gracious lady, we meet again. Queen Mab sent me a dream of angels, so I knew that I would see you."

"Doubtless angels would remind you of me." Lady Macbeth pulled her sleeve over her hand as usual, but she never did it soon enough to preclude the kiss.

The ladies behind her raised their eyebrows. They had classic features, but no warmth in their eyes.

"Meet Lady Regan and Lady Goneril," the queen said, inclining her head in their direction.

Beth bowed. She didn't offer to kiss their hands though Mercutio would have done so. She wondered why Regan was willing to cooperate with Goneril, who had poisoned her because of jealousy over a man. "It is an honor to meet you, lovely ladies. No wonder my dream showed me more than one angel."

Regan smiled an insinuating smile. "Greetings, gentleman of Verona."

Goneril sniffed. "Angels. We're dead enough in our play. Remember this isn't really Mercutio, Regan. Don't make a fool of yourself."

"I know that. I was just being courteous." Regan frowned at her sister.

"Have you met our foolish father?" Goneril asked.

"Er, yes." Beth wasn't sure what she was supposed to say. "He is, well, formidable."

"He is, well, nasty," Regan said. "He always was. It infuriates me that the play is so sympathetic to him."

"It's difficult not to be sympathetic to an old man out in the rain," Beth said.

"The blasted rain it raineth every day in old England," Goneril complained. "He isn't the only person who was ever soaked. The rain has ruined several of my best gowns."

"What a pity." Beth tried to sound as if she agreed.

"Thank you, dear ladies," Lady Macbeth said. "Could you leave us now? I have set aside a modest collation for you in the hall. My husband's handsomest warriors are also there."

Both ladies smiled at their hostess and swept out of the room.

"How on earth are they going to help us?" Beth asked.

"You shall see." The queen smiled her mysterious smile. It certainly was similar to Sita's. "How many characters are now with us?"

"Rosalind and her friends, Toby Belch and Andrew Aguecheek, and Henry V. A motley group. And of course Titania would try to help us, but she's trying to keep the Midsummer World together. It's distressed about Bottom's disappearance."

Lady Macbeth frowned. "Richard is already bringing grief to a world where it should not exist. I wonder where that poor fool is."

"I hope not in his dungeon. That's a miserable place." Beth shivered at the memory of visiting the dank dungeon to save Mercutio, who, it turned out, hadn't been a prisoner after all, but had been collaborating with Richard.

Lady Macbeth shook her head. "The dungeon is too obvious. Richard has probably hidden him in some other play. Likely not a pleasant one."

Beth shivered, which wasn't difficult in that damp castle. "Merlin said we shouldn't look for him yet, but I want to."

"I believe that Merlin is mistaken. You should save Bottom. After all, the quality of mercy is not strained," Lady Macbeth told Beth.

Beth didn't want to think of all the terrible places in the plays where Bottom could be hidden. She was only moderately surprised that Lady Macbeth would quote Portia. Every character seemed to have layers and layers. Like people.

Beth wondered what she herself was like, deep down. When she was Mercutio, would she attack without much provocation? And when she was herself?

What was Bottom like, at bottom? Could Richard win him over, or force him to participate in something evil? Would Bottom understand evil when he saw it? Did she? Why was she working with Lady Macbeth, anyway?

Chapter 13

T HE NEXT MORNING, BETH slept late. When she woke, she saw that the snow was at least a foot deep.

"It's a snow day," her mother announced. "Montgomery County schools are closed. I didn't want to wake you to tell you."

"Thank you." Beth hugged her, but wondered whether she was getting too old to do that.

"How about pancakes for breakfast?"

"Great. Thanks." Beth gave her mother a smile.

"Arnie Silver called and asked that you call him back." Her mother took the pancake mix out of the cupboard. "He's nice."

"Yes, really nice." Beth wondered whether her mother hoped that Arnie would become her boyfriend. "Is it okay if I call him while you're making breakfast? I'll be quick."

"Of course, honey."

Beth went to the living room and dialed Arnie.

"Hello. Silverado here," Arnie said.

"Hey, Long John. It's Beth. I heard you called."

"May I come over in a while and talk?"

"Sure. In about an hour?"

"Fine."

Beth hung up the phone and sighed. How much more would she have to reveal to him?

When Arnie came over, they went for a walk. Beth hoped her mother wouldn't jump to any conclusions. And that Arnie wouldn't.

The air smelled crisp. Most of the neighbors had shoveled their sidewalks. People were walking dogs dressed in jackets, and some dogs had already yellowed spots in the snow. Some big dogs jumped into snow piles, while little ones had to be dragged, or, in some cases, carried.

In places where the snow hadn't been shoveled, it came over the top of Beth's boots and slid down her ankles, making her socks unpleasantly moist.

Snow still covered the tree branches, but Beth didn't see many icicles.

"There's our breath," Arnie said of the little clouds emanating from their mouths. "Proof that we're still alive."

"Did you need proof?"

"Can you see the characters' breath in cold weather?" he asked.

"Yes, in their worlds. But I doubt whether I could see ghosts' breath."

"You've seen ghosts, too?" Arnie's tone showed no signs of skepticism.

"Yes. In Renaissance England. Ghosts like Shakespeare's sister."

"Awesome. I wish I could see them." Arnie walked around a patch of snow that no one had cleared from the sidewalk. "Sometimes in my dreams I see Shakespeare's plays, and I wish I could enter those worlds as you can. I wish drinking orange juice with you would give me your powers."

Beth shook her head. "Be glad you don't have them."

"If you're going through troubles, I wish I could go through them with you," he said.

"I wouldn't wish that on anyone." Beth frowned. Did he care too much about her? She didn't want to turn him down.

"I thought of a question," Arnie said. "If Richard wants to change the endings of Shakespeare's plays, who could he find to write the new endings? It couldn't be just anyone."

Beth closed her eyes. "Oh, no," she said. The answer came to her all too quickly. "Marlowe. I guess I need to visit his ghost. But I don't like him."

"Marlowe!" Arnie's eyes widened. He paused for a moment. "That's logical. But can a ghost write plays?"

"No, but Richard is probably trying to find a way around that." She decided not to tell Arnie that Marlowe hated Shakespeare, because that would be too close to revealing Shakespeare's secret. Only she and Merlin knew that Shakespeare had killed Marlowe because Marlowe had seduced his sister, Judith Shakespeare, and she had gotten pregnant and drowned herself in the Thames. "Thanks, Arnie. For believing me and helping me."

"I wish I could do more." He looked into her eyes.

"Not now," she said. "I'd like to go home now. It's too cold to keep walking."

"I don't mind the cold," he said, "but if that's what you want, we'll do it."

He left Beth at her door. She said a quick hello to her mother, who was working on lesson plans, and hurried upstairs. Arnie was a better companion than Marlowe, but Beth felt she needed to visit the playwright's ghost. She had never met the living Marlowe.

Though Beth didn't like the ghostly banks of the Thames where Marlowe dwelled, she closed her eyes and tried to go there.

She stood enveloped in fog. The temperature was not as cold as it had been in Bethesda, but the air was damper. Dense mists blinded her. Even the fog on the witches' heath had felt more wholesome.

She was dressed as Ben. But she was still a girl, with her own hands and feet. Her many identities began to confuse her. Being a boy had been fun at first, but she wasn't sure it still was. Marlowe could see through her disguise, so what was the point? But she couldn't order a costume change for herself.

She began to walk, though she didn't know where she was going. The banks of the river were steep enough to keep her from walking into the water by accident.

She wondered whether she had made a mistake in coming here. She couldn't ask Marlowe directly about her concerns, because she didn't want to give him ideas for harming Shakespeare.

Beth trudged on. This gray world of the dead chilled her more than the snow. The fog sank like sorrow into her bones. If she was killed as Mercutio, would some part of her go to a world like this? She knew this was the world of ghosts who had been real people, unlike Mercutio, but where was Mercutio now? Could he be in some world like this? At least Hamlet's father had told Hamlet where he was, but she hadn't heard from Mercutio. Maybe he wasn't suffering.

Mercutio, she called out, wishing for an answer. Maybe there was some special place for dead characters. Maybe Hamlet's father knew where Mercutio was. She abandoned her quest for Marlowe's ghost.

"Royal Dane!" she called out. "King Hamlet!"

Beth moved to a different fog, this time on a rocky coast rather than the bank of the Thames. The fog was darker, because the hour was deep in the night, but it wasn't as creepy as the fog in the world of dead human beings. She still looked like Ben, perhaps because she was looking for Mercutio.

A tall ghost in armor appeared out of the fog. Maybe she had made a mistake in diverting herself from her mission. She remembered that this ghost had talked only to Hamlet.

"Please speak, your majesty," she begged the ghost. "I am not your son, but I am trying to help Shakespeare."

The ghost beckoned her to follow him. She wasn't eager to do so, but that was the only way to get him to talk. They moved some distance through the fog. Then the ghost said, "Mark me."

"I will," Beth said.

"Revenge," the ghost intoned in a deep voice. "Murder most foul."

"I know." She tried not to flinch at the harshness of his tone. "It's terrible that you were murdered, but your son avenged you. I want to ask whether you have seen Mercutio in the place where you dwell. He is also a character who was killed, and he is my friend."

The ghost paused, and she feared he would not answer.

"Please, your majesty. Have you seen Mercutio?"

"Mercutio? No." The ghost spoke slowly. "He is not condemned to walk the night nor confined in fast fires in the day. Or at least, I have not seen him."

"Thank you." Beth breathed a sigh of relief.

"Swear to revenge me," the ghost demanded. "Swear."

"Your son has already done that," Beth repeated. "I'm not sure why you are still walking in the night. I hope you find rest."

She thought of her bedroom, and whirled through fog back to her own room.

She had failed at her mission. She hadn't found Marlowe or talked with him. But at least she knew that Mercutio wasn't in Purgatory. Probably. But he hadn't committed foul crimes, as Hamlet's father had.

I'm going to go nuts, caring this much about characters, she thought.

She could have asked the ghost about other characters. She wondered why Lady Macbeth wasn't in Purgatory for her sins. Maybe characters were in Purgatory only if Shakespeare had put them there. Beth was glad she was involved in Shakespeare's works, not Dante's. She wouldn't want to see a lot of characters suffering in hell.

What about Richard? Well, maybe him. But she was afraid that, even there, he would exert power over her.

Time for homework. Could geometry heal a mind troubled by Shakespeare? But should she have looked for Bottom in Denmark? No, she had to focus on geometry.

TRIANGLES AND QUADRANGLES. LOVE triangles and quadrangles. Drama was a class just as much as geometry. If she saw the "real" Viola and Olivia, that would constitute homework, wouldn't it?

Water engulfed Beth. She gasped for breath. Was she in the Thames again? She grabbed onto something. A piece of wood. She pulled herself up for air. The smell of saltwater filled her nostrils, as water filled her lungs. She tried to spit it out. She was treading water in a sea, where she saw nothing but pieces of wreckage. She was Viola. A sea captain would rescue her and take her to Illyria. But he hadn't appeared yet. Beth clung to the wood. She had a brother who was missing and maybe dead, but since she had never seen him, it was hard to care too much about him. As Beth, she knew that Viola's brother Sebastian was doing well.

No, she didn't want to be Viola. She wanted to see Viola.

A wave engulfed her. She spluttered.

Then she stood on dry land, in Mercutio's clothes. What a relief. The scent of wildflowers filled the air. She approached the gate to a mansion.

There stood Viola, willowy and handsome in her male attire. Viola's face was long, and her fair hair was shoulder-length. Her hands moved gracefully as she gestured to Olivia on the other side. Beth's Mercutio hands were much thicker.

Olivia's skin was olive-toned. Black hair, impossibly sleek, streamed almost to her waist. Her features were Mediterranean, and well-shaped. Her brown eyes gazed at Viola.

Neither of them noticed Mercutio.

Beth felt Mercutio-like irritation that they ignored her. After all, she was one of the handsomest young men in Verona, or at least she looked like him. She supposed she should look at Amelia the way Viola looked at Olivia. Viola was pulling back just slightly, but she maintained her disguise better than some actresses who played Viola and had to keep showing how feminine they were.

Mercutio would surely interrupt them.

"Hail, Lady Olivia! Hail, Cesario!" Beth strode over to them.

Cesario/Viola frowned, as if Mercutio were competition.

In a fit of jealousy that Beth knew was absurd, she wanted to compete with Viola for Olivia's attentions.

"What lady is this?" Beth exclaimed. "Are you the Lady Olivia? No wonder Duke Orsino pines for lack of your love. Anyone would do the same. If I cannot kiss your hand, you will break my heart."

Finally noticing Beth, Olivia extended her hand.

Beth kissed Olivia's hand. It was soft. Well, of course a woman's hand would be, especially the hand of a woman who had never had to work. And it was nice that Olivia's hand had never been stained with guilty blood. Olivia's perfume excited Beth's admiration. Maybe she would try to find something like it at Macy's.

"Who are you, fair stranger?" Olivia asked. "I am surrounded by fair strangers."

Viola looked daggers at Beth.

"I am Mercutio, cousin of the Prince of Verona." Beth looked into Olivia's eyes as if they were the most beautiful in the world, though they weren't as huge as Romeo's eyes, which really were the most beautiful. "I have never seen a lady so lovely, neither in Verona nor any other place."

"You are most courteous." Olivia gazed at her.

"What are you doing here, Mercutio?" Viola asked in a tone that was not her sweetest.

Beth remembered that she needed Viola's cooperation, not her enmity. "I am here because Richard III is trying to change the endings of Shakespeare's plays. He is gathering a host of characters, mostly villains, who want to force a change. But of course those of you in comedies, with happy endings, won't want a change and will join with me in opposing Richard."

"Not want a change? I am uncertain about that." Olivia smiled at Mercutio, then at Viola. "Sebastian wasn't my first choice, after all."

"Orsino was mine." Viola's voice was sharp enough to slice bread. "I don't want a change. But how are we supposed to resist Richard? I may be wearing men's clothes, but I don't know how to fight."

"True, but if you join our band of brothers and sisters, we may be able defeat him," Beth said. "Perhaps Queen Mab will bring us a dream that shows us the way. Won't you stand with us, dear Lady Olivia?"

"If you speak so courteously, how can I refuse?" Olivia's voice was warm, maybe too warm.

"Thank you, my friends. I had best go and leave you to your play. I shall return anon, when we have a plan."

Beth bowed and backed off. Darn, she might have done more harm than good. She shouldn't have tried to compete with Viola.

Beth found her way back to her room and returned to geometry. It was simpler dealing with numbers than with people—or with characters.

Chapter 14

BETH LAY ACROSS HER bed and fell into a deep sleep. She woke in the atrium of a villa with marble pillars. The atrium's floor was paved with tiles depicting waves and dolphins. A statue of Romulus and Remus with their lupine mother stood in the center.

Beth could smell bread baking in some nearby kitchen. She heard the cries of crows flying overhead.

Two men in gleaming white togas stood near the statue. They did not see her, and she did not see herself. Was she dreaming?

"I care about nothing but honor," said a man she had never seen before. He had black hair and, not surprisingly, a Roman nose. "I will enter into no more plots."

"I know that you are an honorable man," said the other. "You are the most honorable Shakespearean character of them all. You love your country as much as honor; indeed, loving your country is your honor."

Beth immediately recognized the second speaker as Cassius, and the first undoubtedly was Brutus. No matter how honorable he thought he was, she shuddered at the thought of a man who would stab a friend.

"The honor of Rome is not at stake." Brutus had a rolling voice, an orator's voice, though he had failed to be as fine an orator as Mark Antony.

"Your other country is Shakespeare's world. The honor of our play is at stake." Cassius moved towards Brutus. "If Caesar was a tyrant— and he was—then Richard III is a far greater one. He even kills his allies. He killed innocuous little Mercutio."

Beth bristled at the description.

"There is a movement to change Shakespeare's plays," Cassius continued. "That is, to persuade him to make revisions. Richard III is leading that movement. Can we allow him to control our lives? What honor will we have if he rewrites our play? We are the ones who should rewrite it. I beg you to join with me in opposing Richard's tyranny."

Brutus shook his head. "Why should our play be rewritten? It is based on history. We cannot rewrite history. We must stand by what we have done."

Cassius's voice rose. "Richard's plan is much developed. He has strong powers on his side. The only thing to do is slay him and replace him with honorable men."

"More plotting I cannot bear." Brutus began to pace around the room. "Great Caesar haunts me."

"He haunts us all." Cassius beat his breast. "I still grieve over his death, tyrant though he was. But Richard has no greatness except great villainy. Opposing him is a virtue. I know what my duty is, as a Roman and as a Shakespearean character. We must keep our history true and sacred. If we replace Richard, we can ensure that. The other plays are fictions and lies. They do not matter so much. But our Roman play must stay pure."

"Cassius, you weary me." Brutus continued to pace. "How much of you is honor, and how much is ambition?"

If you don't know the answer to that by now, you're a fool, Beth thought. So Cassius was conspiring against Richard. Of course he would be. Conspiracy was in Cassius's blood. Would he be a less frightening opponent than Richard? But why? Cassius was no less treacherous.

She drifted away to Richard's great hall. She shuddered. She still couldn't see herself in the scene and hoped that Richard couldn't see her either.

As usual, Richard sat alone on his throne. Incense still filled his hall. It almost made Beth sneeze, but she held back the sneeze that would have betrayed her presence.

"Come, Mephistopheles!" Richard chanted, waving his hands over a stream of incense. "I call upon the powers of darkness. Join with me, and we will be doubly strong."

A dark cloud passed through the hall. Thunder rumbled.

Beth covered her ears. A stench permeated the air and made her hold her nose. The odor must be brimstone.

A handsome being in flowing red robes flew into the room through one of the many mirrors. His features were chiseled into perfection, but his eyes were like blocks of ice. An arctic cold, far deeper than the cold of ghosts, emanated from him.

"Hail, great Mephistopheles, prince of many worlds!" Richard said, inclining his head. His face glowed in triumph at summoning a devil.

"Prince?" Mephistopheles laughed. The room shook. "Not a king? So you believe that I am less than you are?"

Richard smiled. "Less well known, I think, for you are Marlowe's character, not Goethe's, and Marlowe is less well known than Shakespeare."

Mephistopheles scowled. "That ranking is a travesty of literature."

"Indeed." Richard's voice resembled a leopard's purr. "I long to communicate with your Marlowe. Could you help me?"

The devil shrugged. "You know that characters cannot summon their creators."

"True, they cannot." Richard smirked. "But you are the most powerful character of all, aren't you? Or Lucifer is. I think you or your master could communicate with Christopher Marlowe, or at least his ghost, if you tried."

"And what would I gain?" Mephistopheles asked.

"More power. And that's most important commodity, isn't it?" Richard made his voice seductive. "I seek to increase Marlowe's power and prestige, and that would surely increase yours. You might become as powerful as your master."

"An appealing prospect." The devil smiled. His smile was as frightening as a blow to the chest.

Beth woke. Great. That was a restful night. What rotten dreams. And the worst thing about them was that when she dreamed about Shakespeare's characters, the dreams usually were true visions. She hoped these weren't, but she was afraid they were.

She turned on her computer and saw that it was five o'clock in the morning. Her room was dark, except for the gleaming screen. She went downstairs and drank a glass of orange juice, though she didn't believe it would protect her. Well, maybe there was a chance it would.

Cassius was a compulsive traitor, she thought, but she doubted that he could defeat Richard. She wondered whether she should visit Brutus and try to win him to her side.

Or would it be better to enlist Mark Antony? Antony was the victor in *Julius Caesar*, but he was defeated in *Antony and Cleopatra*. The ultimate victor was Octavian, who became Augustus Caesar. Maybe she should appeal to him, though she didn't like him much.

She also was afraid that none of the Romans would have much use for Mercutio. Even though he might be their descendant, he wasn't their style.

She remembered that Adam was playing a part in *Julius Caesar* in Shakespeare's London. If she could bring him with her, he might be able to persuade one of the Romans to join her side.

When had she started thinking of it as her side? Beth wondered.

Beth willed herself to be in London, wherever Adam was.

She coughed on tobacco smoke as she walked into a tavern. The smell of ale also assailed her nostrils. The torches on the wall smoked, adding their scents to the strange bouquet of smells.

Adam sat at a table rolling dice with another young man, who Beth guessed was also an actor. They both wore bright-colored though well-worn clothes.

Still coughing, Beth approached them.

"Ben! Good to see you." Adam beamed at her. "Want a roll of the dice?"

"I have no money to waste on that sport," she said.

"No more do I," Adam's companion said. "You've won enough off me. Master Burbage doesn't pay enough to risk losing it. See you tomorrow, Soothsayer."

"Tomorrow, Cinna. *Ave atque vale.*" Adam slapped him on the back. He turned to Beth. "Sit down, Ben."

"If you've finished your drink, let's go outside and talk," she said.

"It is dark, and dark, and dark outside," Adam said, not budging. "It is warm, and warm, and warm in here. Let us stay in the warm a little longer."

"Can we talk here?" Beth looked around the tavern. The smoke made her eyes water.

"There's no one near us." Adam took up his tankard and drank. "Hot cider for my young friend," he called out.

Beth suspected that the cider would be considerably more alcoholic than she was used to, but she was willing to taste it.

"How is your play going?" she asked.

"It's wonderful. Caesar dies excellent well. Brutus is too sure of himself, and Antony's speech could make a lawyer weep."

"I hope I get a chance to see it." Perhaps that would help her decide whom to approach, Beth thought.

"You should. The Soothsayer is magnificent. His warning is heartbreaking," Adam said. "Maybe next time I'll get a bigger part."

A boy whom Beth thought was too young to be working in a tavern, or working at all, brought her cider. She sniffed it. At last an aroma that pleased her. She touched her lips to the tankard, but the cider was still too hot to drink.

She glanced around again to make sure no one was near enough to hear them. The nearest tables were empty.

"If you had to pick a character from your play to work against Richard, who would you choose?" she asked. "Cassius is already working with Richard, but conspires against him, and is trying to persuade Brutus to join him in conspiracy."

"Some people never change." Adam shook his head and drank more ale. "Brutus is undecided, of course."

"Of course. Undecided, but leaning against. Who would you choose?"

"Mmmm." Adam put his hand on his chin as if lost in thought. "Caesar. If one of the greatest generals in history is available, why choose anyone lesser? And he'd probably enjoy destroying Cassius."

"If Richard doesn't do that first. He doesn't exactly welcome conspiracies against him." Beth tasted her cider. It had cooled down, but it burned her throat and hit her chest like a blow. "Darn. This is too strong for me." She pushed the drink away. "Wouldn't Caesar want to change the play?"

"I doubt it. He's too intelligent to want to play around with history. His position is assured." Adam finished his drink. "He's the one you should approach."

"He's the one *we* should approach," Beth replied. "You've been studying Roman manners. I think you'd make a better impression on him than Mercutio would."

Adam raised his eyebrows. "You think I could come, too?"

"Let's see if my power is strong enough to bring you."

"Cool. Very cool."

"Let's walk outside, please, so no one sees us disappear."

"Anyone could disappear on a street at night in Southwark and no one would be surprised," Adam said. "Let's hope we don't return in the midst of a gang of cutthroats."

"Can we go to your room?"

"I have to share it with two other actors. Let's go to the green room behind the stage at the Globe. There's no play tonight. I have a lantern to light our way." He pulled a lantern from beside his bench and lit it with a torch on the wall.

They walked along a Southwark street. Many passers-by also carried lanterns, and no one seemed to dawdle. Some of the alehouses they passed echoed with shouts.

A man bumped into Adam and tried to steal his purse. Adam kneed him in the groin and hurried on, taking Beth by the arm.

An old man cried out, "Pretty girls, fresh from the country, come in and enjoy."

Beth grimaced.

They reached the unlit theater. Adam had a key and took Beth around to a dark room behind the stage, the place where the actors changed clothes between scenes. Togas lay neatly on a table.

Adam hung up his lantern.

"Think Roman thoughts," he urged Beth.

Beth closed her eyes. "Great Caesar, lend us your ears," she said.

They stood in the atrium of a villa that was much grander than any she had seen before. Statues of Greek and Roman gods stood among flowering plants. Some statues were bronze rather than marble. Beth noticed that the bronze statues had more detailed expressions than the marble ones. Some of the statues of men made her blush. Why were the ancients so fond of nude statues?

Adam wore a toga, and so did Beth. Her body was Mercutio's, and she wore Mercutio's rings. She hoped she wouldn't trip on the toga.

Caesar stood at his desk, writing. His face was stern, impassive, commanding. He looked just like his pictures on coins she had seen depicted in history books. Beth was so impressed that she took a step backwards, so as not to impose on him.

Caesar glanced at them.

"What do you want with Caesar?" the great man asked.

"Mighty Caesar, other characters conspire to change the ending of your play," Adam told him. "We beg you to oppose them and put your great strength on the side of Shakespeare, and indeed of Plutarch."

A woman rushed into the room. She was middle-aged, but handsome, in the Roman way. She wrung her hands. "O Caesar, do not listen to them! Change the play, I beg you!"

Darn, Beth thought. This must be Calpurnia, Caesar's wife. But he didn't listen to her, in life or in the play, much to his loss.

"Great Caesar," Beth said, "you have written history. You would not want anyone to tamper with your words. Would you want them to tamper with Shakespeare's?"

Caesar gave Beth a dismissive wave. "Caesar does not need you to teach him his duty, Mercutio." As in the play, Caesar referred to himself in the third person. "Nor you to inspire cowardice, Calpurnia. Caesar has lived his life and he will stand by it. History is on Caesar's side. What little men would dare to tamper with it?"

"Richard III," Adam told him.

"And Cassius," Beth added.

"O, that lesser men should try to change the fates of greater." Caesar shook his head. "They will fail. Caesar will oppose them. I have defeated greater men than they. Pompey was far greater."

Calpurnia glared at Beth and Adam as if they were aiding and abetting the conspirators.

"Thank you, great Caesar," Adam said.

"Great Caesar, thank you," Beth added.

She saw servants bringing dishes to a table beside a couch. She wished that he would invite them to dinner, but she guessed that was not to be.

"Farewell." Caesar did not gesture, but made it clear that they were dismissed.

Adam saluted him and Beth bowed. They both bowed their heads to Calpurnia, who gave them a smile that was all teeth.

As the climbed down the villa's marble steps, Adam stared at Rome spread out before them.

"I've never been to Rome before. Let's look around."

"I've never seen it either, and we'll never see it this way again," Beth agreed. No ruins. No Vandals had come. And no churches, no Vatican City. A whole different place. "And Bottom might be hidden in this play."

"I don't think he would fit in very well," Adam said.

They approached an intact Capitol. Beth stared at the columns. Many were brightly painted, unlike the modern idea of classical architecture.

She wondered whether guards would keep them out, but she saw no guards, which seemed strange. Were the plebs allowed to enter at any old time?

They climbed the steps and entered the doorway. Beth thought of Caesar's last trip there before he was assassinated.

They walked into what must be the Senate chamber. A body lay on the floor. A knife protruded from his back. Not Caesar; Cassius.

Beth gasped and grabbed Adam's arm. She hadn't liked or trusted Cassius, but she didn't want to see him dead.

Beth turned away from the sight. "Who killed him?" she asked. "Caesar?"

"Stabbing in the back isn't Caesar's style," Adam said. "Richard must have learned that Cassius was betraying him and sent someone to kill him."

"That does sound more likely." Her pulse raced. Her heart beat fast. The sight of Mercutio's body lying covered with blood in Richard's hall flashed before her. She choked out a sob.

"Hey, it's OK." Adam put an arm around her. "Cassius was a bad guy."

"Mercutio," she choked.

"He was nothing like Mercutio. And remember, these are characters. The real Cassius died two thousand years ago. He fell on his sword because he was defeated by Mark Antony." Adam patted her shoulder.

"But the characters seem just as real as you and me," Beth objected. "So how can I feel that they aren't real people?"

"I don't know the answer. But remember we saw the bodies of Mercutio, Tybalt, and Richard dissolve into thin air. Cassius's body hasn't done that yet, but I'll bet it will." Adam waved at it. "Go on, dissolve. You're disturbing my friend." He paused. "Sorry. It didn't dissolve. Great. We might be suspects."

A guard wearing armor and a helmet entered the room. He just stared at Cassius and shook his head. "I helped clean up the blood from great Caesar's body," he said. "I have no taste for cleaning up his murderer's blood, too."

"Do you have any idea who could have done it?" Adam asked.

The guard shrugged. "It might have been a wild-eyed, white-bearded old man in strange clothes who stormed into the Senate a while ago. He stormed out again a little while later."

"King Lear!" Beth cried. "Richard must have persuaded him to do it."

"Lear wouldn't have had much use for assassins," Adam agreed. "And he was mad. Look," he exclaimed. "The body's dissolving!"

Beth shuddered. "I don't want to see it. Mercutio, poor Mercutio!"

"That sounds truly strange when you're wearing his body," Adam said.

"I don't care." She wiped her eyes. "Let's get out of here. Back to London."

They landed beside the stinking Thames. Fortunately, it was morning this time. Dawn was fading. Vendors scurried around to get their carts in place.

"Honey cakes! The best way to break your fast!" an old man called.

"Buns are better! And onion pies! Best pasties this way!" an old woman cried.

Blue-clad apprentices on their way to work flocked to the vendors to buy their wares.

"Too bad we didn't eat in Rome," Adam said.

Mercutio would have agreed, but Beth said, "Yuck. How can you think of food after seeing all that blood?"

"Blood sausage!" cried a nearby vendor.

Beth clutched her stomach. "I'm going to be sick. You stay in London. I'm going home."

"We didn't look for Bottom," Adam observed.

Beth got sick all over the street. Two curs rushed over to lap up the mess.

"Let me get you some water," Adam said.

"Not in this world!" She wanted to get away more than ever, now that he had seen her vomit again. She hid her face with embarrassment.

Beth spun back to her room. She went downstairs and poured herself a glass of cold water from the refrigerator.

She sat at the kitchen table. Opposing Richard was dangerous. Was Cassius's death a warning?

Chapter 15

BETH FELT CONFIDENT AS she walked into her history classroom. Mr. Clarke had sent the class an email saying that they were behind schedule, so the reading of *Richard III* was over. Reading *Henry V* shouldn't be hard to take.

A movie screen stood at the front of the classroom.

In the middle of the room, Mr. Clarke fiddled with a projector.

"Reading plays takes up too much class time," he told the students. "We'll watch Kenneth Branagh's excellent version of *Henry V* instead of reading the play aloud."

A few students applauded. Kevin slumped in his desk. Beth guessed that he had expected to read the part of Henry.

The battle scenes were the only part of the play that would be difficult for her. She remembered being transported to a bloody version of the Battle of Agincourt. She closed her eyes and saw bodies without limbs and wounded soldiers screaming for help. Shuddering, she opened her eyes again. She realized that there wasn't enough class time for the whole movie. They would see the bloody part the following day.

She watched the movie, though she knew it almost by heart, and wished that Shakespeare hadn't killed off Falstaff so soon.

That night Beth sat in her room waiting for her mother to come home. She decided to look for Bottom. The last time Bottom had gotten lost, he had been in a forest. Perhaps he had an affinity for forests. Beth decided to revisit the Forest of Arden. That should be pleasant.

She smelled trees, resin, and moist soil. Mossy ground spread before her. Some trees had Orlando's poems to Rosalind pinned on them. Beth smiled. Would she ever be that foolish in love? Well, perhaps agreeing to die to bring back Mercutio could be considered foolish.

She heard a sound in the bushes. Was it a deer? Or a hunter?

An old man rushed out at her. Lear carried a sword. His eyes were red with rage.

"You're the one who wants to keep Cordelia dead forever! Prepare to die, Veronan pretty boy!" He swung at Beth.

She stepped back out of his way. "Peace, old man. I have no wish to fight one so senior to me," she said, but she put her hand on her sword.

"Condescending imp! Coward! I'll silence your laughter." Lear's next lunge barely missed Beth.

She darted to one side. The old king hadn't lost all his strength when he wandered out into the rain in his play.

She wanted to disappear, but what would Mercutio do?

"A good try, old man!" she said. She forced out laughter. "I am the finest swordsman in Verona. You're a fool to believe Richard. He won't care which one of us kills the other." She held her sword in readiness.

Lear charged her. He dealt a blow to her sword, knocking it out of her hand.

Beth jumped to retrieve it. "Nice try," she said. Her voice strove for calm. "May Queen Mab send you dreams of victory over your foes. But I am not one of them."

Lear's next blow struck her shoulder. She fell backwards onto the ground.

"Peace!" cried a voice coming from behind Mercutio. "Arden is a place for peaceful gatherings, not bitter feuds. We find sermons in stones, books in running brooks." A gray-haired man thrust himself between them.

Lear's sword went through the man's chest. He collapsed.

Letting out a howl of triumph, Lear ran off through the trees. He began tearing his clothes off.

Beth groaned. Lear had killed Rosalind's father, the Duke, a truly nice man. And was it her fault?

The corpse disappeared, but Beth wanted to slink out of Arden. She couldn't face Rosalind.

Beth fell on her bed. Yes, being Mercutio was dangerous. When would Richard find someone who would kill her? Should she let herself be killed so no other characters would be killed trying to save her?

"Dinner's ready, honey," her mother called from downstairs. "I've brought home a wonderful veggie lasagna."

Beth dragged herself up from her bed. How many more people would die? she wondered. She couldn't help thinking of characters as people. They talked like people, they walked like people, so they must be people.

BETH CALLED UP HER friends and asked them to meet her at a deli near her neighborhood.

Sita, Arnie, and Kevin all showed up. They ordered sodas from a waitress who was probably old enough to have grandchildren. Beth liked places that hired old women. It was good to hire kids, but if a place hired only kids, that meant salaries were low and the owners didn't expect anyone to work there for very long.

The deli had too many plastic plants, but it was always clean and you could get a good table during the week. The chairs weren't too comfortable, but nobody pushed you to leave the minute you finished eating.

"What's happening?" Kevin said over his chocolate milkshake.

Beth also had a chocolate milkshake. She needed it. She took a sip, then tried to make her voice steady. "Characters are being killed." Her voice broke despite her best intentions. "King Lear has killed Rosalind's father and Cassius. Richard must have egged Lear on."

Sita sucked in her breath.

Kevin whistled. "Cassius is no loss, but why would anyone kill Rosalind's father?"

Arnie scrutinized Beth's face. "Yes, why the Duke? Is Richard trying to intimidate the characters from the comedies so they won't join you?"

"I hadn't thought of that." Beth felt a pain in her chest. She tried to soothe it with more chocolate milkshake. She held the chocolate in her mouth to savor it, but that didn't work. She choked.

Sita finally spoke. "What were the circumstances when Lear killed the Duke?"

Beth stared into her shake. She didn't want to answer that question, but of course it was necessary. "Lear had attacked me. I tried not to fight back, but I had to. I had dropped Mercutio's sword and fallen, and the Duke intervened to save me. Lear killed him and ran off." She fought back tears. "I didn't want anyone to die for me."

Her friends all exclaimed at once.

"You should take me with you! I'd fight for you," Kevin contributed.

Arnie frowned at Kevin. "That's all she needs for a perfect storm." He turned to Beth. "Richard didn't know that anyone would save you. You're the one he's trying to intimidate."

Sita shook her head. "No, he knows how hard it is to intimidate you. He's trying to force you to get killed as soon as possible. He's more afraid of you acting as Mercutio than he is of Mercutio himself. You need to keep fighting back."

"And let Mercutio stay dead longer?" Beth bristled. "Maybe I should die and get it over with."

"Please don't talk like that." Arnie put a hand on her arm. "I don't like this whole mission. I don't want you to die for Mercutio. Who knows what it would do to you in real life? Dying's an experience that could change you forever, even if you do it in another body and return to yours. Assuming you can come back. Do you know whether any other human has died as a character to save a character? At least ask Merlin that question."

A white-bearded man in a sports coat and British walking cap came to their table and drew up a chair.

Beth almost fell out of her chair. Merlin had never appeared to her friends before.

The wizard sat there silent, for effect, while the others realized who he was.

"This is a private conversation," Kevin said.

Arnie stared at Merlin. "I think he has an interest in it," Arnie said.

"How kind of you to join us," Sita said, her voice dripping with sarcasm.

"You're ruining your teeth with those sugary drinks," Merlin declaimed, frowning at all of them.

"What business is it . . . ?" Kevin began.

"Be calm," Beth said. She put her finger to her lips. "Don't let the whole restaurant know you're amazed. This is Merlin. Remember, act calm. Pretend that he's one of our teachers."

"So how are you going to help Beth?" Sita asked the wizard.

"Your friends are unmannerly, but no worse than I expected," Merlin told Beth. "I came to answer Arnie's question. Yes, in fact a human being did come and die as King Arthur so that King Arthur could go to the Blessed Isles and sleep instead of dying."

Kevin's mouth hung open.

"Thank you for your response, sir." Arnie inclined his head. His voice was as courteous as if he were Sir Galahad. "But going off to centuries of sleep is not the same as living. I believe Beth is trying to bring Mercutio back to life. And my next question is, what happened to the human being who sacrificed his life for King Arthur?"

"He lived," Merlin said, picking up Beth's milkshake, frowning at it, and putting it down again. "He is known today as Sir Thomas Malory."

Of course, Beth thought. The man who wrote perhaps the most famous book about the life and death of King Arthur.

"That's a pretty fable," Sita said, "but there's absolutely no reason why we should believe it." She put a spoon into her soda, pulled out a bit of ice cream, and ate it. No one else had paid attention to their food since Merlin had sat with them.

"Beth, you should not share these secrets with your friends," Merlin chided her. "You used to be discreet."

Beth ignored his scolding. "I suppose you know that Richard has had both Rosalind's father and Cassius killed. I'm worried about Mercutio. I'm worried about Bottom. And I'm getting worried about myself. Just missing death by a sword is a bit intimidating."

Merlin shrugged. "I have told you that you would not die. Not as Beth Owens. I do not know what you would experience dying as Mercutio. It doesn't matter what Richard does to the other characters. They'll all be resurrected sooner or later. What does matter is what he does to the plays. Worry less about Mercutio and Bottom and more about the plays."

With that, the wizard tossed down some money to pay their bills, rose, and walked about of the deli.

"How nice," Sita said. "He treated you to a chocolate milkshake in exchange for dying in another world."

"That was really him?" Kevin asked. The power of speech had returned to him.

"That was really he." Arnie always used proper grammar.

"Why are you so antagonistic to him?" Beth asked Sita. "Are you still angry that he didn't choose you instead of me?"

"Of course I'm angry that he didn't choose us both." Sita ate more ice cream.

"What he said changes nothing," Arnie said. His brows furrowed. "I still think what you're doing is too dangerous, Beth."

"He's right," Kevin chimed in. "You shouldn't do it."

"You're wasting your breath," Sita said. "She will."

Beth drained her milkshake. "It's my choice. I choose Mercutio. And Bottom. And Shakespeare."

"That's an excellent speech." Arnie's voice rose, which it seldom did. He glanced around the restaurant and lowered his voice. "But Shakespeare's work has endured all these years without your help, and I believe it can continue."

"I hope so." Beth wished they understood the pressures on her. "I don't want to be conceited. But I have to believe Merlin and try to do my part. I'd appreciate whatever help you have to give." She changed to a brisk tone. "Kevin, has Richard tried to communicate with you lately?"

He shook his head. "No. I guess he was just using me for the reading of that play."

"Don't count on it." Sita finished her shake. "Let us know when he reaches out and touches you again. Come on, Beth. Let's walk home. We've had enough excitement for this afternoon."

Beth hoped that was true. She didn't know what excitement was waiting for her in the other world. She rose and left with Sita.

"Where should I return when I travel?" she asked Sita as they stepped over a slush-filled curb and crossed the street. She watched out for black ice. Stepping on it could cause a nasty fall.

"Richard doesn't want you to go to the Forest of Arden, so perhaps you should go there." Sita rolled her eyes. "Or maybe he does want you to go there and is just pretending he doesn't."

Beth groaned.

"Wait up, please."

They turned. Arnie ran across the street. "You should find out where Mercutio is. He has to be somewhere, even if he's unconscious."

"Beth isn't a missing persons bureau." Sita frowned at him. "Doesn't she have enough to do?"

"Arnie's right." Beth avoided a patch of ice. "I do want to find him."

Chapter 16

BETH HURRIED TO THE auditorium for the drama club's second practice of *Twelfth Night* on the stage, and their first of several dress rehearsals. She adjusted her costume. The breeches were tighter than she liked, but they were the appropriate style. Her doublet held in her breasts.

She thought Sita's breeches and doublet looked better on her. Sita always looked impossibly stylish. Her new haircut was perfect for Feste.

Arnie's doublet needed pressing and his hair needed combing, but his tone was just right for Count Orsino.

As Cesario/Viola, she asked him how he would feel if he knew another woman loved him as he loved Olivia.

"Make no compare between that love a woman can bear me and that I bear Olivia," he said. He waved his hand dismissively.

"Aye, but I know ... " she said. She strove to look at him with love, but not too obviously.

"What dost thou know?"

Viola had to turn her face so he wouldn't see the love she attempted to hide. "Too well what love women to men may owe." She strove to keep her voice sounding slightly masculine. "In faith, they are as true of heart as we." He wasn't Arnie. He was the man she loved.

Orsino had the last line in the scene as he bade her go to Olivia again. "My love can give no place, bide no denay."

Arnie exited stage left. Beth walked to the back of the stage. A light plunged from the ceiling and crashed just two feet away from her. She jumped. "What!" she cried out.

She tried not to collapse. She could hardly believe what had happened.

Ms. Capulet leapt onto the stage and ran to her. She took hold of Beth's arm to steady her.

Arnie rushed in and grabbed her other arm. He was shaking as much as she was.

Kevin also ran onto the stage. "Beth? Are you okay?" His face was white as chalk.

"Were you working the lights?" Ms. Capulet demanded.

Kevin nodded. "Something slipped."

"It certainly did." The teacher glared at him. "I want to have some words with you."

Sita dashed over and thrust her face close to Kevin's. Her voice was low, but Beth could hear her. "Was that deliberate, or is Richard acting through you without your knowing it?"

Kevin's face reddened. "Deliberate? Are you crazy? I'd never hurt Beth."

"Come aside, all three of you." Ms. Capulet's voice was strained, and there was little of mercy in it. "Stay here, Arnie."

Arnie squeezed Beth's hand, then let go.

Ms. Capulet led the others to her office.

Beth fell into a chair. Her breath still came out in audible gasps.

As soon as the teacher had closed the door, Kevin said, "I didn't do anything. It was an accident. The light was loose."

"I checked the lights early this morning." Ms. Capulet's voice was as grim as Hamlet's father's. "Nothing was loose."

"I didn't do anything." Kevin's voice rose. "Don't blame me. I like Beth. We've been friends since first grade."

He looked so miserable that Beth felt sorry for him. "I know you're my friend. I don't blame you," she said.

"I do," Sita said. Her voice was cold and hard as a weapon.

"Let me handle this," the teacher told them. "Kevin, I'm certain that the so-called accident was Richard's doing. Why were you working the lights anyway? That's not your job."

"The guys who are supposed to do them didn't show up. So I thought I should try. The idea just came to me. I want to learn everything about the theater, so I should try to work the lights."

Sita snorted.

"So how did you feel when the idea came to you?" Ms. Capulet asked. "Was there anything different from how you had felt when you walked into the auditorium?"

"I felt a surge of power. Like I could learn anything I wanted, be anyone I wanted to be." Kevin's eyes widened. "That felt great. Was it wrong?"

The teacher groaned. She looked him in the eye. "Normally, that feeling would be good. But it sounds as if Richard sent you that feeling."

Kevin rubbed his eyes. "Great. Now if I'm feeling good, I'm supposed to worry that Richard is using me?"

"Possibly. Especially if you are doing something anywhere near Beth." Ms. Capulet's voice lowered. "It's frightening that Richard is able to use a person in this world. You have to examine everything you do."

"Do I need an exorcist or something?" Kevin trembled.

"No." The teacher touched his shoulder. "Once Beth has defeated Richard in the other world, you'll be fine. All we need to do is help Beth."

"So now Kevin's my responsibility?" Beth exclaimed. The weight of all her responsibilities sat like a rock on her shoulders. "I have to save Kevin from trying to hurt me?" She let loose a long, loud, "ARRRGH!"

"Or Kevin could be locked up for his own good," Sita said, putting her arm around Beth.

"Thanks a lot." Kevin scowled at Sita.

"No one's going to lock you up," Ms. Capulet said. "But you must be very aware of everything you think and do. All of you." Her look included Sita. "Remember who the real enemy is." She turned to Beth. "Are you able to rehearse now?"

Beth nodded. "I'm all right. The show must go on."

They returned to the auditorium. Sita sang "the rain, it raineth every day" the whole way.

The other kids were waiting for them.

Amelia rushed to Beth. "I heard the light almost fell on you. Are you all right?"

"I was just a little bit unnerved. I'm okay now," Beth said.

"Hey, Belcher," Arnie said, poking Kevin in the arm. But Arnie's gaze was fixed on Beth.

"The noble Sir Toby probably has a hangover," Frank said. "Let's get on with the show."

AFTER THE REHEARSAL, BETH went to the drama classroom. She wanted a few minutes alone. She sat in her usual chair and gazed at the poster of Shakespeare on the wall.

"I'm trying to do my best for you," she said.

She spun, and landed in a forest. Sunlight streamed through the trees. Little white butterflies played in the sunbeams. A red squirrel with pointed ears dashed from one tree to another.

Beth thought it was the Forest of Arden, but she wasn't sure. "Bottom!" she called out. "Bottom, are you there? Bottom?"

Two young women strolled into the clearing. One of them was Rosalind.

Beth wanted to hide her face. She wondered whether Rosalind knew what had happened to her father.

"My affection hath an unknown bottom, like the bay of Portugal," Rosalind said.

"Or rather bottomless, so that as fast as you pour affection in, it runs out," said the other girl, who was undoubtedly Rosalind's cousin Celia.

"Love is bottomless," Beth said, bowing, remembering that she was Mercutio. "Though bottoms have something to do with it. But I must not be crude, sweet ladies. For, pardon me, I do see that you are so beautiful that you must be ladies. Nor do I have leisure to speak of love. For our world is indeed Bottomless. Nick Bottom the weaver is missing and the Midsummer world grieves for him. I have come to search for him because he might find this forest congenial."

"We have not seen him, but you should ask our good fool," Celia said.

"This forest is not congenial." Rosalind's voice was hollow. "Some wretch killed my dear father, who was so brave in exile."

Beth noticed that Rosalind's eyes were red. "Whoever did that foul deed, I am sure King Richard instigated it," Beth said.

"I know that well." Rosalind sighed. "My heart is weary, but I shall work against evil. I would like to know who struck the blow on behalf of that vile king."

"Be leery of Lear," Beth said, and hurried away in search of Touchstone.

She came upon a man in motley. He sat on a log with his arm around Audrey.

Beth bowed. "Good day, lady fair. May I ask whether this gentleman is the noble Touchstone?"

Audrey gave Beth a suggestive look, but put her finger to her lips.

"I am Touchstone," the fool said. "In the forest I touch stones a-plenty. In the court I touched pearls and velvet, but here I touch bark and clods of earth. Here no one covets my stones and bark, so I am happy, or so I say."

"I am seeking Bottom the weaver. Have you seen him?"

"I have seen the bottom of stones, with grubs attached. I have seen the bottom of trees, with more grubs. I have seen the bottom of streams, with little fish. And I may have seen other bottoms." Touchstone pinched Audrey, and she giggled. "But I have not seen the bottom of a weaver."

"Excellent jests, but Nick Bottom is missing from the Midsummer world, and the rain it raineth every day there," Beth said. "I am certain that Richard III has kidnapped him and hidden him in another play. I thought it might be this one."

At the mention of Richard, Touchstone jumped up and pulled Audrey with him. "I have nothing to do with courts, and especially that king's court. If other courts might be full of toadies and braggarts, his is filled with murder."

Touchstone hurried Audrey away, but as they disappeared among the trees, Audrey turned and blew a kiss to the one she believed was Mercutio.

Beth returned Audrey's air kiss. No luck. She had been foolish to hope that Richard had hidden Bottom in a congenial world. The poor player was probably in some world where he was lost indeed.

Beth returned to her classroom. She watched the poster of Shakespeare, but of course it didn't move.

Beth tumbled through fog to the banks of the ghost Thames. Fog surrounded her so deeply that she felt as if she were dead already. There was nothing but gray.

She shivered and started walking to try to warm herself, but her steps moved slower and slower. Her legs felt paralyzed.

An icy hand touched her shoulder.

Beth screamed. She was immediately embarrassed because she didn't approve of girls screaming at every little thing, but this was too much.

A hollow laugh sounded behind her. "Girls do not usually scream at my touch, except with delight."

She spun around.

Marlowe's ghost stood before her. His shoulder-length hair was trimmed, as well as his mustache and thin beard. He would have been handsome except for the blood dripping from the eye that dangled from his gory eye-socket.

"Has Richard III approached you?" she asked.

"What a civil greeting. No preamble, no niceties. You come from a savage age. But not savage enough for me." Marlowe laughed again.

"Why would such an illustrious writer listen to Richard?"

"Why, indeed." He mocked her. "Who better to rewrite Will's dabblings?"

"You wouldn't. You mustn't." Beth scarcely knew whether to use an angry voice or a courteous one. "As a playwright yourself, you should believe the written word is sacred."

"Ha! Sacred! Did Will believe that?" Marlowe clenched his fists.

Beth stared at him. "Of course he did."

"Sacred." His voice mimicked hers. "You believe that anything can be sacred. I lost such childish beliefs in my time. I cannot imagine anyone from the future having such quaint ideas."

"Shakespeare did."

"Shakespeare did *not*," Marlowe snarled. "Your loathesome cur of a Shakespeare destroyed my works, and I will destroy his, play by play, verse by verse." Blood oozed from his eye socket.

Beth averted her eyes from the blood. "No one destroyed your works. They still exist."

"You lie, Shakespeare's lickspittle." Marlowe's icy hand grabbed her arm.

Beth winced and tried to pull away, but the ghost gripped her. Her body chilled. Every part of her felt as if it would dissolve. Her guts revolted. "He didn't hurt your work," she insisted in an enfeebled voice.

Marlowe pushed her to the ground. "He mangled my plays. He gave them foolish, happy endings. He redeemed every character. He added jests. He ruined my life's work."

Beth sucked in her breath. Lying on the ground felt better than being in Marlowe's clutches. "Your plays don't have happy endings. No one has changed them. Someone is lying to you. It must be Richard III."

"Why should I believe you?" More blood poured out of the ghost's eye socket.

"Because I live in the future. Your plays are dark. They made me shudder."

"So they should. Life is dark. Death is darker." Marlowe's voice sounded more despairing than Hamlet's father's ghost's. "Shakespeare sent my Faust to heaven. I'll send his fairies to hell!"

"No, you mustn't!" Beth leapt up and confronted him. "You have no right to tamper with his plays. He didn't change yours. Your view of life is so bleak that you believe every lie you hear."

"Hear me, little girl!" Marlowe bellowed. "His heroes will hang themselves. Every one of them!"

"No!" Beth screamed.

"Beth!" Ms. Capulet shook her. They were in the drama classroom. "What happened to you?"

"Marlowe." Beth's voice shook. "Richard has gotten to Marlowe's ghost. He believes that Shakespeare has changed his plays, so he will try to ruin Shakespeare's. Could Marlowe's ghost do that?"

"If anyone could, he could." Ms. Capulet clutched Beth's shoulder. "You must stop him."

"That's a great homework assignment. Thank you so much." Beth pulled away from her teacher. "How am I supposed to do that? For Arthur's sake, Merlin, appear and listen to me."

As if he were an ordinary human being, Merlin walked in through the classroom door. He was dressed in a wool turtleneck and wool pants, as if he were a teacher.

"Arthur, indeed!" He frowned at Beth. "Summon me properly. Say 'For *King* Arthur's sake.'"

"I'm so sorry that I was too informal." Beth summoned up her every bit of rebellious teen sarcasm. "I've just seen Marlowe's ghost, and he swore he would change the endings of Shakespeare's plays because Richard has told him that Shakespeare changed the endings of Marlowe's own plays."

Merlin trembled. The sight made Beth lose hope. The wizard so rarely displayed fear.

"Marlowe?" Merlin's voice cracked. "The one being who might be able to do it? If he weren't already dead, I'd say we should kill him."

"I'm not killing anyone." The word "kill" disgusted Beth. "We have to convince him that his plays are intact. Can't I bring the latest editions of them to his world?"

"No, you cannot, you foolish girl." Merlin frowned at her. "How can you imagine that a book could travel to the land of the dead?"

"If I can, why not a book?" Beth frowned back at him. She was fed up with being called foolish.

"If you can find a book made of flesh, certainly you can take it." Merlin glared at her. "Only fleshly beings can move to that world."

The thought of a book made of flesh made Beth gag. "Then what can I do?"

"Tell Shakespeare," Merlin said. "Perhaps he can communicate with his fellow playwright."

"Are you kidding?" Beth scoffed. "Marlowe would carve him up and eat him for dinner if he could. We must protect Shakespeare from Marlowe. I'd never suggest that Shakespeare talk to him."

"You may have a point," Merlin conceded. "I wonder whether you could communicate with any of Marlowe's characters."

"No, thanks. I once saw Tamburlaine, and he ordered me killed, and tried to kill Adam. But Richard saved us."

"Richard did what?" Merlin screamed. "So you're the one who introduced Richard to Marlowe's plays. That's why Richard was able to communicate with his characters, and ultimately with him. You've tampered with the worlds."

"You're the one who sent me traveling in the first place, and you didn't save Adam when Tamburlaine was trying to kill him." Beth spat out the words. "Stop blaming me. I can't control everything that happens to me."

Ms. Capulet spoke up. "This argument is getting us nowhere. Calm down, both of you." She dared to speak to Merlin as if he were one of her students. She had never used that tone with him before.

Merlin stared at the teacher as if she had gone mad. "You mortals have no sense of awe. You use the word 'awesome,' but when you meet a being who is awesome, you become over-familiar." He shook his head. "Beth, remember who killed Richard the last time. You should visit Lady Macbeth."

"He didn't stay dead," Beth complained. "I'll speak with her, but remember that she killed him only for a moment. Why didn't he stay dead?" She paused. "Because Lady Macbeth only killed Richard, not Mordred. Mordred brought Richard back to life."

Merlin paled. "Mordred." He intoned the name as if he spoke of a devil. "You realize that Lady Macbeth could not kill him." He made a sign to ward off evil.

The door to the prop closet opened, and Sita emerged. "That's brilliant," she said. "Someone has to kill Mordred."

Merlin whirled around and glared at Sita. "No one can do that! How dare you sneak around and listen to my words! Leave the room this instant!"

"If you have so much power, you should have known I was present." Sita spoke in a voice that lacked not only awe but also respect. "You can't kill him, or you would have done it long ago," she said. "You must have tried and failed."

"Yes." Merlin's voice hollowed. "I have tried and failed. No one knows how to kill Mordred."

"Didn't King Arthur do it?" Sita asked. "Or almost do it? But you can't summon him, can you? Or you would have."

"No. I can't summon Arthur." Merlin's voice broke. His face turned gray. He put his hands to his head and moaned.

"So who can kill Mordred?" Sita asked.

"I can't." Beth shuddered. "I don't want to kill anyone."

"Arthur," Merlin groaned.

"It's cruel to remind Merlin of his broken heart," Beth said.

"Get over it, Beth." Sita's voice was harsh. "We can't always be kind if we're going to defeat Richard."

"Sad but true," Ms. Capulet said. "Now we know what must be done."

"Don't talk about killing that way." Beth sucked in her breath. "Not even about Mordred."

"Beth, do you feel strong enough to visit Lady Macbeth?" the teacher asked.

"Why? Because she's willing to kill?" Beth sighed. "That's one skill I don't want her to teach me." She paused. "I won't ask her how to become a killer, but visiting her isn't too upsetting."

Beth's head spun. She stood in the Macbeths' bare garden. The weather was good, at least for that place. Of course the sun didn't shine, but the breeze was mild. The garden smelled as if someone had done spring cleaning and taken away the odor of mold and replaced it with the scent of new grass. Yes, there was a patch of green grass. Beth sat on a stone bench with legs carved in designs of wolves and bears.

Lady Macbeth entered through the garden gate. "Good day, Mercutio," she said. "You bring the balm of Verona's air with you."

Beth forced herself to rise and kiss the queen's hand. She escorted Lady Macbeth to the bench, and waited until she seated herself. Then, when the lady inclined her head, Beth sat beside her.

Beth felt tired of being Mercutio. Who would want to wear a sword all the time? she thought, as she made sure it was out of the way. And it was tedious to always have to kiss ladies' hands.

"Thank you for giving me leave to sit, lovely lady," she said. "It is your beauty that brightens this garden."

"You must be weary of these courtesies, but you must keep up your part." The queen smiled at Beth. "Please don't feel that you have to jest or mention Queen Mab unless someone else joins us."

"Thank you." Beth rejoiced at being released from the burden of thinking up jests. She would tell some of what she had learned. "Richard has enlisted the aid of Christopher Marlowe's ghost. Marlowe believes that Shakespeare has altered his plays, and he's willing—no, eager—to mutilate Shakespeare's."

Lady Macbeth sucked in her breath. "Marlowe? I don't want to learn how much darker he could make our play. It's quite dark enough."

Beth silently agreed.

"We must act with even more speed than I imagined," the queen said. "Screw your courage to the sticking place."

"If I'm Mercutio, I suppose I have more than enough courage, if not sense," Beth said. "But what can I do?"

"Kill Richard." Lady Macbeth used the tone she had used in the play when she urged her husband to kill King Duncan.

"What good is that?" Beth objected. "You've killed him already, but he didn't stay dead. What about killing Mordred? You know more about killing than I do. Could you do that?"

Lady Macbeth rubbed her hands and moaned. "I cannot slay him. I do not have the power." She shivered and pulled her sleeves over her hands. "You have not yet found Bottom, or you would have told me you had. I tell you that you must find Bottom."

Beth sighed. Not another mission. "I suppose you're right. I'm not used to visiting so many worlds in one human day. And I can't believe I'm talking about killing someone. I don't believe in killing. I don't even eat meat."

"Are you a man?" Lady Macbeth demanded.

"You know I'm not." Beth refused to be intimidated by Lady Macbeth's tone.

"Then unsex yourself. Put a little dire cruelty in your heart, at least toward Richard. And find Bottom the weaver." Lady Macbeth rose and walked away.

Beth didn't even try to kiss her hand in parting.

She bade farewell to Scotland and thought of the Midsummer world.

Beth traveled through a storm. She arrived in a downpour. No, maybe a hurricane. Blinding rain drenched the ground, turning it to soupy mud. Winds battered and bent the trees. There was no light in the fairy world. It was far darker than Lady Macbeth's garden.

Beth almost wept at the sight of sodden fairies hiding under bushes. Only Queen Titania stood in the open. Her wings were folded, but her smile was brave.

"Greetings, dear Beth," she said, though Beth still wore Mercutio's form.

"Can't you stop the rain?" Beth asked, ducking under a tree, even though she knew that might not be the smartest thing to do in a hurricane.

"Not always." Titania sighed. "Sometimes it is too much for me."

"I'm so sorry I haven't found Bottom yet." Beth's spirits were damper than the weather. Her wet clothes clung to her. Her boots squished.

Titania touched her hand, which gave it a little warmth.

"I know it's a difficult task, dear." Titania's voice was heartbreakingly brave.

"Weren't there any clues about where he might have been taken?" Beth asked.

Titania shook her head. "I suppose any clues would have been washed away. But you might ask the mechanicals who were his fellow players."

"Thank you. I should have thought of that." Beth wandered off through the woods. Lightning hit trees, and they fell, just missing her. The wind howled. At least, she hoped the howling came from the wind, and not from anything worse.

She was Mercutio, so she waved her sword at the wind. "I laugh at you, wind and rain," she said. "For you are only a dream sent by Queen Mab." The rain continued. She felt more like King Lear than Mercutio.

She stumbled over a root.

"Ouch," it said.

No, it was the foot of someone hiding under a bush.

Beth peered to see who it was. No fairy had a foot that big.

"Master Quince?" she asked.

"Unfortunately," he moaned.

A chorus of moans from other players hidden in neighboring bushes answered him.

"I'm so sorry that you're stuck in this rain," Beth told them. "Do you have any clues about where Nick Bottom might be? I'm hoping that I can help you if I find him. Was he an ass when he disappeared?"

"No more of an ass than usual," Quince replied. "We were rehearsing a woeful comedy about fairies when he left. He exited pursued by a bear."

"What!" Beth exclaimed "Why didn't anyone say that before?"

"I didn't want to be suspected," Snug the joiner cried. "A lion didn't eat him! If anyone did, it was a bear. When I played the part of a lion, I only roared! I was monstrous fierce, but I didn't eat anyone."

"I'm sure you didn't," Beth said. "I don't believe he was eaten by a lion."

"It wasn't a bear, it was a boar," Starveling the tailor said.

"It was a boar with terrible tusks," Snug said. "It wasn't a lion."

"Yes. I believe he was pursued by a boar," Beth said. Richard again. Where did he hide Bottom? She didn't believe Bottom was dead. "Why don't you keep on rehearsing through the rain? You can say your lines under the bushes. That might keep up your spirits." She didn't think that was a particularly good solution, but she couldn't think of any others.

Could Bottom have been taken to *A Winter's Tale*, where one character exited pursued by a bear, and was never heard from again? She had read that play only once. She suspected that Bottom's exit was only a red herring—or a red bear—and he wasn't in that play after all.

She thought of her warm, dry classroom, and spun back out of the rain.

She opened her eyes and saw Sita and Ms. Capulet waiting expectantly. "Don't ask," Beth warned them. "No, I didn't find anything that could help us. But I'm desperately tired. Isn't it time to go home?"

"It's time for geometry," Sita said.

Beth moaned. Maybe a little wind and rain wasn't so bad after all.

Chapter 17

A T HOME AFTER SCHOOL, Beth peeled carrots and washed broccoli to sauté when her mother came home. That would be a nice surprise for her mother.

Then Beth went upstairs. She had time for a journey to London. She hoped she wouldn't wind up in the Thames.

She almost smashed against a tall building, and wound up on London Bridge. She could scarcely see the river from the bridge because there were so many tall buildings on it. The sun was setting, but the buildings obscured her view.

She was Ben again. Sometimes changing roles so fast dizzied her. Her vision blurred.

"Honey cakes! Fresh baked honey cakes," an old woman called. "Honey cakes with cinnamon. Only a penny, but worth more."

Beth had bought one of the woman's honey cakes once before, and it had tasted good. She had paid tuppence then. The woman had lowered her prices. Beth thought a snack before dinner wouldn't hurt her.

"I'll take one," she said, reaching into her pocket for a penny.

"A growing lad like you needs two," the old woman coaxed her. "Do you have tuppence?"

"Not now, thank you," Beth said. She paid and took a bite out of the honey cake.

Someone grabbed the cake out of her hand and knocked her down.

She saw a grubby boy her age or a little older. They recognized each other. He was the boy who a few months earlier had tried to get her arrested for a theft his gang had committed.

"You!" they both exclaimed.

He kicked her, and she fell.

"This is the turd what left us holding the bag," he said to another boy.

The other boy moved to kick her. She grabbed his leg and threw him off balance.

The first boy was about to kick her when someone gave him a roundhouse kick, knocking him to the ground. Someone in Renaissance London knew karate.

Hands pulled Beth up. "Run," a familiar voice said.

Beth needed no urging. They both ran down London Bridge to Southwark. They barely managed to avoid vendors' stalls and carts drawn by horses and oxen. They had done nothing wrong, but escaping was the safest move since the boys were bigger than they were.

When they passed huge Nonsuch House with its heads of executed prisoners stuck on pikes, Beth and her rescuer stopped to catch their breath.

Beth looked at the face of her rescuer. "How did you get here?" she asked Sita. Sita was also dressed like a boy—like Beth, a well-to-do boy with a fine linen jacket.

"I'm not here." Sita darted away. She ran among passers-by and was lost in the crowd.

Beth hoped that Sita wouldn't be in danger because of her brown skin. It was a good thing that Sita was dressed as a boy.

Beth saw a cluster of large birds near the river bank. She moved closer to get a better look. The reddish birds were sinking their beaks into a man's dead body. She gagged and turned away.

"Hope I don't get et by those red kites," said a passing beggar, shaking his head.

Beth put her hand over her mouth. She wanted to get as far away as possible because the boys were probably pursuing her. Shakespeare lived in London, but so did danger. Ordinary danger, not magical danger. The people in London were real, so they could hurt her. Or even kill her. Or Sita.

Beth opened her eyes in her bedroom. Her side ached. She pulled up her shirt and saw a large bruise. She felt her ribs. None of them were broken. That was good, because she had no idea how she could have explained the injury to her mother. Beth flopped down on her bed to rest.

What was Sita doing? Beth wondered. Why hadn't Sita told her about having the power to time travel? Was Sita also working against Richard? She must be.

The landline phone in the living room rang. Beth dragged herself down the stairs to answer it. She wished she was using her smartphone and didn't have to go far to talk.

"Are you all right?" Sita asked.

"Just bruised." It was so good to tell someone. "Would you mind telling me how you got there?"

"Not now. My little sister might listen in. See you tomorrow."

"Okay."

Beth hung up. A hard day. And now, geometry homework. She wished that the street boys of London had to do homework, too. Their lives must be bleak, with no prospect for advancement, but she felt little tenderness toward them anyway.

"HONEY, I'M HOME," BETH's mother called out.

There still was a normal world to return to, Beth thought with relief. She walked downstairs and gave her mother a cursory hug—anything more intense might have seemed suspicious.

"I'm feeling lazy, so I got a pizza," her mother said.

"Pizza would be great. I'm starving. I've got some vegetables ready to sauté after we eat pizza."

They both sat at the table and opened the pizza box.

"Mushrooms and pineapple! Thanks, Mom." Beth grabbed a slice. "Don't you miss having pepperoni? It would be OK if you had that on your half sometimes." She bit into the pizza and felt intense pleasure. Talk about comfort food.

"Sometime I will." Her mother took a bite. She scrutinized Beth. "You're looking just as stressed as you did when you took that seminar on Shakespeare. Are you working too hard? Or is something else troubling you?"

Beth chewed longer than she needed to. Time for the big lie. "Nothing's troubling me, except geometry. I can't wait 'til I finish math for good."

Her mother continued scrutinizing her. "Are you sure that's all it is? When you came downstairs, it looked as if you were in pain. And you've been preoccupied."

"I got a little sore in gym class. It's nothing to worry about." Beth fished for an excuse. Earlier in the winter, Ms. Capulet had told Beth's mother than Beth was grieving because a boy she liked had been killed in an accident. The drama teacher had glossed over the point that the guy was Mercutio and that Richard III had him killed in front of Beth. "Remember the boy who died a couple of months ago?" Beth hung down her head so her mother wouldn't see that this explanation was only partly true. "I guess I'm thinking more about him."

"Oh, honey." Her mother took her hand. "I should have realized that was the problem. Do you want to see a grief counselor?"

Beth gulped. Not a counselor she would have to deceive. "No thanks. I'll be all right. I just think about him sometimes."

Her mother persisted. "It might be good to talk about him. You've been deeply affected. It's better to talk about your pain instead of holding it in."

"I talk about him with Sita. She met him, so she understands." Beth evaded her mother's attempts to look into her eyes.

"Sita is a good friend, but she isn't trained in dealing with grief. I can easily find a good counselor. Just try one session, honey."

"Please, Mom." Beth took another piece of pizza. She managed to smile. "I'm going to be okay. I'll think about what you said and let you know if I want to see a grief counselor."

"All right." Her mother patted Beth's arm, then took another piece of pizza. "But please think about it. I want you to be happy."

"I know you do. Thank you." Beth bit into the pizza and savored the extra cheese. She thought she was just as happy as she could be for someone who was preparing to be killed in another world.

Chapter 18

BETH DIDN'T SEE SITA before rehearsal the next day. They had a scene together, where Feste and Viola meet in Olivia's garden. When Beth said, "I saw thee late at Count Orsino's," she paused before saying "Count Orsino's" to give the line extra meaning.

Sita grinned as she said, "Foolery, sir, does walk about the orb like the sun; it shines everywhere."

Beth gave her a look that said, *you bet it does.*

When they had finished that scene, Ms. Capulet said, "Let's rehearse the scene where Malvolio is trapped in the cellar. I wish this stage had trapdoors. That would make it so much easier to stage the scene." She stared at the stage as if a trapdoor might suddenly appear. "We'll have to use scenery to hide him instead. Frank, get behind that wall, and try to sound as if you were in a dark hole."

"I will, despite my objections to using the word 'dark' as a pejorative." Frank grinned.

Sita and Kevin came to center stage and taunted him. As Feste, Sita called herself Sir Topas, and spoke to him.

"Never was man thus wronged," moaned Frank. "They have laid me here in hideous darkness."

The scene continued. "Sayest thou that house is dark?" Sita asked.

"As hell, Sir Topas," Frank's voice was a strangled cry, even more desperate than Beth had expected.

"I really am in a dark hole!" he called out. "Help! What happened?"

"That's not in the script," Amelia said from the wings.

Sita stared at Kevin. Beth's chest muscles tightened.

"I'm in a pit! Is there a pit under the building? Get me out!" Frank cried.

"Hang in there," Ms. Capulet told him. "We'll get you out as soon as we can." She looked at Beth.

"*Merlin*," Beth whispered. "Help!"

A white-bearded man dressed like a janitor walked through the auditorium and behind the stage.

Frank staggered out from behind the scenery. "What happened? Is the building falling apart?" He wiped his forehead.

"It isn't," Ms. Capulet said. "Let's take a break, everyone. Frank, would you like something cold to drink?"

Beth reached into a cooler of soft drinks that the teacher had provided for breaks and brought Frank a ginger ale because she had seen him drink them often.

He sat down on the stairs leading to the stage, took the drink, and gulped it down.

"Are you all right?" Sita asked him.

Frank glared at the group. "No one wanted me to play Malvolio. Is this some idiot's idea of a joke? I could have been injured. I didn't believe that this could happen at James Dean. My father warned me about things like this. Who's out to get me?" He looked from person to person. "Was it you, Kevin? You're the one who almost dropped the lights on Beth."

"No, man, I wouldn't do a thing like that." Kevin looked as if he also wanted to sink through the floor.

Beth realized they all had guilty expressions on their faces because they could guess what had happened.

Ms. Capulet approached Frank. "I'm sorry this happened, but no one here is out to get you."

"You had to know." He looked at her sorrowfully. "How could anyone have done that without your knowledge? I never dreamed you'd participate in a thing like that."

"You don't know what a 'thing like that' is." Ms. Capulet tried to reassure him. "Come to my office, and I'll explain. Beth and Sita, you come too."

"You can't tell him!" Beth exclaimed.

"Beth, I am not going to have my theater class charged with perpetrating a racist attack." The teacher pursed her lips. "I have to tell. Come along."

They went to the drama teacher's office.

Frank sat down. Beth and Sita remained standing.

Ms. Capulet removed a stack of books from her chair and settled in it. "I know you will find it difficult to believe me, but this incident falls rather into the realm of the supernatural."

Frank gave her a disgusted look. "A poltergeist at James Dean High School? Give me a break. Can't you think up anything better?"

"It's not a poltergeist," the teacher said. "How did you get out of the hole?" she asked.

"A janitor who looked too old to be working pulled me out. I don't know how he got the strength." Frank shook his head.

"I don't suppose you'd believe that he was Merlin?" Ms. Capulet asked.

"Merlin the magician? That's crazy." Frank gave her a disgusted look. "Why don't you tell me the truth? Are you afraid my father will sue? He'll tell the school board."

Sita leaned towards Frank. "You've known me a while. I hope you don't think I'd participate in a racist incident. Frank, it really was Merlin. You were attacked by Richard III."

"Come off it," Frank said.

Ms. Capulet frowned. "Merlin, it's time," she intoned.

A white-bearded man in a janitor's uniform came in.

"You are being tedious, Frank," the old man said. "Do you remember me?"

"You're the one who pulled me out of that weird hole." Frank smiled at him. "Then you disappeared before I had a chance to thank you. Thank you very much."

"Your thanks are accepted." Merlin nodded. "To say that I disappeared is precisely accurate. I did not walk away, I vanished. And you were not in any normal hole created by human hands. You were taken to an evil place out of this world. I saved you because I am Merlin."

Frank shook his head. "This isn't happening."

"Of course it is." Merlin sharpened his voice. "I seldom appear to mortals, and I hope that you are worthy of my effort. Even though I saved you, no doubt I have to do more to prove my identity."

Frank, Beth, and Merlin stood on a muddy ground where knights in armor and on horseback rushed at other knights. Abruptly, they were back in the classroom.

"That's the short version," Merlin said. "Are you going to demand a longer one?"

Frank's eyes were wide as saucers. "No, I've drunk the Kool-Aid. I guess I believe you." He kept staring at Merlin. "What the hell is this all about?"

"In brief," Merlin said in his usual superior tone, "Beth has been time traveling to Shakespeare's London and the worlds of Shakespeare's characters on a mission for me. Richard III is trying to take over and alter Shakespeare's plays. He can't injure her because she is a human being, not a character like him. But he can frighten her. That idiot, Kevin, had a dream about Richard and decided it would be clever to agree to be Richard's agent so he could spy on Richard. Richard is using him without his knowledge to make trouble in Beth's world. Kevin can't undo that pact as easily as he got into it. Do you understand?"

"O-okay," Frank drawled. "More things in heaven and earth, Horatio. A lot more."

"Precisely," the wizard said. "Now, if you'll excuse me," his voice was heavy with sarcasm as usual, "I have other things to do."

"I'm not sure you do have other things to do," Beth said. She was still annoyed at Merlin. "You're focused on this mission, and I doubt that there are any others that are as important to you."

"Talking tough to impress your friend, are you?" Merlin's eyes narrowed. "You are not impressing me."

Frank shook his head. "You're right that I can't tell anyone about this, or I'd be taken to drug counseling before the words were out of my mouth." He turned to Beth. "So you're on a mission to save Shakespeare's plays?"

She nodded.

"Count me in if I can do anything to help," Frank said.

"There are already too many teens involved in this mission." Merlin frowned. "It's dangerous. I don't want to have to keep rescuing them. Beth is the only one I authorized." He stomped out of the office.

Beth wondered, not for the first time, whether Merlin's thinking was racist, but she hesitated to challenge the one thousand year-old wizard. She was feeling overwhelmed by dealing with Richard anyway, and didn't want to be responsible for anyone else getting hurt. "It really is dangerous," Beth told Frank. "Please don't let that make it sound more appealing to you. I'm just stumbling along trying to figure out whether I'm doing the right thing, and so is anyone else who gets involved, or tries to."

"Let me know if you want me to stumble with you." Frank said. He smiled at her.

Beth smiled back.

"I'm glad that is settled," the teacher said. "I'll see you at tomorrow's rehearsal, Frank."

"You bet," he said, and left.

"I need you girls to stay a few more minutes." Ms. Capulet turned to Beth and Sita. "You seemed to be giving each other some private message while you read your lines. That must not happen in a rehearsal."

"I'm sorry," Beth said.

"It won't happen again," Sita added.

Beth groaned and dropped into a chair. "I know what I have to do," she said.

"I'm sorry, but it might be best." Ms. Capulet shuffled through her papers as if denying responsibility.

Beth thought of Richard. Her stomach protested. She felt as if she were hurtling through a chamber of pins sticking into her head.

"Greetings, dear Beth," Richard said.

Beth shook her head in an attempt to banish the pain. The many mirrors on the walls of Richard's hall gleamed into her eyes as if she were staring at the sun. Somehow she had managed to get there in her own body, not Mercutio's.

"The sun of York," Richard said, chuckling.

"Stop attacking my classmates," Beth demanded.

"Please, address me in a manner befitting my station." He continued to project false joviality.

Beth inclined her head. "Your majesty, I humbly request that you refrain from attacking my classmates." Her tone mimicked his.

"You are leading a conspiracy against me, but you expect me to refrain from hurting your friends?" Richard shook his head. "That's hardly likely, is it?"

"You started attacking my friends long before I began working against you," Beth said. There was no use pretending that she wasn't working against him. They both knew she was, and knew why.

"Poor Kevin," Richard drawled. He wiped an imaginary tear from his check. "It must be so painful for Kevin to know that I'm using his brain to enter your world and do damage. You would show more concern for your friends if you stopped plotting against me."

Beth felt herself redden with anger. "Don't you know that Mordred is using you? You should drive him out. He's not helping you."

Richard's laugh was nastier than ever. "Destroy the better part of myself? You truly are a child if you believe I would do that. Give up, Beth. You are on the wrong side of history. The tide is turning against you and your cohorts. You don't belong in my world, and you can't change it."

"Thank you so much for your advice." Arguing with him was useless. She wondered why she had tried.

"Look into my mirrors before you leave, dear girl." He gestured towards the mirrors.

In one mirror she saw Iago, making a mock bow.

In the next mirror she saw Lear, who looked angry enough to charge through the mirror and attack her.

In the third mirror, she saw Bottom, smiling and bowing.

Beth gasped. She tried to see what his background was so she could determine which play Richard had placed him in. But the background blurred and Bottom disappeared.

"I do not comprehend your fondness for that clown," Richard said. "But it is your attachment to him that has prompted me to move him away from his original world. Any suffering caused by that is your fault. Repent, and save Bottom, or who knows what might happen to him?"

"Do you think I'm foolish enough to believe a word you say?" Beth raised her voice as loud as it could go without shouting. "You wouldn't release him, no matter what I did. I'll have to find him and free him myself."

"Always so self-reliant, aren't you?" Richard picked up a sweet and nibbled it. "What a tedious quality in a girl."

"Good-bye." Beth wished herself away.

She slumped in her chair in Ms. Capulet's office. Fortunately, her teacher kept soft drinks there, too, and gave her a ginger ale. Beth drained it.

Sita squeezed her hand.

"No luck, of course." Beth could barely speak the words.

"I have to go now. I have Advanced Placement Spanish." Sita rose and moved to the door.

"Let's walk home together later," Beth called after her.

"Okay," Sita said and was gone.

"I'm too tired to talk," Beth told her teacher.

"Take another drink with you," Ms. Capulet said, offering Beth an orange soda.

Beth gulped it down greedily. She wondered whether it had the same magical properties as orange juice.

"If you see Arnie, please tell him to come to my office," the teacher said. "I'm going to have to ask him to keep an eye on Kevin. They're good friends, aren't they?"

"Yes. Good idea," Beth said.

She could hardly wait for the school day to end. She lurked by the entrance in case Sita tried to avoid her. Kids eager to leave school hurried past Beth. Some of them chatted and laughed. A few members of the chorus sang a song she didn't know. One of the girls in her geometry class stopped to ask how Beth did in the last test. Beth shrugged. She wasn't sure.

Wind blew in every time the door opened. Beth sneezed, but she persisted.

Finally, Sita approached, moving fast.

Beth matched her pace. They walked into the wind. It blew so hard that it messed even Sita's perfect hairdo.

"What were you doing in England?" Beth demanded.

"Having a spot of tea and a crumpet." Sita grinned at her.

"Be serious. How did you get there?" It hurt that Sita didn't open up.

"I can't believe it." Sita didn't slow her pace. "After all the secrets you've kept from me, you flip if I have a few secrets of my own. You'll find out in good time."

Beth bit her lip. "Did you get there on your own power, on Merlin's, or on someone else's?"

"It's hard to be on the other side, isn't it?" Sita didn't smile. "I helped you. Isn't that enough?"

"I guess it has to be. Thank you." Beth fought back tears. "But whatever you do, don't listen to Richard."

"I'm not a fool like Kevin. Don't worry. I'll see you tomorrow." Sita turned to go down her street.

A few tears dripped from Beth's eyes. It was too cold for her to linger, so she hurried home.

Chapter 19

BETH FOUND A CROISSANT in the breadbox and wolfed it down. Tea and crumpets, indeed.

She went to her room. She felt alone, but she must be brave. Facing Richard was bad enough, but facing coldness in someone she loved was worse. She had faced it with Sita, so she might as well face Shakespeare.

She whirled through a wind full of ink-covered pages that hit her in the face. She tried to grasp them but could not.

She stood outside a door that she thought might be Shakespeare's. He had moved since she last saw him. Lingering wouldn't make her any more welcome. She knocked.

"Who disturbs my peace this evening?" Shakespeare opened the door. When he saw Beth dressed as Ben, Shakespeare paled. "Why have you come?" he asked. "What more is there to say?"

She steeled herself to bear his dislike. "I'm sorry to disturb you, but there is more. Richard III is causing great trouble in many worlds."

Shakespeare walked heavily to the lone chair and sat down. He indicated that she should sit on a stool. Though this room had a view of a tree, which was an improvement, Shakespeare had the same simple table, chair, bed, and stool that he'd had earlier. Books, parchment, and a pen lay on the table. So did a candle and a mug of something that smelled like ale.

She sat. The room had a musty odor, as if whoever cleaned it had not visited for a long time.

"Is this madness?" Shakespeare's voice shook. "How can my characters act on their own devices? Or girls from the future appear? Has someone drugged my ale?" He put his hands to his head. "Please don't trouble me."

"I'm sorry, but I must. Richard III is gathering together a band of characters who want to force a change in the endings of their plays." She colored because she guessed that Shakespeare wouldn't believe her.

"Do you know that madmen approach me in the street and tell me that Hamlet's father's ghost will kill me or that I shall be damned for letting Romeo and Juliet die?" He shook his head. "How do your words differ from their ranting?"

She realized that, though Shakespeare's ghost had seen Richard kill Mercutio and menace her, the living Shakespeare had never seen Richard outside his own play. Richard, as Shakespeare's character, did not have the power to summon his creator. Most of Richard's harassment of her had been because he believed she had the power to bring them together, but for Shakespeare's sake she had resisted Richard.

Tears formed in her eyes. "I don't know how to persuade you to believe me. You seem to believe that I came from another time. I don't want to tell you too much about that because I don't want to violate the bounds of time. If you can believe that Merlin sent me here, can't you also believe that he has sent me to the worlds of your plays and that I have seen the characters living on in those worlds after the plays have ended?"

The playmaker stared at her. "There are no such worlds. Merlin is deceiving you. Perhaps he has given you hallucinations, as he showed me battles and court intrigue. If you see such strange visions, use them as stories for your own writing, but do not believe them."

The tears that had been threatening to fall poured from her eyes. "Please believe me. Richard is dangerous. He wants to injure you. If you have any dreams or visions telling you to make your plays darker, please resist that message."

Shakespeare averted his gaze. "I have had such dreams, terrible dreams of my characters changed into monsters, so that even the good and gentle ones injure one another. I now drink little ale and less wine to ward off those nightmares." He groaned. "Can you see into my very soul? Must you strip the flesh from my head and peer into my skull? A man cannot exist without some private space to call his own."

Beth sobbed. "I'm not trying to look into your soul. I'm trying to help you."

"Perhaps you are my nightmare," Shakespeare said. "You may be a curse brought on by my sins."

"No!" Beth screamed at him. She felt as if her own soul was shrinking. "I'm not a nightmare. I love you, because I love your work. Please, please believe me. Merlin, please tell him to believe me!"

Merlin did not appear.

"Not Merlin again!" Shakespeare shook his head violently. "He has harrowed my soul too often. Seeing you is terrible enough, if you are indeed a real being."

Beth trembled. She covered her eyes. "You hate me." Her voice became shrill. "I love you, but you hate me and call me a nightmare. I've studied your plays, I've acted in them, I've dreamed of becoming a famous actor. I want to preserve your plays. You can't understand, but I'm risking my life to preserve them."

She felt a touch on her shoulder.

"Your flesh seems real." Shakespeare stood next to her, but he pulled back. "Do not sob. Would you truly risk your life to preserve my plays?"

Beth took her hands from her eyes, and looked into his. She knew how tear-stained and miserable her face must be. "Yes," she said. Perhaps it was better to say no more.

"I do not want to wrong you." Shakespeare handed her a linen handkerchief. "Please dry your tears. I shall try to listen."

Beth wiped her face with his handkerchief. She wished she could take it back to Maryland with her. "I have seen many things that are beyond imagining," she told him. "Please believe that Richard exists somewhere and is your deadliest enemy. Merlin told me that you based Richard on Mordred. Is that true?"

Shakespeare nodded. "That much is true. You could not have guessed that if Merlin had not told you."

"That was a terrible mistake," Beth said. "Is there any way that you could take Mordred out of Richard's character? Then Richard might be an ordinary villain, with no unique powers."

"Are you asking me to rewrite the play?" Shakespeare began to pace around the room. "I wrote it years ago and have not thought much about it since. I have written better."

"Was there magic involved in the writing of it?" Beth asked. "Could you simply hold the manuscript and wish the magic out of it?"

He shook his head. "I no longer have the original manuscript. It was burned in a small fire at the theater. But the folio has been published. I don't know how I can release whatever devil there might be in it."

Beth wondered who had been behind the burning of the manuscript. Was it an accident?

Shakespeare paced. "I cannot call a priest to exorcise the folio, for summoning a priest would land me in the Tower." He shuddered. "I cannot bear the thought of the rack."

"Of course not!" Beth exclaimed. "I wasn't asking for you to do that. I don't believe in exorcisms anyway. You are the author. If anyone could remove Mordred's presence, it would be you, not a priest. Perhaps Merlin could help you time travel back to the time when you wrote it."

"No!" Shakespeare shouted. "I am wary of the supernatural, and weary of it."

Beth thought of the witches on the heath. They no longer seemed horrible to her. She wanted to say that the witches might have useful suggestions, but she understood that telling Shakespeare that would agitate him further.

"I know this may sound strange since I just asked you whether you could make changes in a play," Beth said, "but please be wary of suggestions that you should change them, especially of suggestions that you should make them darker."

"I have had enough of the dark," Shakespeare told her. "I already regret writing *Titus Andronicus*. I was younger then. I was trying to shock audiences, but I do not want to whet their taste for too much blood, at least not for blood-letting without thought of the toll it takes. If I write more plays, many of the evil deeds will be reversed, and the deaths may not be true deaths."

That fit what Beth had learned about Shakespeare's later plays, but she refrained from saying so.

She hesitated. "I don't know whether I should tell you this, but Richard is trying to find a way to enable Marlowe to rewrite your plays and make them darker."

Shakespeare let out a terrible cry. He sank into his chair. "Not Marlowe! He would if he could. But how could he? He died so early."

"Maybe I shouldn't have told you that." The sight of his sorrow hit Beth like a blow to the stomach. "I don't suppose there's any way you could communicate with him and reason with him?"

"Marlowe!" Shakespeare sounded like Macbeth seeing Banquo's ghost. "I killed him. That was my greatest sin. No, no, I could never face him, or, God preserve me, his ghost." He shuddered. "He must hate me now, and would never heed my wishes."

That was true, Beth thought. "I'm sorry to distress you," she said. "Please be calm. Many people love your work. It must be preserved. I can't believe it could be changed, even if someone tries to change it. Maybe all my fears are exaggerated. Just believe this: People love your plays."

"I hope that love will sustain the plays," Shakespeare said. He strove to calm his voice. "I must believe that, or I could write no more."

"Believe it!" Beth put all her fervor into her voice.

"I will." Shakespeare sighed. He glanced in the direction of his chamber pot. "Would you mind leaving? After so much agitation, I must answer the call of nature." He laughed. It was a weak laugh, but a laugh nevertheless.

Beth smiled. How like Shakespeare to turn from agony to a jest.

"I will exit," she said, and walked out of his door.

She flew through a volley of papers and returned to her room. She lay on her bed and went to sleep without taking off her clothes.

Chapter 20

ETH WOKE UP WHEN her mother came home, and sleepily ate a vegetarian chili dinner. The chili warmed Beth, but she worried that the beans would make sounds in school the next day.

"It's not like to you to be so tired at dinner," her mother asked the third time Beth yawned. "Are you coming down with a cold? Are you working too hard?"

"I'm fine, Mom." Beth endeavored to make her voice sound cheerful. Why did she have to have such a solicitous mother? Heroines were supposed to be orphans or have cruel stepmothers. Her mother was too exemplary. She never even got drunk or yelled. Your mother should give you some justification for being annoyed at her.

"Would you take some Vitamin C? And maybe some B-12? I think you might be coming down with something." Her mother looked ready to rush out of the room to bring vitamins.

"Sure," Beth said. "I'm not sick, but those won't hurt me." She smiled to hide her resentment at being scrutinized. She noticed that her mother was twisting her napkin. "You're the one who looks worried."

"It's nothing to worry about. I probably shouldn't even tell you." Her mother's face was covered with guilt as if a dose of real-life problems would scar her daughter for life. "The college has a budget shortfall, and I won't get a raise this year. But we'll be fine," she reassured Beth.

"I'm sorry, Mom. That's not fair. You're the one who works hard." Beth got up and hugged her. "We'll be okay."

"I'm not sure we can take a vacation this summer." Her mother bit her lip. "Except for a few days at the beach. I had hoped to take you to see some national parks."

"The beach is great. I love the beach. No worries, Mom." Beth went back to her chili. She knew her mother desperately wanted to give her a perfect youth. She couldn't tell her mother that she was traveling a lot as it was.

"You're a wonderful daughter." Her mother beamed at her.

"Thanks, Mom. You're pretty nice yourself." A wonderful daughter who was as full of secrets as a cake was of sugar, Beth thought.

When she went back upstairs to do her homework, Beth spent a little time on French. She didn't have to spend much time on history because she had already researched Renaissance England thoroughly. Her class was going to finish discussing *Henry V* the next day. She wondered what that king was doing to oppose Richard.

She spun through air that was chilly but fortunately dry and found herself on a battlefield that was so close to a field full of sheep that she believed it was in England. She could hear the sheep bleating as shepherds drove them away from the army.

King Henry V paced in front of his tent. Pennants waved from it. His army stood at the ready. Soldiers tested the sharpness of their swords and drank from their flagons. Some prayed.

Heavy, white-bearded Falstaff, sweating though the air was cold, stood beside the king. In the plays, Falstaff died, scorned by the king, shortly after Henry came to the throne, but in this world they both lived again and Falstaff apparently could talk with Henry.

"I have challenged Richard to single combat," Henry proclaimed.

"No, Hal, you mustn't!" the old man warned him. "Just pull some trick on him. Let me sneak up on him with a band of our old friends. You can come if you want, in disguise."

"A dishonorable plan." Henry gave his old friend a look of disgust. "I shall never be Prince Hal again. Take your foolery and go."

"I can't leave you, Hal. Your arm could be broken. You could no longer lift a goblet of sec. Your teeth could be shattered so that you could no longer chew a leg of mutton." Falstaff wiped his brow. "For the love of life, Hal, don't fight him in single combat," Falstaff pleaded. "You could be wounded in any of your parts. You could be killed."

"A coward dies a thousand times before his death, but the valiant taste of death but once," Henry said stiffly, adjusting his armor.

"Not so! A brave character can be killed again and again," Beth said. "I know that."

"Don't become a coward, Mercutio," Henry said scornfully. "Don't listen to this pathetic old tosspot. I don't listen to him anymore."

"You should," Beth said. "He is giving you good advice. There must be some way other than single combat. Richard is fuller of tricks than a dog is full of ticks."

"The Eye-talian is right," Falstaff said, nodding his head. "Don't believe that Richard will fight you fair. You'd defeat him if he did."

"I shall listen no more." Henry donned his helmet. "For England and Saint George!" he cried, striding forward. "I challenge Richard of York to fight me."

Beth could see a man in armor striding towards Henry. The man carried Richard's boar shield. His helmet was closed. He looked taller than Richard, with broader shoulders. Her heart sank.

"Don't do it, King Henry!" she called out. "I'm not sure this is really Richard."

"Honor won't save you or mend you!" Falstaff exclaimed. His voice choked.

Henry reached his opponent and raised his sword. A mighty blow knocked Henry's head, helmet and all, from his shoulders. It fell on the ground and rolled several feet.

"Hal! My king! My friend!" Falstaff sobbed.

The opponent took off his helmet. He was Othello.

"General Othello!" Beth cried. "How could you stoop to impersonating Richard? How could you kill a man who didn't even know whom he was fighting?"

Othello wiped his brow. Tears began to fall down his cheeks. He picked up Henry's head.

"Poor, noble king. It grieves me to kill you," he wept. "I am a wretch. But this is the only way I can undo a worse murder, killing my innocent Desdemona. At least Henry was armed and stood a chance against me." He carried the head to Falstaff, who cradled it and sobbed.

Beth gagged. Blood poured from the head and soaked Falstaff. Her stomach heaved.

"Oh, Othello, you are on the wrong side. You are making more mistakes, not amending the ones you've already made," she said. She felt compassion as well as anger toward him.

Othello shook his head. "I must make amends to my poor Desdemona. Please tell Henry's wife that I regret having to kill him."

Falstaff would have to do that, because all Beth wanted was to be gone. She bowed to the unfortunate Othello and spun back to her room.

Chapter 21

BETH ASKED SITA TO come for a sleepover, but Sita agreed only to go out after school. They sat in the deli, where Sita ordered a turkey burger and Beth ordered a veggie burger.

The deli was decorated with hearts because Valentine's Day was coming soon. Hearts always made Beth feel a little sad that she didn't have a boyfriend. Did loving Mercutio count?

"I wanted to ask you something," Beth began.

"That's fine if you're talking about this world, not so fine if you're talking about the other world," Sita said. She played with the ends of her scarf, a beautiful concoction of multicolored strands of wool.

"I'm worried that Amelia might be interested in me," Beth confided. "She plays the part of Olivia so well. She really looks into my eyes. And she sometimes keeps it up after practice. I hope she doesn't mean it seriously."

Sita frowned. "Don't get so nervous. Amelia doesn't want to date you."

"How do you know?"

"Because I'm dating her." Sita looked directly into Beth's eyes.

Beth gasped. Then she thought, oh no, that was the wrong reaction. "Oh! I don't mean that's bad. I'm just so surprised. You never said anything about liking girls that way." She felt hurt, as if she had been cheated. "You should have told me. I'm your best friend." She hesitated. "Or maybe I'm not. Maybe Amelia is." Yes, the pain in Beth's chest told her, she was hurt. Jealous. She didn't want to kiss Sita, but she had counted on being her best friend.

"I don't know who's best," Sita smiled. Not her Lady M smile, but a gentle one. "You're a really good friend. We matter to each other. And she's my girlfriend-type girlfriend. She's great, too. I love you, and I'm in love with her."

Beth tried not to cry. "I love you, too. I'm attracted to boys, but I don't feel as close to any of them as I do to you. Why didn't you tell me? Didn't you trust me to still be your friend?"

"I trust you," Sita said quietly. "I just didn't want to talk about being lesbian to anyone for a while. But I thought you'd understand because of your mother."

Beth nodded. "Yes, she's a lesbian, too. I didn't know whether you realized it. She hasn't dated anyone since I was a baby because she wanted to concentrate on being a mother, and on her work. But she told me long ago. I wonder whether she's guessed about you?"

Sita grinned. "I'm sure she has. Don't worry, Beth. I'll always be your friend, no matter whom I date. I hope that you and Amelia will be friends."

"Sure." Beth was grateful for the arrival of the burgers. "I'll try harder to be friendly. She seems nice."

"She is."

Beth took a bite out of her burger, which wasn't one of the best veggie burgers she'd ever had. She spread on more mayo. Amelia was so good-looking. What would it be like to kiss a girl? She could try that out as Mercutio. But that would be dishonest, wouldn't it? She'd rather kiss Mercutio. What was it about Amelia that had made Sita fall in love with her? Sita had never fallen in love with anyone before.

Whatever Sita said, she must like Amelia better than she liked Beth. The thought made Beth feel lonely.

"When did you fall in love with her?" she asked.

"We took an English class together last semester," Sita said. "She loves poetry so much and reads it so beautifully. She writes it, too. But we didn't start going out until this month. Everything's going fine, except that once I had cat hair on my clothes and had to go home and change. I just have to be more careful about things like that because of her chemical sensitivity."

"Do you like poetry better than drama?" Beth asked. She couldn't keep the resentment out of her voice.

"No, I like drama best." Sita rubbed her hands like Lady Macbeth.

"You're certainly good at it." Beth decided to venture further. If Sita was going to be this open about her life, maybe she'd be more open about the other world too. "And you're good at secrets, at least your own. What were you doing in Shakespeare's England?"

"I reveal only one secret per day," Sita told her, and continued eating.

"Does that mean you'll tell me tomorrow?" Beth couldn't resist pushing her.

"Tomorrow and tomorrow and tomorrow," Sita said. "Would you like some fries?"

"All right." Beth decided to content herself with fries for the moment. "But be careful in the other world. King Lear has killed Rosalind's father and Cassius."

Sita raised her eyebrows. "You don't know whether I can visit the world of Shakespeare's characters without your help. You know only that I can visit Renaissance London."

"And you aren't telling me anything more?" Beth asked.

"You still haven't offered to take me to the characters' world." Sita's voice sharpened.

Beth realized that Sita still held a grudge about that. "Should I?" Beth asked.

"I was the one who saved Bottom from Richard last time," Sita pointed out. "Maybe I could find Bottom now." She finished her burger.

Beth paused. "You did. But going there might be more dangerous for you than for me, because you're Asian American."

"That's Merlin's excuse for excluding me." Sita's eyes flashed. "I didn't think you'd use it too."

Beth spilled her drink, then started wiping it up. "I just meant that it would be more dangerous for you than for me."

"More dangerous than planning to die as Mercutio?" Sita gestured to the waitress to bring the bill.

"No," Beth admitted. "But would you go as a boy?"

"I thought I might go as Mercutio's girlfriend. You could protect me." Sita grinned. "Unless the idea of my being your sweetheart makes you uneasy. I don't want to go as your servant."

"Of course not." Beth tried to conceal her discomposure. "You could go as Mercutio's male friend."

"I think Mercutio might be more likely to have an Asian mistress than an Asian male friend," Sita said.

"Maybe. Come however you want." Beth thought a girlfriend was less likely to come to blows with anyone, and since she had to die as Mercutio, that was good. "What name do you want to use?"

"There's nothing the matter with Sita. I'll keep that name. When shall we travel?"

"I guess we should go to my home now." Why not? Things keep getting stranger all the time, Beth thought.

The bill came and they pulled out their wallets.

On the way home, Beth worried. Could she bring Sita to the world of Shakespeare's characters? Beth hoped that she couldn't manage it. Everything would be simpler if she didn't have the ability. Sita had fallen into that world once, but it seemed more dangerous than ever now. Beth didn't want to endanger her best friend. Her probably-best friend. At least taking Sita to another world was something Amelia couldn't do. How far had they gone? It must have been all the way. But there was no reason to be jealous. It was a high school romance. Beth would be Sita's friend forever, and high school romances almost always didn't last. Not that she wanted Sita to be hurt.

Beth saw Sita grinning and guessed that Sita could almost read her thoughts.

"Don't be disconcerted," Sita said. "This experiment will just give us more practice with Shakespeare's gender mix-ups."

"Sure," Beth said.

"I'm not trying to flirt with you in real life," Sita said. "I just think it would be funny to do it in another world."

"I guess so." Beth wasn't too sure. Would Mercutio find Sita attractive? Any guy would. And he'd probably see her as exotic, forbidden fruit. Great. How was Beth supposed to think of her best friend that way?

They went to Beth's room, and Beth concentrated so hard it gave her a headache. She didn't want to go to the Forest of Arden because Lear might be hanging around. Or he might be in Rome. She tried to picture herself and Sita in Italy, during a later period.

Beth felt herself flung from winter to summer. She couldn't tell whether Sita was spinning with her.

Beth felt firm ground under her feet. She stood beside an unfamiliar river that was not so wide as some she had seen. Statues lined the sides of the river. Churches towered above them. A huge palazzo dwarfed the other buildings. Donkeys pulled carts of food. In the distance, men were singing.

Sita stood beside her. She wore a gray velvet gown and a matching cloak. Her hair was long and looped over her ears. A pearl hung from a chain on her neck. She had a red *bindi* on her forehead, though the twenty-first century Sita did not. She looked even prettier than usual. Gorgeous, in fact.

A heavy-set, bearded man in gaudy clothes approached them.

"Ho, Mercutio!" he greeted Beth. "It's good to see another Veronan in Padua. See how wealthy I have become." He thrust forward his hands, which were covered with rings on every finger.

Beth frowned. "Wealth does not give you the dignity of birth, Petruchio. You should address me with more respect."

Petruchio roared with laughter. "Fine lord Mercutio, cousin of the Prince of Verona, I see you're doing well. What a pretty girl!" He eyed Sita up and down.

Sita bared her teeth at him.

"Sita is mine, and I shall thank you not to stare at her in that manner." Beth drew herself up to Mercutio's full height. She doubted that the world of *Taming of the Shrew* was Bottom's hiding place. "If you were a gentleman, I might fight you."

Petruchio laughed again. "Where did you find her? Off a ship in Venetia? I'd go there myself if there were more like her. But if you hope to wive it wealthily in Padua, you'd better hide her."

Beth frowned. "I have no need to find a wealthy wife. My own wealth is sufficient."

"Ha! You will marry a woman with money. The rich always do." He leered at Sita. "And if he discards you, dark beauty, I could find a place for you."

Beth put her hand on her sword, but before she said anything, Sita spoke. "I should so like to meet your wife, Signor Petruchio. I admire her greatly. She would tear you limb from limb if you brought another woman home."

Petruchio laughed. "My wife is obedient. Shall we hold a contest, Signor Mercutio, to see whether your girl is as obedient as my wife?"

"I am not such a fool as to bet against you, Signor Blowhard," Beth said. "My wench obeys me though she scorns you."

Sita bared her teeth again.

"Women who can rage can also fire up in other ways," Petruchio said. "Let's drink to that!" He pulled out his flask.

"I think you have already had sufficient wine this morning," Beth said. "We have come for two reasons. Have you heard of King Richard's plan?"

"Hush!" Petruchio put a finger to his lips. "I have. I like the ending of my play very well, but Kate might want it changed."

"I am sure she would," Sita said, too sweetly.

"We are also seeking Bottom the weaver," Beth told Petruchio. "Have you seen him?"

"I have seen many bottoms." Petruchio laughed. "Thin bottoms, fleshy bottoms, dimpled bottoms. But not Bottom the weaver."

"He might be hidden in your world nonetheless," Sita said. "Bottom, come hither, come hither!" she called out in a voice that was sweet as Titania's, but almost as shrill and penetrating as a dog whistle.

They paused.

"He is not here," Sita said.

"I'd come if you beckoned me," Petruchio said.

Beth pulled out her sword and flourished it. "That is enough, Petruchio. We shall leave."

They swept away.

They stood on a rocky promontory near a castle. Denmark. They both wore heavier cloaks.

Sita pulled a hood over her head. "Your wench is so impressed with your gallantry, Lord Mercutio," she said.

Beth tried not to blush. "You know I have to play the part."

"You could call me your lady fair. People would still guess that I was your mistress. You don't have to say 'wench.'"

"I'm sorry. I'm just trying to guess what Mercutio would say. You're right. He would say 'lady fair' or 'fair Venus' or the like."

"At least you won't feel you have to speak that way to Hamlet," Sita said.

"I don't know what he'll say to you," Beth warned. "He's not exactly a feminist. Here he comes now."

Hamlet walked slowly towards them. He wore only a shirt and breeches, with no protection against the cold. He stared out to sea, then finally approached them.

"Greetings, Mercutio," he said. "Can we talk alone? I do not trust women."

"My lady is trustworthy, but we can talk alone if you wish," Beth told him.

Sita inclined her head to the prince, then went off by herself and began calling Bottom.

"Bottom the weaver is lost, no doubt through a plan of King Richard's," Beth said. "We are trying to find him. My friend can imitate Queen Titania."

"Women can be many selves," Hamlet said with a look of disapproval. "I have decided to join with you. A man must stand against evil. How can I help?"

"When I know, I shall tell you," Beth said. "Nothing rash. King Henry V invited Richard to single combat, and Richard sent Othello in his place. Othello killed Henry."

"Oh, what noble creatures have fallen," Hamlet moaned. "Henry to death and Othello to serving a man far less noble than himself. How can a man survive this world without being corrupted by it? Is it vanity to believe that one can survive with honor?"

"I don't know," Beth said. "We can try. Thank you so much for your willingness to help."

"Am I to fight Lear?" he asked. "Can I kill another graybeard, indeed a whitebeard? Killing old Polonius almost drove me mad. Could I talk to Lear as madman to madman?" He sighed, much more heavily than other people sighed. He exuded melancholy.

Muttering to himself, Hamlet strode off into the castle.

Beth longed to find Sita. To be near another human being who could feel happy. Beth walked along the promontory.

Someone flung herself at Beth and almost knocked her down. To her astonishment it was a middle-aged woman, a good-looking one, in a brocade gown.

"Stay away from him!" the woman cried, beating Beth on the chest. "How dare you enlist my son in your evil band! The play must change! I will save my son's life!"

"Queen Gertrude," Beth said, pulling the woman off her. Even though Beth had Mercutio's strength, the task was difficult. "I know the end of the play must grieve you . . . ."

"It's monstrous! Let me die, but my son must live, marry, and have children of his own." Gertrude still clung to Beth's tunic.

"Who told you that it might be possible to change the ending of the play?" Beth asked.

"That nice man from Italy. Very distinguished-looking. He was a soldier. He explained everything. I know that I must keep my son from helping you." She glared at Beth.

"Iago?" Beth groaned.

"Yes, that was his name. Honest Iago. He didn't tell me what to do. He simply made suggestions."

"That's how he manipulates people," Beth said. "He's the one who persuaded Othello that Desdemona was unfaithful, though she loved only Othello. You can't believe a word Iago says."

"I do believe that I can save my poor Hamlet," Gertrude insisted. "I can't let anything stand in my way."

Sita appeared out of the dark. "Foolish queen," she intoned in her Lady Macbeth voice. "Why do you think the ending would be happier? Richard is trying to give all the plays darker endings. Who knows what he would devise for your play? Perhaps you would be the one who kills Hamlet, or he would be the one who kills you."

Gertrude shrieked. "No, no! That could never happen."

"It could," Beth said, "if you help Richard. Please don't oppose us. Let Hamlet help us if he will. It's true that your play could be even more heartbreaking than it is."

"Is there no hope?" Gertrude sobbed. She tore her hair.

"You have another life now, in whatever world this may be," Beth said. "The play cannot be changed, but you can still see Hamlet and speak with him."

"I try, but he is still so filled with misery." Her voice was heavy with grief.

"Try to comfort him as best you can. That's all I can say," Beth told her.

Then she and Sita spun away from Denmark's darkness.

In Beth's room, they sat on the floor.

"Too sad." Beth ran her hand over her forehead.

"Try to think of something else," Sita said.

"Are you going to come out?" Beth asked.

Sita shook her head. "You do know how to change the subject, don't you? Not yet. I'm not ready to tell my parents."

"Do you think they'll have a problem?"

Sita nodded. "Most likely. They won't cast me out of the house, but they'll keep asking me 'Are you sure? Are you sure?' "

"Well, are you?"

Sita nodded and moved to a yoga position. "Yes. I tried dating Arnie, the nicest boy I know, but I kept thinking about girls. I knew they were the ones I wanted to date. Then I met Amelia and she started asking me out. And that felt just right."

"Do you feel weird about coming to my place for a sleepover? Is that why you haven't come here lately?" Beth asked.

"I knew I was going to tell you soon, and I didn't know how you'd feel. If I do come out to other people, they'll ask whether you and I are going out."

Beth shrugged. "Like that's a problem? All we have to say is we aren't."

"Thanks." Sita squeezed her arm, and Beth squeezed Sita's arm back.

Chapter 22

BETH WALKED WITH TREPIDATION into the auditorium. Today she would see Amelia for the first time since learning that Amelia was Sita's girlfriend. Beth hoped that her voice and face would be normal. Everything was normal. Except that Sita must like another girl better than she liked Beth. No, it was wrong to think that way. It was a different kind of caring.

It wouldn't matter if one of her other classmates had a girlfriend. But Sita? Was it so wrong to want Sita to like her best? Would Sita tell Amelia everything she knew about Beth? Would Sita have all her sleepovers with Amelia now? Would Sita think sleepovers at Beth's house were boring because they just talked? Would Sita think Beth was boring if she talked about guys?

"Why the long face today, Bethster?" Kevin asked. He adjusted the pillow around his waist that he wore to give him the feeling of being Sir Toby. "Viola shouldn't be moody."

"I'm mooning over Duke Orsino," Beth said. She turned to Arnie, who was tying his shoelace. "Oh, Duke, my Duke, why can't you see that I am a woman?"

"Because you're such a good actor," Arnie said. "And maybe Orsino needs glasses." He straightened up and peered around the auditorium as if he couldn't see what was in front of him. "Who's the girl around here?" He stared at Kevin. "Is it you?"

"Yes," Kevin squeaked in a high voice. "Sir Toby is really a woman in disguise."

"It would be fun to have an all-girl performance of *Twelfth Night*," Amelia said, walking up to them. "Or an all-male one, like in Shakespeare's day. I've heard there was an all-woman performance of *Julius Caesar* in New York. I'd love to have seen that."

"Me, too," Beth said. "Hi, Amelia."

"That's Olivia to you," Amelia said. Her voice didn't sound any different, but Beth was sure that Amelia knew that Beth knew.

Sita swaggered over and sang. "But when I came alas! to wive, With hey, ho, the wind and the rain, By swaggering I could never thrive, for the rain it raineth every day."

"Better that it raineth than it snoweth," Kevin said. "Fewer problems getting around."

"Pick up your scripts if you still need them, though you shouldn't need them by now," Ms. Capulet ordered. "Get on the stage, Feste and Viola. Let's go through your scene."

Beth climbed onto the stage. She didn't mind the scene with Sita, but the scene with Olivia would come all too soon. She was an actor. She could do this. And she could do it without blushing.

She also wondered whether there would be any more stage "accidents." She tried not to appear apprehensive. Don't look nervously around the stage, she told herself. Viola isn't worrying whether something might fall on her or the ground might give way under her feet.

Sita's eyes sparkled more than usual when she said, "Now Jove, in his next commodity of hair, send thee a beard!"

Beth enjoyed replying, "By my troth, I am almost sick for the want of one." And in an aside to the audience, said, "though I would not have it grow on my chin." Thank goodness Mercutio did not have a beard, she thought. She certainly didn't want one. Nor did she particularly want to kiss a man who had one.

All too soon, it was time for Olivia to appear.

Amelia poured out Olivia's growing passion. She was good at the part, Beth thought.

Beth enjoyed telling her, "You do think you are not what you are."

And hearing Amelia reply, "If I think so, I think the same of you."

Beth replied, "Then you think right. I am not what I am." Thank goodness that in Bethesda she could be who she was. It was tiring not being who she was. That is, it was nice to be an actor, but not so much fun to have to seem to be a man in a world where people believed it and might seek to fight with her. Men fought too much, she thought, not for the first time.

"I would you were as I would have you be," Amelia said.

Beth couldn't help wondering whether Amelia was jealous of her friendship with Sita. Would Amelia try to coax Sita to see less of Beth? Beth suppressed her thoughts. She should just live Viola while she was acting, not think about her own life. That was what her art demanded.

_*_

BETH RUSHED FROM CLASS to class, trying to ignore the dull ache in her chest. What upset her most? she wondered. Sita's caring more about another girl bothered her, but she felt sure that Sita was still a good friend. Something else pressed her spirits down. She decided to talk to her drama teacher.

She walked to the familiar messy office. It was good knowing she was welcome.

"Come in, Beth," Ms. Capulet said. "I'm looking at a book about earlier productions of *Twelfth Night*. Would you like to see it? There are some wonderful photos. Did you know that Laurence Olivier played Malvolio and Vivien Leigh played Viola in a 1955 production? In 1940, Helen Hayes played Viola." Ms. Capulet extended the book to Beth.

"That's great. Thanks." Beth glanced at the photos, but she couldn't keep the tears out of her eyes.

"Shakespeare doesn't like me," Beth said. Her voice broke. "He doesn't want to see me. I'm trying with all my strength to help him, but he can't stand the sight of me because I remind him of terrible things in his past." She couldn't tell her teacher that Shakespeare had killed Marlowe, because that was Shakespeare's secret that Beth must never tell.

"This is so hard for you." Ms. Capulet gave her a sympathetic look. "You are being taxed almost beyond your strength. But remember that loving great people from the past must always be a one-way love. They loved the world enough to create their works, but they can't love us individually."

"But Shakespeare does know me." Beth sniffed. "That's just the trouble."

"But he can't understand all that you are doing for him and his works. Of course that's hard." Ms. Capulet's tone was soothing, as if Beth were a child. "I wish it wasn't so hard. All I can say is to try not to think about how he reacts to you."

"But I need Shakespeare to communicate with Marlowe's ghost. He doesn't like the idea. He doesn't like the supernatural." Beth handed the book back to her teacher.

"That's understandable." Ms. Capulet paused. "Wouldn't it make more sense for you to try to summon Shakespeare's ghost and ask him to communicate with Marlowe's ghost?"

"You're right. Why didn't I think of that?" Beth dried her tears. "Thanks. I'll try." Seeing Shakespeare's ghost wouldn't be nearly as satisfying as seeing the living Shakespeare, but the ghost probably couldn't sadden her as much either.

Beth closed her eyes. That wasn't necessary for time traveling, but she was uncomfortable being watched while she disappeared for a minute or two. She usually did it alone. But when she came back from her travels, it might be good to have her teacher there.

Where would Shakespeare's ghost be? Beth wondered. The last time she had seen him, he had appeared in a mirror in Richard's great hall, but she didn't want to go back there.

She whirred through dark spaces and thudded onto a hard floor.

She sat on the stage at the Globe. The theater was empty. It was night, and she could see stars over the place where the groundlings stood during a production.

Shakespeare's ghost hovered on the stage in front of her.

She felt glad that he was in a more comfortable place than Marlowe's foggy station near the Thames. It was fitting that Shakespeare's ghost would live on a stage, though she had thought he might be in Stratford. The Globe had burned down before Shakespeare died, but apparently that didn't matter. This was a Globe in another world.

"Why did you summon me?" the ghost asked her. His voice was like the living Shakespeare's, but hollower.

Beth tried to keep her voice from shaking. Even the most benign ghost was so awesome—truly awesome—that she could hardly speak. "Do you remember when Richard III had Mercutio killed?"

The ghost sighed. "Ghosts do not forget. We forget nothing."

Beth shivered. She wasn't sure she wanted to forget nothing after she died.

"Richard III is trying to wreak havoc with your plays. He can't do it, but he has found a way to speak with Marlowe's ghost to persuade the ghost to do it."

"Marlowe!" The ghost cried. It was a piteous cry, a cross between a moan and a shriek. "His name cuts me like a sword. My own damned, blood-stained sword."

"I'm sorry I needed to mention him." Beth felt as if she had shrunk to leprechaun size. "But he believes that you tampered with his plays, so he wants to tamper with yours."

"Madness!" the ghost intoned. "Madness! I never touched his plays."

"I wonder whether there's a way you could tell him that," Beth ventured.

"Marlowe!" Shakespeare's ghost shrieked. "Talk to Marlowe! Torture! No!" He began to fade.

"I don't want to torture you, but please just think about it," Beth said before he vanished.

She spun away and opened her eyes. She saw the familiar poster of James Dean in her drama teacher's office.

"These travels are wearing me down," she said.

"I'm sorry." Ms. Capulet's brow furrowed. "Is there anything I can do?" She handed Beth an orange soda. "Perhaps the whole experiment was a mistake. I don't want you to be hurt. Is there any way to discontinue it?"

"It's too late now." Beth took a sip of soda. "I'd never forgive myself if anything happened that I could have prevented."

"I'll never forgive myself if I've scarred you." Ms. Capulet's face sagged. "And I'll never forgive myself if my students all wind up with years of tooth decay because I keep giving them soft drinks. I hope you brush your teeth frequently."

"Sure." Beth rolled her eyes. How mundane could you get? It was a good thing that she hadn't told her teacher that she was going to die as Mercutio.

She walked out of Ms. Capulet's office and saw Kevin standing in the hall.

"Hi, Beth." His grin was not as broad as it had been. "Isn't there anything I can do to help you?"

"Thanks, but I can't think of any . . ."

A scream came from Ms. Capulet's office.

Beth thrust open the door. The book on *Twelfth Night* performances had burst into flames, and the piles of papers on her teacher's desk were catching fire. Ms. Capulet was tearing the tabs off soft drink cans and pouring the drinks on the fire.

Kevin rushed into the room, tore off his leather jacket and beat the flames on a pile of papers. Beth hurried to knock papers and books that had not yet caught fire off the desk and away from the flames. Ms. Capulet splashed soda on Kevin's jacket to keep it from burning.

The school's fire alarm went off. The sound of students and teachers thudding down the halls to leave the building reached the room, but the three of them kept working. They extinguished the fire, but a pile of ashes sat on Ms. Capulet's desk.

"I wasn't looking for a muse of fire," the drama teacher said, quoting the chorus at the beginning of *Henry V.* "We should exit the building along with everyone else. I'll call the principal and tell her the fire has been put out."

She grabbed her cellphone and dialed while they proceeded to the corridor and marched out in an orderly fashion, joining the kids who were moving along nervously and saying, "Where's the fire?" "I can smell the smoke?"

Beth could hear Ms. Capulet mumbling into her phone and apologizing profusely.

"We can go back to my office," the teacher said.

Beth and Kevin turned around and followed her.

Once they were in the office, Kevin threw himself in a chair. "I didn't do anything. Did the fire happen because of me? Should I go off to a desert island or kill myself? I can't stand being used for all these attacks. Someone could get hurt."

"Be calm," Ms. Capulet told him. "You know perfectly well that you can't go to a desert island and shouldn't hurt yourself. Eventually Richard will stop using you. I just don't know when."

Kevin clenched his fists. "If I ever see him, I'll knock his . . . ."

"Stop posturing," the teacher said. "I hope you never do see him, and it would dangerous to attempt to hurt him. Just try to be calm, and do what you did just now. If you see that you can help put out a fire, do it."

"But there was nothing I could do once the light fell or when Frank plunged into a pit," Kevin objected.

Ms. Capulet opened her window. "Don't sit here in the smoke any longer. I'm not going to. Please be calm."

"It's tough, Kevin. But everything will work out," Beth said, because she thought she had to say something. But she wasn't at all sure that things would work out. She wasn't even certain that she trusted Kevin.

Arnie appeared in the doorway. His face sagged. "Hey, Connelly," he said. "Let's go to our next class together, okay?"

"At least you don't think I'm some kind of demon, do you?" Kevin demanded.

"No. But I'm assigned to be your guardian angel." Arnie grimaced.

"Just don't grow wings. I hate birds," Kevin said, hitting him on the shoulder.

Beth remembered turning the boys into birds to save them from Richard. Kevin evidently bore a grudge.

"Could we all go to the movies tonight? A Friday night out? The new movie *Teen Misery?*" Arnie asked. He looked at Beth while he spoke.

"Great! How about it, Beth?" Kevin brightened. "Let's ask Sita, too. And Frank."

"Why not ask the whole cast?" Arnie did not sound as if he wanted to ask everyone.

"Just those of us who know what's going on," Kevin said. "We could go out and brainstorm afterwards."

"I was thinking of relaxing for the evening," Arnie said.

Beth realized that Arnie meant no one would want to share thoughts with Kevin because they didn't know whether Richard was tapping into his mind. She felt torn. She didn't want Kevin to guess that what they were thinking, but she also was afraid that Arnie proposed keeping the group small because he wanted to have more time with her.

She could say that she had more work to do, but a break from time travel sounded like a relief.

"Sure, let's ask them," she said. She was curious about whether Sita would be busy. "You text them."

The incident with the burning book was too much smaller than the others, Beth thought. She was afraid that meant the next incident would be much more dramatic.

They went to their history classroom. Mr. Clarke lectured about Henry VIII. Beth knew a great deal about that king, but it was always interesting to hear about his many wives and his break with the Catholic Church.

"Was Henry a good king?" Mr. Clarke asked. "England experienced a period of prosperity, with no wars. Yet there was a religious schism that led to future wars. Did he make the right decision when he broke with Rome to ensure that he had a male successor to the throne, if that was his true reason?"

Beth contemplated writing a paper on that subject. She imagined the points for and against.

At the end of the class, the teacher said, "Now for the subject of your first papers. All the students on the right side of the classroom will write papers on *Richard III*. All those on the left side will write about *Henry V.* You may choose to write about the plays' historical accuracy or lack of it, or, if you wish, other aspects of the plays."

Beth sucked in her breath. She sat on the right side of the classroom. She would have to write about *Richard III*. A wave of nausea passed through her. She knew that once Mr. Clarke gave out an assignment, he was too rigid to change it. She wished she could write about Henry V, Henry VIII, or any other Henry, rather than Richard.

More time with Richard. Just what she needed.

Arnie gave her a look of sympathy.

Chapter 23

BETH MET ARNIE AND Kevin at the theater, a Megaplex that showed six movies at a time. There was a crowd of kids, but Arnie had purchased the tickets online.

"Sita and Frank were both busy," he announced.

"Too bad," Kevin said.

"Too bad," Beth echoed. She wondered whether Amelia would monopolize Sita's weekends.

They loaded up on popcorn and soft drinks and went into the theater. Kevin had hidden in his backpack a less expensive drink purchased elsewhere, and Beth wished she had done the same. Arnie sat between Beth and Kevin, giving Beth the aisle seat that they knew she preferred.

They saw Frank with an attractive African American girl whose name Beth didn't know. He waved to them.

The movie was about kids who didn't fit in because they were fat. It had some comic moments, but Beth sometimes felt tears come to her eyes. She wondered whether Frank got discriminated against for being heavy, or whether he had experienced so much racial discrimination that he felt the other kind was not as bad.

After the movie, Kevin went to the men's room. Beth was going to go to the women's room, but Arnie said, "Wait a minute, please?"

She stood with him just outside the women's room. There must be a line in there, but it didn't reach out to the hall.

"What would be the easiest way to kidnap Bottom?" Arnie asked. "Think about it."

"Oh." Bells rang in her mind. "Persuading him to play the part of a kidnap victim."

Arnie nodded. "So he's cooperating and doesn't understand what he's doing. But remember his desire to play all the roles."

"I'm following you." Beth groaned. "He'll have Stockholm Syndrome, or he'll pretend to. They'll tell him to play the part of one of the kidnappers. Good thinking. But we still don't know what play he's in."

"I've looked on the Internet," Arnie said. "The only plays with kidnapping that came up were *Cymbeline* and *Pericles*."

"Boring!" Beth shook her head. "I don't want to have to visit them. I don't believe he's in them. I think Richard might be trying to waste my time. Is taking Bottom just a red herring?"

"Is Kevin a red herring?" Arnie asked.

"Am I a what?" Kevin came up behind them. His voice was far from pleased.

"Sort it out among yourselves. I have to go to the women's room," Beth said, dodging into that room. There wasn't a line, so she went into a stall. Doubtless Richard was seeding their path with red herrings, if you could seed a herring, she thought. She imagined a field with red herring tails sticking out of the earth.

"Herrings fresh and dried!" someone shouted.

Beth stood on a street in old London. She was Ben again. Oh no, not a time travel while she was in the women's room. She willed herself back to the theater, but she was on the fishmongers' street, and the smells were much worse than those in the clean theater bathroom. Fish, fish, fish stank enough to make her puke.

"Herring, cod, pike!" cried one vendor with a tub of swimming fish. "See how fresh!"

"Oysters! Mussels!" called another. "Ready for your table!"

Beth put her hand in her pocket and found that she was supplied with a handkerchief. She put it to her nose and hurried to get off the street as soon as she could. She wished she had a pomander to cover the odors.

Someone behind her grabbed the ends of her handkerchief, pulled it tight over her mouth, and tied it. She struggled and kicked behind her, stepping on her attacker's foot, but one person grabbed her arms, another grabbed her legs, and someone else pulled a hood over her head.

They carried her away, still struggling. She hoped that one of the fishmongers or their customers might help her, but no one did.

Did her talk with Arnie about kidnapping cause the attack?

Someone threw her in a cart and covered her with a blanket. The cart moved along, and she felt every bump on the London street. The ride took forever.

She tried to will herself back in the movie theater, but the endless ride continued.

She silently called to Merlin, but nothing happened.

Did Richard have the power to bring her to London and have her kidnapped? Beth wondered. Or did she just happen to wind up on a London street when kidnappers were abroad? The bumping bruised her, and bruises from old London would show up on her in real life. She wished she didn't know that she could even be killed in London. Really killed, not like dying as Mercutio. She wished herself to be Mercutio in the world of one of Shakespeare's plays, any of them, but nothing happened.

The cart finally stopped. People picked her up and carried her, none too gently. They threw her down on a floor.

Someone pulled the hood off. She had landed in a gray stone room. Two men stood by her, one large and silent, but the other, a man with a salt-and-pepper beard, laughed at her.

"Ben, aren't you? I saw you in a tavern once. You wanted to act at the Globe, but Master Shakespeare would have none of you. You've got your wish, Ben. This is Blackfriars, and all our actors are boys. Aren't you grateful to us?"

He tore the handkerchief off her mouth.

"No!" She tried to shout, but her voice sounded more like a squeak. "You kidnapped me."

"'You kidnapped me.'" The man, who was ruddy and rangy, mocked her words. "All of our boys are kidnapped. Queen Elizabeth signed a decree letting us kidnap boys to act in our company. She's dead, but the decree still stands."

Beth gasped. "That can't be true!"

"Tell him, Henry," the other man said.

"It's true," said a pale boy of about thirteen who stood in the corner. "They kidnapped me, too. I've heard that my father has been suing to try to get me released, but the courts haven't heard his plea yet."

The thin, bearded man laughed nastily. "They'll never hear it. Forget about your father."

Uh-oh. Beth remembered reading something about the practice of kidnapping boy actors, and how angry Shakespeare was that audiences preferred seeing boys act instead of his trained, and mostly adult, actors. Hamlet complained about it in his scene with the players. And Blackfriars, where she was being held, was a former monastery, now a theater.

The thin man thrust a script at her. "You have to perform tonight, Ben. You'll play the part of Lady Mary. Now's your chance. If you do well, you'll get good rations. If not, there's a beating in store for you. Learn your lines."

She took the script. The men left the room and shut the door behind them.

She saw that the script, like most actors' scripts of the time, had only her lines and her cues.

She stared at Henry. "How long have they held you?" she asked.

"Five months." He choked on the words. "I'm longing to go home." His voice hadn't matured yet. "You look old to be able to play girls' parts."

"I'm just lucky, I guess," Beth said.

Please, let me go back to the movie theater, she thought. Merlin, can you see me? I haven't asked for your help in a while, but can you help me now?

Nothing happened.

Bottom might have been willing to play a kidnap victim, but she was not willing to be one, Beth thought.

She read the script. It was hard to tell from just one person's lines, but she thought it was much inferior to Shakespeare's work. No surprise there.

"Do you have a father who could sue to try to get you back?" Henry asked. "Because my father is trying, they don't sell me the way they sell some of the other boy actors."

"Sell them?" Beth's stomach turned.

"Like whores," the boy said. "I hope they never do that to me. Or to you. You're handsome, so they might."

Beth gagged. Get me out of here! She called silently.

"Better learn your lines, though. We'll be on stage together tonight," Henry said. "I could help you, if you aren't used to acting."

"Thank you." Beth said. She tried to keep back tears at the thought of Henry's longing for his father and his father trying to get him back. Renaissance English law was worse than she had imagined.

"Please, let's practice now," Henry said. There was a tremor in his voice.

He read.

CUE: from PATIENCE, LADY MARY'S DAUGHTER: Will they kill us, as they have slaughtered so many others?

Beth's line was:

LADY MARY: Yes, my child, the evil, witch-guided priests will murder us as they have so many others.

"I can't read that line," Beth exclaimed. "This is anti-Catholic propaganda."

"You're a papist!" Henry cried, pulling away from her.

"I'm not a Catholic, but I believe in religious freedom. Both sides are guilty of persecution."

"You're a freethinker!" The boy backed into a corner. "Never speak that way again, please!"

Beth groaned. She desperately had to go to the bathroom. She eyed the smelly chamber pot in the corner. She concentrated hard on the bathroom at the theater.

She was in the clean stall. She did what she needed to do.

When she left the stall, tears were streaming down her eyes.

"Beth, are you all right?" Kevin yelled from the other side of the bathroom door.

"Yes," she called back while she washed her hands. Evidently she had been in the bathroom a long time. She used a paper towel on her eyes, but it didn't do much good. She fled into the hall and almost ran into Kevin and Arnie. She didn't see anyone else near them.

Her words came choking out. "I was in London. I was kidnapped. Did you know that the Blackfriars company kidnapped boys to be their actors and held them against their will? It's terrible."

"Bastards!" Kevin clenched his fists.

Arnie put his hand on her arm. "That is awful. You can't keep going to London alone. It's too dangerous. Let's go get milkshakes and calm down."

"Okay." Ordinarily she would have protested at the idea that she shouldn't go to London alone, but that advice sounded better to her now.

"Take care of yourself, please." Arnie put his whole arm around her. Fortunately, Beth had to put on her coat, so she could squirm away from his arm without offending him.

Arnie held back for a minute while Kevin strode on ahead of them. "Keep drinking lots of orange juice," he whispered. "I've kept it up, and I think it's changing me. Maybe someday I'll have magical powers, too."

Beth shuddered. "Don't wish for them," she said.

When Beth returned home that night, she said good-night to her mother, then went to her room and sat on the bed. She wished for Merlin to come.

The wizard appeared through the window, though it was closed because the weather was so cold. He wore a late eighteenth century gentleman's garb with a powdered wig.

"It has been a while since you have called me," he said. "I suppose you have found yourself in a situation that you can't handle alone."

"Didn't you hear me calling you from London?" Beth asked. Her voice was shrill.

"No. I am not always listening. Do you think I am always tuned to you like a radio?" He frowned. "I can do that only when you time travel with my assistance and I know what you are doing."

"I didn't time travel willingly." Beth shook. "I was pulled into it somehow."

"That is serious." Merlin's voice sank. "I am not sure what force pulled you to London. I must advise you to stay away from there now if you can."

"I thought you might be able to reach Adam and ensure that he meets me when I go there," Beth said.

"Perhaps, if you let me know when you are going."

Beth's heart sank at the word "perhaps." "Just perhaps? Not definitely?"

"I think you should confine yourself to being Mercutio in the world of the plays for the time being," Merlin told her.

"If I can do that, I will." Beth longed for sleep. She wanted to be in a world where she couldn't be killed. At least not as her real self. She shut her eyes.

"You're closing your eyes and slumping over. No doubt that is supposed to indicate that all you want now is mortal sleep. Have you no stamina?" Merlin said accusingly.

"This mortal flesh is weary," Beth said.

"Go knit up your raveled sleeves of care." After this sarcasm, Merlin vanished.

Beth pulled the covers around her and hoped to dream no more, at least that night.

But instead of falling asleep, she fell into a wind that blew her into a fog. She hoped this wasn't the land of the dead. She landed in a bunch of gorse and scratched her knee. The heath. She hadn't seen the witches in a while. Perhaps they could help her.

"Hail, Mercutio!" intoned three familiar voices.

Beth had almost become used to their appearance. Almost. Maybe it was normal to be eerie. The smell of their cauldron was another matter. Holding her nose would do no good because the stench was so bad that it invaded her mouth too. Even her ears felt as if they had been bathed in the noisome potion.

"I was kidnapped in London. Strange things keep happening in my high school. I'm afraid," she said.

"Afraid!" A chorus of laughter followed.

"Afraid! Now she's afraid!" They laughed again.

"She has agreed to be killed as Mercutio, and now she is afraid!" the first witch muttered.

"How can I fight Richard?" Beth asked. "It seems impossible."

"Women bring peace," the first witch said.

"Some women." The second witch laughed.

Not Lady Macbeth, Beth thought. Though the Lady seemed helpful now, peaceful wasn't a word Beth would use to describe her.

"Ghosts to ghosts," the third witches screeched.

"Who knows the answers?" the first witch chanted.

"Who knows the questions?" the second witch chanted.

"Everyone must die someday," the third witch said.

That seemed obvious. "Can't you explain?" Beth asked, though she knew they wouldn't.

"Two minus one is one," the first witch sang.

"Which two are you talking about?" Beth asked.

"Double the boar, or uncouple it?" the second witch sang.

Then the witches laughed and disappeared.

Beth stood alone on the heath. An owl hooted. Two minus one is one. Were they saying that Richard minus Mordred would be less formidable? Could they be separated? If only. Beth went home and to bed.

Chapter 24

WHEN BETH WOKE IN the morning, the sun shone into her bedroom but she could barely prod her eyes open. She staggered out of bed and down the stairs.

She called up Sita. "Hi." Beth's voice was unsteady. "Would you like to come over tonight for a sleepover? I'm sorry for the last-minute invitation."

"No problem. I'll ask my mother, but I'm sure I can come."

Beth was only a little nervous. At least Amelia didn't monopolize Sita's weekend time.

Beth fumbled her way into the kitchen, where her mother was drinking coffee.

"I've asked Sita for a sleepover tonight. I hope that's all right."

Beth's mother beamed. "I'm so glad that you're seeing your friends. Sita is such a nice girl," she said.

The phone rang.

Beth hurried to the living room. She was so tired of not being able to use her smartphone. She didn't want her mother to hear what she was saying. She hoped this call wasn't from Sita, saying she couldn't come over after all.

"Hello." Beth knew her voice sounded feeble.

"Hello, Beth," a man's voice said. "This is Adam. Our mutual friend talked to me. I need to tell you that I can't come to London with you anymore."

Beth gasped. "Why not? Where are you now?"

"New York. I was turned down for a part. I want to live in Old London, at least part of the time. If I have to choose, that's where I always want to live. I'm allowed to act in Shakespeare's company. What more could I want? So I can't risk getting in trouble with the people who live there by doing things like getting you out of that last place where you were. I'm sorry, but that's how it is. I hope you understand."

"I understand," Beth said, because she had to. She set down the phone. She knew that Adam cared more about his acting than anything else. But she felt abandoned anyway. Old London was far from perfect, but she didn't like being banished from there. And if Adam was going to spend his time there, she might not see him again. She sighed. Now she understood was why Shakespeare thought exile was such a painful punishment.

SITA CAME OVER THAT evening and acted the same as ever. They ordered pizza and chatted with Beth's mother a little while. The pizza tasted better when Sita was there. Then the girls went up to Beth's room.

"Thanks for asking me over," Sita said, plopping down onto a cushion on the floor.

"I'm glad you still have some Saturday nights free." Beth sat on a cushion next to her. "And doing things you normally do will help keep your parents from guessing before you're ready to tell them."

"That's thoughtful. Thanks." Sita smiled.

"I also wanted to ask again whether you can tell me more about why you're time traveling. Is anyone helping you, or talking to you?"

"Talking." Sita kept up her guard.

"Renaissance London has become too dangerous for me. I think you'd better stay away, too." Beth shivered. "I was kidnapped last night by the Blackfriars players. Their young actors were coerced to play. I almost became one of them."

Sita whistled. "That is scary. Yes, you'd better stay away. I haven't been there in a while either."

"Do we have to have secrets from each other? I can't tell you other people's secrets, but I'm trying to tell you mine." Beth gave Sita an imploring look. "Who's the person who knows what you're doing? Not Merlin?"

Sita shook her head. "Ms. Capulet."

"She has the power to send you time traveling?" Beth almost fell off her cushion.

"No way. It's my own power. If it's coming from someone else, I don't know who. But I tell her what I'm doing." Sita grinned. "So don't worry. I'm reporting to a responsible adult."

"One who can't help you if you get in trouble," Beth pointed out.

"Says the girl who was kidnapped last night."

"Says the girl who knows it's dangerous," Beth said. "Have you told Amelia any of this?"

Sita choked with laughter. "Are you kidding? That would be a great way to start a romance. 'Honey, my friend Beth spends a lot of time in Renaissance London and in a world where Shakespeare's characters live. I'm trying my best to join her.' Would you tell that to a boy you wanted to date?"

Beth joined in Sita's laughter. "No. But you might tell her when you get closer."

"I might." Sita rubbed her chin. "After about three years, if I was certain that she could handle it and would never tell. Then again, I might not. We can't keep spreading the secret."

"Thanks." Beth smiled. She could trust Sita. And they shared a secret that Amelia didn't know. That reassured Beth.

They talked long into the night and slept a little, like most sleepovers. Beth thought Sita was just as glad as she was that things were back to normal, at least in this part of their lives.

"Would you like to try time traveling together?" Beth asked in the morning.

Sita grinned. "Would birds like to fly? I thought you'd never ask."

"We have to try to find Bottom."

"I knew you wanted me for my skill-set. Who else can sound like Titania?"

"Not fair. I've always wanted you to come. But Merlin forbade it."

"Where shall we go? What do you think is the best place to look for Bottom?"

"I've been thinking." Beth opened her computer to a full text of *Dream*. "He wants to be a dramatic actor. So I think he's hidden in one of the best dramas. Are you sure you've searched *Hamlet* completely?"

"I didn't hear him. Maybe we should try *Macbeth*."

Beth shook her head. "Lady Macbeth is worried about his disappearance. She should know if he's in her area."

"Are you sure she'd know? Let's try it. I wouldn't mind seeing the queen again anyway."

"You already play her so well that you're scary," Beth said, but she thought it was only fair to let Sita visit Macbeth's Scotland even if they didn't have much chance of finding Bottom there. Sita had seen Lady Macbeth only once, in Richard's hall, the time that the Lady killed Richard.

Beth concentrated on *Macbeth*. She spun through gray clouds and howling winds. Ravens flew with her. She felt a wing brush her cheek.

She landed inside Macbeth's castle. She knew it by the smell. It smelled of old blood and sorrow. The dampness on the castle walls felt like tears. It was night, but few torches shone on the walls.

Sita stood beside her, turning her head this way and that. "Look," she whispered, pointing in the distance.

Beth peered through the dark hallway and saw Lady Macbeth, wringing her hands. Beth heard a faint moan. "Out, out damned spot."

"We came at a bad time," Beth whispered. "I don't think the queen would want us to see her like this. Let's leave."

"Let me call Bottom first." Sita let out her strange fairy call, "Bottom, come hither, come hither," which was so high-pitched that it almost hurt Beth's ears.

There was no response.

Beth concentrated on Denmark. Bottom might be there after all.

She spun away from the ravens through a cloud of seagulls. They landed inside Elsinore castle this time. Beth was glad because the castle was warmer than the promontory on which it stood. She heard music and laughter nearby.

"King Claudius must be holding a banquet," she said.

"Good," Sita replied. "I'm hungry."

"I don't think I want to eat at his table." Beth shivered.

"It's fine if you don't drink the wine." Sita grinned. "I don't really want to join the party. I'm just joking."

A pale young woman with long blonde hair and a tear-stained face stalked past them without noticing them.

"Ophelia isn't enjoying the feast either," Beth said. "Why don't you call Bottom now?"

Sita called, "Come hither, Bottom, come hither," again and again.

After a pause, Sita shook her head. "No response," she said. "But I hear voices outside."

"It's probably just the old king's ghost. But I guess we'd better find out who it is."

They slipped carefully to a window so they could see without being seen. The cold air hit them. "Maybe it wouldn't be so bad to go to Claudius's banquet after all," Beth whispered.

Beth saw Hamlet talking with King Lear. She recoiled. Lear meant danger, and she wasn't ready to die yet.

"Yes, a hawk is different from a handsaw," Lear said in a serious tone. The expression on his face was calmer than Beth had ever seen it. "The wind is blowing, but it is not so cruel as the wind in my land."

"Wind is an illusion of the air," Hamlet said. "The air is nothing. How can nothing move? We just imagine the wind."

"You haven't felt the wind and rain in my country." Lear sighed. His sighs were even deeper than Hamlet's. "It is cruel hard for any who venture in it. The wind must chill the poor people of Denmark, who have no shelter."

"Who is poor?" Hamlet asked. "Is a man poor if he lives in a wooden shack but he still has both parents, and they love him? I say he is not poor, but rich."

Lear shook his head. "You have never felt hunger."

"I hunger for justice," Hamlet said. "But am I blessed?"

"Blessed?" Lear asked.

"I forgot. You lived before my religion was founded. Pardon me," Hamlet said. "But even in your time, people knew about justice."

"Justice?" Lear's face reddened. "There is no justice."

"There may be, if you are willing to die for it," Hamlet said. Despite the cold, beads of sweat broke out on his face. "Is justice more important than life?"

"You were a good son." Lear patted Hamlet's shoulder. "Never regret that you gave your life to bring down your father's murderer."

"And you should be grateful that you finally recognized which of your daughters loved you and that you reconciled with her," Hamlet said.

"Grateful?" Lear shouted in a deafening voice. "Grateful that my Cordelia was killed? Never!" He drew his sword and waved it around.

"I will do all in my power to bring her back, and I'll kill anyone who stands in my way!"

Beth shivered. Sita put her hand on Beth's arm.

"Your play is noble, and it reminds many children to love their parents and parents to love their children," Hamlet told him. "No other love is more important than those loves."

"Where is your rage?" Lear shouted. "Have you lost your rage? Rage against Shakespeare, who forced you to die for avenging your father's death."

"I was ready to die," Hamlet protested. "I am a martyr. I had no other claim to sainthood, so martyrdom is good."

"Fool!" Lear yelled. "Only life is good. Martyrdom is dust, bones and dust."

"Everything must come to dust," Hamlet retorted.

"Not the young! Not the young and good!" Lear jumped up and paced across the castle terrace. "Shakespeare killed Cordelia, and I must save her!"

"No one can be saved, only avenged," Hamlet said. "The evil characters in your play died, so Cordelia was avenged."

"No! She was not!" Lear screamed.

His scream was so loud that Beth tumbled from the window onto the balcony.

"Mercutio!" Lear yelled. "The prattling Veronan who is keeping me from saving Cordelia!" He drew his huge sword.

"You should listen to Hamlet, noble king," Beth stammered, trying to stand.

"Enough blood has been spilled," Hamlet said, trying to hold Lear's arm.

Sita leapt in front of Beth. She stared into Lear's blood-red eyes. "You would not kill a woman, would you?"

Lear paused, sword in the air. "Only my worthless daughters Regan and Goneril," he said.

"Let's go!" Sita demanded.

Beth still hadn't gotten to her feet, but she wished to be back in her room.

They spun through Denmark's chill to Bethesda's. Snow was falling outside Beth's home.

Beth sat on one cushion and saw that Sita was still on the other one.

"I'm supposed to die as Mercutio," Beth said. "But I'm afraid to. I'm not doing my job."

"You're not dying in front of me!" Sita grabbed her hand. "I hate the idea of you dying. Who knows what it would do to your mind?"

"Is that why you're coming to the world of the plays with me?" Beth asked.

"Of course, I care more about you than about Bottom," Sita said.

"I'm glad." Beth relaxed. Tension flowed out of her body. People cared about her.

"Are you very much in love with Amelia?" Beth asked.

"Yes." Sita rolled over on her cushion. "I'm so happy."

"Congratulations." Beth could almost say that sincerely because she felt their friendship was secure. She wondered when she would fall in love. With someone other than Mercutio, that is.

Beth's mother's voice came through the door. "Are you up, girls? Would you like some French toast?"

"Thank you, Professor Owens," Sita said. "We'll help you make it."

Beth realized that if she was going to die in the other world, she'd have to go there alone. She didn't want Sita to have to see her die. Or get attacked for trying to prevent it.

Chapter 25

AFTER SITA HAD LEFT, Beth contemplated writing her paper. What would be the least painful way of writing about Richard? Her head began to hurt and she took some aspirin. She thought she was taking too many. Maybe if she got cut she would bleed to death.

She knew so much about Richard that she couldn't tell. There was no way she could write that Shakespeare had based Richard on Mordred. Should she write about how different Shakespeare's Richard was from the real Richard? She could find papers from the Richard III Society and analyze them. Not plagiarize them. Or should she compare Richard with Macbeth or some other villain? Should she try a psychological approach and say that Richard was weak? Would that lessen his power over her?

The aspirin didn't work. Her head ached so much that she wanted to close her eyes, but she was afraid that if she did she would see Richard.

She could write about one of the other characters in the play! She jumped up and danced around the room. She could write about Queen

Margaret's history and Shakespeare's use of her in the play. Margaret of Anjou had ruled England when her husband, King Henry VI, went mad (or so it was said). She had led the Lancastrian armies against the Yorkists. Richard's older brother, Edward, defeated Margaret, and she was gone from England before Richard became king. When Margaret was queen, she had founded Queen's College, Cambridge. No doubt she had disliked all the House of York, but her raving at Richard was one of Shakespeare's inventions.

Beth smiled. She could say how clever it was to introduce Margaret into the play.

She spun out of control and landed in Richard's hall. Incense made her choke and the mirrors nearly blinded her.

"Do you think you can escape me by writing about Queen Margaret?" Richard scoffed at her. "What a pathetic dodge."

Beth reeled. Richard was intruding in her brain more than ever.

"What did you do to me?" she yelled at him. "You don't have the technology to put electrodes in my brain. How can you see what I'm thinking? Get out of my head right now!"

Richard laughed at her, and continued laughing like a hyena. "I shouldn't admit this, my dear Beth, but I can only do that occasionally, and only when you are thinking about me. I congratulate myself that I could do it this time." He smirked. "I am sure that you must think of me more often than I am able to see into your brain. You are much too open. Write about the formidable Margaret all you like. Indulge yourself with thoughts of women in history who had some power. But don't imagine that you can erase me from your mind so easily."

"Good-bye. I refuse to listen to you." Beth whirled back to her room.

She dug her nails into her hands. She would do anything to get him out of her mind, Beth thought. She wondered whether Richard had been able to influence Mr. Clarke's choice of assignment, but she doubted that. Could she be going mad? No, she thought, I'm not mad. I'm angry.

She tried to concentrate on Margaret of Anjou. She liked Margaret because that queen had the chance to call Richard a devil. Beth's computer screen froze a few times, but she just rebooted and refused to believe that Richard had anything to do with her computer problems.

ON MONDAY MORNING, BETH decided to time travel again. Now traveling felt more like a duty than a pleasure. She went to school early and entered the empty drama classroom. She gazed at the poster of Shakespeare.

She spun past columns and felt the warmth of a new day. That is, a very old day. She had landed in Ancient Rome. For some reason that she could not fathom, instead of being Mercutio she was now a boy whom no one would notice. She wore a shining white toga with a purple stripe. She hoped she could keep it clean. There were sandals on her feet. The sandals were more comfortable than the boots she had worn in other plays. The sun beat down on her, and she wished she could stay in Italy for a while. She stood on a street from which she could see hills covered with the pines of Rome.

What would she call herself in Rome, if she was there long enough to be asked her name? Lucius might be a safe choice.

Julius Caesar stood on the summit of the nearest hill.

Beth looked for a path and scrambled up the hill to see him. Running in sandals was an art she had not yet learned. Pebbles scraped her feet. The scent of pines invigorated her. As she neared the top of the hill, she could see that only a few guards had accompanied Caesar, and they stood some distance away from him, though they watched his every move.

Someone walked ahead of her—a massive man trod steadily. She recognized him.

He came in view of Caesar. "Hail, Caesar," he said, saluting him.

"Hail, Othello," Caesar replied. His voice was calm, even stoic, and so was his face. "Caesar knew that you were seeking him, so he has let you find him alone, not amidst the crowds of Romans who follow him. Caesar has ordered his guards to witness what happens, but not to intervene. Here is Caesar. Caesar opposes changing the endings of the plays." He extended both arms, displaying his weaponless hands but not offering them for touching.

"Mighty Caesar," Othello said, his voice just as dignified and stoic as Caesar's, "I have come to challenge you because I must. If you stand with those who block me from saving my wife from my misguided wrath, I must fight you. I am not a man who would stab you in the back."

"You must stab Caesar in the chest, then." Caesar's voice was cool as ever. "Caesar is prepared this time."

"I cannot do that unless you fight!" Othello exclaimed. "I have murdered once, and can never bear to murder again."

"Caesar will not fight you, noble Moor," Caesar said. "Caesar bears you no ill will. But Caesar stands against softening the plays. We cannot change our destiny. If you demand to change the endings, you must do it over Caesar's dead body."

"No!" Othello groaned. "I cannot! God witness my agony! I cannot kill this brave man. Caesar, you are an excellent general. I am a general, too. You must fight me."

"Caesar is a great general, and more than a general," Caesar said. "This is Caesar's strategy. You cannot kill Caesar unless you murder him."

"Oh, most unhappy day!" Othello moaned. "I have no fear. I would face you in combat, and you might kill me. But I cannot act like the ignoble Cassius and stab you when you are unarmed. Yet perhaps I should give up my honor for Desdemona's sake." He raised his sword, but he remained standing at a distance from Caesar.

A woman with flowing brown hair and light olive skin swept into the clearing.

"No!" she cried, flinging herself on Othello. "No, my beloved husband. Do not kill a noble man in my name." She clung to him.

Tears formed in Othello's eyes. "My beloved! I have wronged you so terribly. I must do anything I can to change the ending of our play. I cannot bear what I have done to you."

Desdemona stood straighter and looked him in the eye. "You are strong and brave. Be even stronger and braver, my love, and bear what you have done. I accept our ending, and so must you. Remember the days of our love without grief. I love you too much to let you lower yourself to fight on the side of evil men."

Othello embraced her. "It must be as you say. I cannot kill Caesar and I must live with what I have done. Your forgiveness overwhelms me." He turned to Caesar. "Hail and farewell, Caesar," he said. Othello and Desdemona walked away. Beth scurried out of the path to let them pass. Desdemona's endless love sickened Beth.

A faint smile crept over Caesar's stern countenance.

Beth wondered whether he smiled because he believed that he had outwitted Othello, or because Calpurnia's pleas could never have changed a decision of Caesar's.

The answer didn't matter. One of her problems was solved. Othello had left Richard. Beth hoped that others would also.

"Beth!" someone called. Suddenly recalled to the classroom, Beth looked around her.

Ms. Capulet stood just inside the doorway. Her face was pale as a marble statue. Her eyes welled as if she were going to cry. "I've heard that Merlin has planned for you to die as Mercutio in Shakespeare's world. You mustn't do that! I'd never have agreed for you to time travel if I had any idea that Merlin would be so careless with your life."

Beth had never seen her teacher so emotional. "Who told you about that? Sita?"

"Yes, she finally told me. I can't believe you'd try to do that."

"I know what I'm doing. I have to do it to bring Mercutio back to life."

Ms. Capulet took a step closer to Beth. "You don't have to do it! You mustn't do it. I won't let you do it."

Beth scowled. "What can you do to stop me? Give me an 'F' in drama class?"

Ms. Capulet gasped. "I've never heard you talk like that. Please consider how much anguish you would go through. The experience could scar you for life. You already are hurt. I can see it in your eyes."

Ms. Capulet reached out her hand, but Beth backed away from her.

"Mercutio is my friend. I'm going to do it."

Beth walked out of the classroom. She was afraid enough without listening to anyone else's fears for her.

"Beth!" Ms. Capulet called, but Beth kept walking and didn't answer her.

Chapter 26

ETH WOKE UP THE next morning ready to do more than go to school. She couldn't travel to London. But she could still time travel for a few minutes before breakfast. She wanted to do something, not just wait for things to happen.

She spun through rain, but the rain wasn't water. It was raining blood. Not a good sign, Beth thought.

She landed in King Richard's courtyard, with its fountain that spurted red water just for effect. She hoped that was all the rain had been.

She was Mercutio, looking at the guards in boar-emblem uniforms. They nodded to her. It seemed that they hadn't been told to regard her as an enemy, even though she had once been held in Richard's dungeon as a ruse to confuse Beth. But Beth as Mercutio was an enemy. She felt an urge to run into Richard's hall and attack him, but she knew that would only get her killed. She was supposed to die as Mercutio, but she wasn't suicidal. She wanted a little more time. Just to find Bottom, of course. Not because she wanted to live.

She headed out of the courtyard and through the wall to the orchards and town outside Richard's castle. The wattle houses looked in good shape. People, pigs, and cows walked through the streets. Carts carried barrels towards the castle. Women scolded children for running through the mud.

Beth had a memory that must have been Mercutio's, of being a child tripping a woman carrying a cheese so that she fell in the mud. Then he had given her the money to buy a new cheese.

"You again!" A harsh voice assaulted her. "Haven't I killed you enough times already?"

It was Tybalt, Juliet's hot-blooded cousin who had killed Mercutio in the play and had killed him again, in Richard's hall, in front of Beth. But then Romeo had run into the hall and slain Tybalt again.

How dare Tybalt be alive while Mercutio was still dead! Rage heated Beth's whole body.

"The outcome will be different this time, Prince of Cats," she snarled, drawing her sword. "Last time you slew me from behind, Prince of Cowards."

Tybalt sneered. "I can kill you any way I want."

Beth felt her blood sing with anger. As she rushed at him, she hated the very smell of Tybalt. He was perfumed, but it was a stale perfume. He had killed Mercutio. She didn't care about swordsmanship. She bent low and ran as if she were playing football. His sword grazed her shoulder. She rammed hers into his groin. He yowled, and fell backwards, hands grabbing his bloody crotch. She pulled out her sword and thrust it into his neck.

He was dead. Tybalt was finally dead.

She pulled out her sword and looked at the bloody wreck of a body. The smell of blood filled the air and choked her.

She vomited. She, Beth Owens, had killed someone. She was Mercutio, but she had killed Tybalt partly as Beth, not just as Mercutio. She was a killer. Her head spun. She wanted to die.

People crowded around.

"That was no fair fight," a working man cried.

"Stay away from the brute," a young woman said, pulling back her little boy, who tried to get nearer to see the body.

I am the brute, Beth thought.

Tybalt's body disappeared. But she still gagged. She wished herself home.

She landed on her bed and began to sob. She had killed a man. She was a killer. Yes, he had only been a character, but it was still a killing.

Her mother knocked on her door.

"What's the matter, honey? May I come in?"

Beth said nothing. But her mother opened the door.

"What is it?" Her mother walked over and put her hand on Beth's shoulder.

Beth tried to stop crying, but she still choked out little sobs. She couldn't tell her mother what she had done. That would sound insane.

"Is it still grief over that boy who died? Don't you think you need to see a grief counselor?"

"No." Beth wiped her eyes with her pajama sleeve. "I had a terrible nightmare. I dreamed that I killed someone. I hadn't thought I could ever do that, even in a dream."

"You aren't to blame for your dreams." Her mother patted her. "It sounds awful, but we don't know what dreams mean, Freud notwithstanding. Everything is all right. You wouldn't really kill anyone."

Beth sniffled. "Thanks, Mom," she choked out.

"There's time for me to make you pancakes before school. Would you like that?"

Beth nodded. "That would be great, thank you."

"I'll do that right now. Don't worry. Don't let the dream ruin your day." Her mother left.

Beth held her head. I don't deserve such a nice mother, she thought. She doesn't know that I really am a killer. And a brutal one. I can't let myself keep on acting like a nobleman who lived in an age where swords solved things.

No, she thought. I can't use that as an excuse. Mercutio didn't do this killing. I did. I killed a man.

Beth went to the bathroom. She scrubbed her hands.

She got dressed. The smell of pancakes wafted up from the kitchen. She had to go downstairs and smile. Her mother would never know what Beth was capable of doing.

Chapter 27

BETH CUT THROUGH THE high school parking lot on her way to her first class. She longed for play practice. She wanted to be another character. Not herself. And not Mercutio. Just a simple character in a play that was really a play, not another world. Just the world of the stage. She didn't deserve to have such a good life. She was a killer. Maybe she deserved to die.

She heard the screech of brakes. A guy yelled. She saw that an old VW had come within inches of her. She jumped back.

"Beth! Are you okay?" Frank leapt out of the driver's seat. "Did I hurt you?" His face looked the way she felt when she remembered killing Tybalt.

He put his arm on her shoulder.

"No, I'm all right. Your car didn't touch me. You stopped in time," she reassured him. "Don't worry." She remembered that Frank was the only guy she knew who was old enough to drive.

"Thank goodness." Frank exhaled. "I don't know what happened." His tone was a cross between astonishment and apology. "All of a sudden, I couldn't control the car. It seemed to move straight towards you, and the brakes wouldn't work until the last second."

"That is strange." Beth looked at the car and saw Kevin getting out of the passenger's seat. His face was even more distraught than Frank's. Kevin looked as he might if she had actually been hit.

"Beth!" Kevin almost wailed. "I hope this wasn't my fault."

Frank looked at him coldly. "Oh, really? I hope it wasn't too. We need to talk about this, but I've got to get my car parked. You stay out here, Connelly. I'll bring you your books."

Kevin paled. He held his stomach. "Beth," he gasped again.

"Let's get out of the parking lot," Beth said. Her head spun. Was even being near Kevin dangerous for her? A guy she had known since first grade? Did he cause Frank's car to swerve? Kevin must be responsible. She couldn't imagine that Frank would want to kill her or that Frank would be dumb enough to let Richard use him. Not after he had seen how Kevin had been used.

"You're shaking," she said, as they walked towards the side of the next building, which was the auditorium.

"You are too," Kevin said. "Frank's a good driver. He wasn't pulling the car over. He didn't turn the wheel. This has to be my fault. It's horrible. I'm ready for an exorcist."

"It's okay. Don't blame yourself," she said, wondering whether she meant it.

Frank charged over to them. "This is too much." He glared at Kevin. "You're never riding in my car again. I don't want to kill my friends because you're sitting beside me."

Kevin put his hands over his eyes. "I didn't mean to do it."

"Yeah, the devil made you do it." Frank shook with anger. "I don't care why you did it."

Other kids were staring at them.

"We're making a scene," Beth told her friends. "Why don't we go to Ms. Capulet's office to talk?"

She wasn't eager to see Ms. Capulet after their last discussion, but who else could deal with Kevin? Ms. Capulet didn't know what Beth had just done in the other world. She was a killer there, and she thought she might deserve to die there. But she didn't want to die at home, too.

They marched to the drama teacher's office. Other students still turned to stare at them, so there must be something odd about their grim faces.

Beth didn't know whether she felt sorry for Kevin or just angry. She was glad for him that he hadn't killed her, even by accident. She didn't want him to feel the misery she felt at having killed. But her killing Tybalt was no accident.

They knocked on Ms. Capulet's door, and she told them to come in. Frank entered last and slammed the door.

"I've had it!" He was shaking with anger. "Connelly has to be shut up or something. I drove him to school this morning. In the parking lot, my car swerved out of my control and almost hit Beth. I'm not going to kill a friend and go to prison for manslaughter because Kevin has this little problem of making a deal with a centuries-old homicidal maniac."

Kevin's face reddened. "I'm sorry," he stammered.

"Beth!" Ms. Capulet grabbed Beth's hand, as if to reassure herself that Beth was alive. "I'm sorry I started this whole business of encountering Merlin and time traveling. I had no idea it could lead to this. We can't jeopardize your life."

"I don't much want to die in any world, but I sure don't want to die in this one." Beth shook.

"I should just go kill myself." Kevin's voice broke.

"Stop it," the drama teacher told him. "Don't make everyone feel guilty for being angry at you. Of course you shouldn't kill yourself. If you keep saying that, I have to send you to a counselor. I don't know what to do. I don't think canceling the play would do any good, especially since this accident happened outside the theater."

"You could throw Kevin out of the cast," Frank said. "We don't even know whether he's partly willing these things to happen."

"I'm not!" Kevin's voice was shrill. "But I'll leave the play if that would do any good."

"No, that's not the solution." Beth was surprised at how firm her voice sounded. "As Ms. Capulet said, this accident happened outside the theater. Were you feeling anything out of the ordinary before it happened?"

"A little giddy," Kevin said. "What should I have done? Asked Frank to let me out of the car because I felt dizzy?"

"Apparently that is what you needed to do," the teacher said. "Whenever you feel that way, stop whatever you are doing and tell one of us about your feeling. Perhaps that can prevent another accident."

"Do you want to take that chance?" Frank asked Beth.

"I do," Beth said. "It's my life."

"We don't even know that it's just your life," Frank reminded her. "I was cast into a pit. And I'm the one who might have gone to prison if anything had happened to you."

"I know how terrible you would have felt," Beth said, remembering how she felt about killing Tybalt, though it had been done of her own will and she had faced no consequences. "But I promise that I'll do everything I can in Shakespeare's world to stop Richard. All any of us can do is do our best." She tried to smile at Kevin. "I believe that Kevin will try, too."

"I will. Thanks for giving me another chance, Beth." Kevin didn't look any of them in the eye.

Beth knew the misery would spread. Arnie would blame himself for not spending every minute keeping an eye on Kevin. Sita would be angry. She would probably bawl Beth out for not watching what was happening around her every minute.

Beth realized that she looked forward to that bawling out. She loved her friends. She wanted to stay in her world. The bloom had definitely worn off time traveling.

She went to the girls' room and scrubbed her hands.

Chapter 28

BETH RAGED MORE THAN ever at Richard's interference with her life. That evening she did her homework because she was afraid that she would be too tired to do it after time traveling. When she had finished her last assignment, she thought of the place she needed to be. The last place she wanted to be. Richard's great hall. She willed herself not to appear as Mercutio, not because she might kill Richard but because she might hurt some innocent bystander.

She spun through incense and choked on it. When she landed in his great hall, she coughed. She appeared in Ben's clothes.

"Have you caught a cold, dear Beth?" Richard asked with mock tenderness. "You should wear warm clothes in the winter."

She sneezed. "I don't have a cold. Your ridiculous incense is making me sneeze." She strode closer to his throne than usual. "Stop tormenting Kevin," she demanded. "He doesn't want you to use him. Stop it."

Richard arched his eyebrows. "You refused to help me, so I am using your weaker friend. That is your fault."

"He can't do anything for you but upset me," she said.

"That is the point, of course." Richard sipped from his golden goblet. "What is your breaking point? I have long known that hurting your friends is the best way to break you."

Beth felt her blood surge. "I'm not breaking; I'm angry."

"I'm touched. If the only thing you can do is come here and rail at me, you are powerless." He smiled as if her anger delighted him.

Beth thought how he resembled a hyena. How had she ever compared him to a wolf?

"I will give you a boon," Richard said, in his tone that was supposed to indicate magnanimity. "I will show you where that idiot Bottom is."

Richard gestured towards one of his mirrors.

Beth stared at it, and she saw Bottom alone on a stage. He was dressed in clothes like those she had seen Hamlet wear.

"To be or not to be," Bottom boomed. "That is the question. But why am I asking this question? I am."

Bottom grabbed a long-haired blonde wig and put it on his head. He sang, falsetto, "Tomorrow is St. Valentine's Day, and in the morn betime, I'll be a maid at your window and be your Valentine." He picked up a bouquet of flowers and dropped them on the stage. He staggered around the stage as if he didn't know where he was. "I'm mad. Good people, do you see that I am mad? But do not worry. I am not really mad. The girl who I am playing kills herself, but I won't kill myself, I promise.

"But there are no good people," Bottom moaned, looking all around him. "There is no audience." He tore off the wig and threw it down. "I am all alone. Maybe I will go mad. Quince? Snug? Where are you? Where are my friends?" He kept looking around the stage. His voice became more and more distressed. "What good is it playing all the parts if I am alone? Where is the forest? Where is my home?"

"Free him!" Beth cried. "Don't leave him trapped alone on the stage."

"What will you give me for his release?" Richard asked. "He could be released at any time, if you would summon Shakespeare for me. If not, worse things could happen to your beloved clown. Far worse."

"Bottom! Hold on!" Beth called.

"He can't hear you, and he couldn't hear your Indian friend, either," Richard said with a smirk. "You can bring her here and see. He's on a soundproof stage, utterly isolated. Which is the worst punishment for an actor."

"Let me play the part of the queen," Bottom said. "Unsex me! I will be the cruelest queen who ever lived. I will order my husband to kill and kill again! Let me be the murderer! I will be a fearsome murderer. Tomorrow and tomorrow and tomorrow I will kill! But do not worry, good people. I am Bottom the weaver, and I will not kill anyone. Why is this blood on my hands? I did not kill anyone. Why won't it come off? I am afraid of blood." He washed his hands again and again. Tears formed in his eyes. "Where is the lady with wings and all her fairies?" The witches appeared before him. He shuddered and covered his face. "No, you are not fairies. You are not Moth. You are not Peaseblossom. Your cauldron is nasty. I can't wash my hands in it. Why are my hands blood-stained? I am a weaver, not a butcher. This isn't human blood, is it?"

Beth knew that all she could do was bring Sita. She wondered whether Sita could come if she wished for that. She concentrated on Sita.

Sita stood there before them.

"Ah, a voice from the East," Richard said in a mocking tone. "Apparently you have mystical powers. Swami Sita, are you?"

"Don't talk to my friend that way," Beth demanded.

"How touchy you are," Richard replied. He turned to Sita. "Bottom the weaver is trapped on a stage. Your good friend Beth believes that you have the power to release him. But you won't be able to do that this time. I have built a special soundproof stage that will keep him from hearing you."

"We'll see," Sita said. She called out to Bottom in Titania's voice. Beth thought Sita's call was haunting enough to wake the dead.

But Bottom continued to rush around the stage. "I'm so alone," he cried. "Is it nobler to endure the slings and arrows of outrageous fortune, or to take arms against a sea of troubles and by opposing end them? Quince? Where are you? Don't leave me here alone!"

Sita stopped calling. Her shoulders sagged.

"One girl with magical powers isn't enough to stop me," Richard proclaimed, "and neither are two."

"We know where Bottom is," Beth said. "We'll find a way to get him out."

Richard responded with mock applause.

"Go home, Sita," Beth said. She wanted to make sure that Sita got home.

Sita vanished.

"You won't leave your friend with me?" Richard laughed. "She would be perfectly safe, but your concern is touching. I fear that you will leave too."

"You kidnapped Bottom for the same reason that you killed Mercutio," Beth declared. "Yes, to try to crush me, but also because you hate comedy. You want to take the joy out of everything."

"How perceptive of you, dear Beth." Richard chortled. "Yes, I hate comedy."

A thought hit Beth. Merlin also hated comedy. He wouldn't bother to help save Bottom.

But why did Merlin hate comedy? Did he have an ancient fear of ridicule? And was Mordred the part of Richard who hated comedy? Merlin and Mordred both came from a legend of heroism in which comedy played little part. What else did Merlin and Mordred have in common? If Merlin hated and feared Mordred, did Mordred fear Merlin as well as hating him? Why couldn't Merlin defeat Mordred?

Without giving Richard the satisfaction of a reply, Beth spun through the mirrors. She tried to land in the one that trapped Bottom, but she only bumped against it.

She came out of her computer screen and landed in her computer chair. She wondered how she could release Bottom.

She went to the bathroom and washed her hands. Then she wiped the tears out of her eyes. She told herself that crying about being a killer wouldn't do her any good. She wondered what kind of person she was. Could she kill again? If she had killed a character, could she kill a living human being? She didn't want to know.

Chapter 29

THE NEXT MORNING WHEN Beth woke, she braced herself. She had to help Bottom.

Reluctantly, she thought of time traveling. She wasn't sure where she would go, but she thought of the Midsummer world.

She spun through a downpour and found herself, dressed as Ben, standing in a sodden clearing. Fairies danced in the rain. It was a brave attempt, but the expressions on their faces were far from happy. They were trying to sing, but the rain almost drowned out their voices.

King Oberon stood next to Queen Titania under a giant yew tree.

"This rain is a curse." His voice was sharper than a fairy's voice should be, Beth thought. "Why can't our magic stop it? Can't you do something?"

"I'm sorry, dear," Titania said in a placating tone. She touched his wing. "I believe it will rain until we can find Bottom."

Beth stepped forward. "Richard III is holding Bottom in a stage-like box. Bottom can't escape, but perhaps one of you could go to Richard's world and free him. We humans tried and failed."

"Richard's world?" Titania shuddered, and all the fairies shuddered with her. "I am afraid to go there, but if I must do that to free Bottom, I will."

"You will do no such thing!" Oberon demanded. "Richard might pluck your wings off."

Moth, Cobweb, Peaseblossom, and Mustardseed shrieked. "Don't go!" they cried. "Sweet fairy queen, don't go!"

"She won't go," Oberon said. "I command it. Titania, you won't risk your life for that ass. There must be a way to solve this that doesn't involve my wife." He stomped off.

Titania's eyes teared up. "What can I do?" she moaned. "Oberon is jealous of Bottom."

The sight of Titania so sad made Beth want to cry, but she thought the land was already damp enough. "Don't cry, please. There must be another way to free Bottom," Beth said. She was annoyed at Oberon's jealousy, but she didn't think there was anything she could do about it.

Chapter 30

BETH FORCED HERSELF TO go to the final dress rehearsal. It was evening, and the auditorium was lighted as it would be on the night of the real performance. Beth looked around to make sure that Kevin was nowhere near the lights.

For once, she would rather be home in bed. She didn't want to see a lot of people. She felt that because she had killed, she should be playing Lady Macbeth instead of Viola.

"Get that torment out of your eyes." Sita's tone was sharp. "You're acting in a comedy. Your only worry is that Duke Orsino doesn't know that you're a woman who loves him. Snap out of it."

Beth couldn't speak, but she nodded. She closed her eyes for a moment. She had landed on the shore of Illyria. She would pretend to be a man. She knew better than ever what it was like to act that part when another woman was attracted to her. She climbed onto the stage.

At the end of the rehearsal, Ms. Capulet applauded. "Yes!" she exclaimed. "Everyone was just right. You're a perfect Viola now, Beth."

"Thank . . ." Beth began to say. But her vocal cords were paralyzed. No sound came out. She felt the stage shift under her feet. She tried to move, but her legs were like blocks of wood. Her hands moved. They began washing each other, faster and faster, and wouldn't stop.

She tried to cry out, but she couldn't. She choked for breath. Was she going to die in the real world?

She could barely see the people she knew who were rushing to help her. They touched her, but she didn't feel them.

Merlin, in janitor clothes, leapt onto the stage. He pushed the others aside and shook her.

Weak as a rag doll, Beth fell on the stage. She was no longer paralyzed, just weak. "I'm all right," she said. She took Ms. Capulet's arm and let the teacher help her up.

"This is serious. Very serious." Merlin looked grim. He turned his head. "Look backstage!" he exclaimed.

Arnie rushed backstage. He let out a yell.

The cast ran backstage, Beth let her teacher help her get there.

Kevin stood on a stool. He was trying to put a rope around his neck. Arnie reached up and struggled with him.

Lupe screamed.

Beth felt as if her heart had stopped.

"Stop, Connelly!" Arnie cried. He grabbed hold of Kevin's arm and tugged at it.

Frank and Sita lunged to help Arnie, and collided with each other.

"Kevin Connelly, take that rope off this minute! And come down from that stool!" Ms. Capulet demanded in a grade school teacher's voice.

Kevin dropped the rope, fell off the stool, and landed on top of Arnie, who wound up holding the rope.

Everyone rushed to them and tried to pull them up.

"Why the hell did you stop me? My ankle is broken!" Kevin sobbed.

Arnie struggled for breath. "Better than your neck, you damn idiot. Are you crazy?"

Kevin looked at Beth. "Are you all right, Beth?" he choked. "Can't you see? Can't everyone see? All my life is now death and destruction. I'm doomed."

"No, you aren't." Beth threw her arms around him. "We'll solve this. Please don't try to kill yourself again."

Chaos reigned in the backstage area. Lupe sobbed. Frank kept saying, "Damn!" Amelia looked as if she was going to faint.

Beth noticed that Merlin had disappeared.

"Kevin, I'm taking you to get an X-ray," Ms. Capulet said. "I won't tell the doctors in the emergency room what you were trying to do, but I have to tell your parents. That is required by the law. You will be referred to a psychiatrist. I can't be responsible for keeping you alive."

"Please don't tell my parents," Kevin pleaded. "I won't do it again. What can I tell a psychiatrist?"

"You can make up something, but you have to go. Perhaps an anti-depressant will help you get through this difficult time," Ms. Capulet told him.

"No, no. I'm a terrible liar." Kevin rubbed his ankle.

"You need a rest," Ms. Capulet said. "We'll discuss this on the way to the hospital. Arnie, help Kevin to get up. You can come with us." She turned from Kevin to the group. "As of now, *Twelfth Night* is postponed until Sir Toby is in better shape."

Beth heard a few groans from members of the cast.

Kevin moaned. "It's all my fault. I'm ruining things for everyone."

"We could all do with some rest," the teacher said. Arnie put an arm around one side of Kevin while Frank put an arm around the other. They limped away.

"Take care, Kevin," Beth called after him.

"Are you really okay?" Amelia asked Beth in a shaky voice.

"As okay as I can be," she said.

Lupe still sobbed.

Amelia asked Sita, "What is going on? I think you know what it is."

"I can't tell you. I hope that's all right." Sita touched Amelia's arm.

"For now." Amelia turned to Lupe. "Stop crying," she said. "I'll go home with you. It looks like we're the outsiders."

"Thanks for your understanding," Sita said to Amelia.

"Hey, Beth," Sita said, putting her hand on Beth's shoulder. "Bad dress rehearsal, good play. Let's go to Ms. Capulet's office."

Beth staggered off to the office. Then she sat down at her teacher's desk and put her head on her arms. She shook at the thought that Kevin might have died.

SITA SAT BESIDE HER patiently. Or maybe not so patiently. Beth raised her head.

"Maybe you need to go talk to Amelia?" she asked.

Sita frowned. "You mean you want to time travel without me. Go ahead. Richard was able to make you act manic on our auditorium stage, so who knows what he could do there? But you don't need my help." She jumped up from her chair.

Beth didn't reply. It was true that she wanted to go alone. If there was danger, she didn't want to put Sita at risk.

"Oh, you're being silent now? All right, I'll go talk to Amelia. But all I can tell her is that my friends are crazy. Let me know if you hear anything about Kevin." Sita stalked out.

Beth closed her eyes. Her chest muscles ached. She felt more despondent than ever. She wondered what would happen to Kevin. What would happen to all of them? And what about the play?

Twelfth Night! If Richard was preoccupied with the high school production, what might he be doing in the real play?

She wished herself in Illyria, but hoped that she didn't have to almost drown to get there.

She spun through a hail of bottles and mugs. The world smelled like a tavern.

She stood in Olivia's hall, dressed as Mercutio, but no one seemed to see her. Sir Toby and Sir Andrew were sloshed, singing a drinking song so incoherently that she couldn't tell what the words were. Something about being merry. Seeing the real Sir Toby's red face made her wonder how Kevin was doing.

King Lear charged into the hall. "I have heard that your play of half-wits opposes changing endings and saving my Cordelia!" he shouted. "You must die!" Flourishing his sword, Lear rushed at skinny Sir Andrew.

Maria threw an ale pot at Lear's head. It hit his sword, broke, and doused him. Lear stopped and tried to rub the ale out of his eyes.

"Curse you, fools," he choked, ale dripping down his face.

Sir Toby grabbed the old man from behind and dragged him out of the hall. "Out of our play, you madman," Sir Toby bellowed.

Lear must have left, because Sir Toby returned, rubbed his hands, and said, "More ale, Maria."

"I would have stopped him if you hadn't," Sir Andrew protested. "I am brave."

"So you are," Sir Toby said. "I still think my niece should have married you, but I won't make a fuss about that as long as we can drink all we want."

BETH SPUN THROUGH A torrent of papers and wound up back in Ms. Capulet's office, where she knocked over one of the stacks of paper and a stack of books. King Lear hadn't succeeded this time, but he would try to kill her if they met. Who could prevent that? While she restacked her teacher's books, Beth thought and thought. The answer finally came to her.

Beth closed her eyes and spun to an England that existed long before Shakespeare's time. She whirled past Druid stones and crop circles and great forests of yew. She smelled salt air.

In her Mercutio form, she landed on white cliffs. Maybe they were the cliffs of Dover. She hoped she didn't have to see Lear's friend whose eyes had been gouged out. She was tired of bleeding eye sockets. She wondered whether Shakespeare had thought of Marlowe when he wrote that. He must have.

She heard screeching and saw gulls flying around the cliffs.

"Cordelia," Beth whispered. "Cordelia."

She did not see the lady.

Instead, King Lear charged through the brush. He drew his sword and yelled, "Dare to come to my land! Your days are over!" He rushed at her.

She kept her sword in its scabbard. "I do not want to fight such a venerable old man," she said. "Please don't fight, noble king! I do not want to hurt you." But if she had to die as Mercutio, she might as well do it now.

"A thousand curses on your head! I don't want you to spare me!" Lear extended his great sword.

A slight young woman with a sweet face dashed to the cliffs. "Do not fight, Father," she said. She threw herself down beside him and clutched his legs.

"Stay away from the swords, sweeting," he begged her.

"Put down your sword," she said.

Lear moaned. "I must save you, Cordelia. Shakespeare let you die. I must fight for another ending."

"We cannot change endings, Father." Cordelia rose and kissed his cheek. "I know that you love me and you know that I love you. That is enough."

"Cordelia! I saw you dead." The tears streamed down his withered cheeks.

"I am sorry you had that sight, but let it be, Father. Please." She clasped his hand.

He groaned and dropped his sword.

Beth looked out over the gray English Channel. One more enemy wooed away from Richard.

She wished herself back to the drama teacher's office.

Chapter 31

ETH SAT ALONE. SHE took an orange soda out of her teacher's cooler. The drink refreshed her. Nothing would be solved, she thought, unless she could better understand what had happened between Shakespeare and Marlowe. She had a suspicion that she wanted to confirm.

She needed to see what had happened when Marlowe was killed. Merlin would never help her revisit that day. She didn't know whether she had the power to do it herself, but she had to try.

She had read that days before Marlowe was killed, he had been accused of writing a handbill inciting people to kill Dutch Protestant refugees. The handbill had been signed "Tamburlaine"; that was the evidence. Not much, since Marlowe wasn't stupid enough to use the name of one of his characters in a pamphlet that could get him arrested. Obviously, someone had tried to implicate him. The government had issued a warrant for his arrest. He had presented himself to the Privy Council on May 20, but the council said he must await their pleasure before they heard the case.

That was all very peculiar, since many people said that he was a government spy working for the queen's secretary, Walsingham.

Beth concentrated on the time and place of Marlowe's death—Deptford, England, May 30, 1593, the house belonging to Eleanor Bull, a widow. Beth pictured a white house. She thought and thought until she had a headache. She pictured Marlowe's handsome face, his flowing brown hair, his thin mustache and beard, and his piercing eyes, still intact.

Beth spun through a May breeze. Flowers bloomed in the English countryside. Daffodils, like those Wordsworth saw centuries later. She landed in a room with a table and chairs. Four men sat there. One of them was Marlowe.

She hid behind a curtain, mindful of how Polonius ended. This was England, so she could get hurt. Permanently.

The men were drinking ale.

"What can you tell me about my case?" Marlowe asked them. "What does Walsingham say I should do? Do you have any word, Poley?"

One of the men shook his head.

"Or you, Skeres?"

"No idea," another man said.

"Or you, Frizer?" Marlowe demanded.

"Walsingham says nothing," the third man said.

"Nothing, Frizer? Why nothing? Won't he protect me?" Marlowe raised his voice.

"Why should he protect you?" another man said.

"Has he broken yet another promise? Have I been dealing with the devil?" Marlowe bared his teeth. "He won't find me an easy man to cheat, by God."

"How dare you call such a lofty man a devil, you shoemaker's son!" One of the men sneered at him. "You atheistic papist!"

"If I find devils, I shall call them out, and you are just the devil's henchmen!" Marlowe exclaimed. "Do I know too much? Is that Walsingham's problem."

Frizer drew his dagger.

A knock sounded at the door.

"Murder, is it? I won't go quietly." Marlowe seized the dagger and cut Frizer's head, but Frizer dodged and the wound was minor.

Someone pounded on the door.

Skeres grabbed Marlowe.

Shakespeare burst into the room. He was armed with a sword. "Marlowe!" he cried. "Unhand him, you cur."

A dazed Marlowe stared at Shakespeare.

Shakespeare rushed at Skeres. Skeres ducked, and Shakespeare's sword pierced Marlowe's forehead above the eye.

Marlowe collapsed, blood-covered and dead.

Shakespeare fell to his knees. "Kit!" he cried, and shook himself as if in a dream. He stared at the three men. "What happened? Why were you holding him? I was coming to challenge him to a duel, but this was no duel."

Poley extended his dagger towards Shakespeare. "If it isn't another playwright. This must be playwrights' day in hell."

Skeres grabbed Poley's arm. "Don't be foolish, Poley. How would we explain two of them dying?" He turned to Shakespeare with a toothy grin. "This is the queen's business, Shakespeare. Forget you ever saw it. Forget you came here. You wanted him dead anyway, so you have your wish. If you talk, you won't live long enough to see your next play staged."

Shakespeare groaned. "Fortune has toyed with me. And you cowards have sullied my soul as well as this day."

Poley sneered, but Skeres said, "There's patronage in this for you. You are a wise man."

"Would that I were braver and less wise. Marlowe betrayed my sister, but he would not have betrayed the queen. He had his own sort of honor." Shakespeare closed Marlowe's remaining eye. Then, weeping, he rushed out of the room.

Beth's heart pounded. Shakespeare had killed Marlowe, and Marlowe had seen him do it. But Shakespeare had intended to attack the men holding Marlowe instead.

Shakespeare's memory of the day was mistaken. And Beth could guess who had muddied his memory.

In a rage, she spun back to Ms. Capulet's office.

She stood up. "Merlin!" she yelled. "Come here right now!"

Merlin walked out of the computer screen. He wore a flowing white robe.

"How dare you summon me as if I were a servant, you insignificant girl?" he bellowed.

"You can't intimidate me the way you intimidated Shakespeare!" Beth didn't shout, but she shook with anger. "I've seen what happened the day Marlowe was killed. Shakespeare was trying to save Marlowe but killed him by accident. You talked Shakespeare into having a false memory of killing Marlowe in a duel, didn't you? His guilt gave you more power over him. I'll tell him the truth."

"You were not authorized to go back to that day!" Merlin's face whitened to the color of his robe. "You are not allowed to meddle with history."

"But you are?" She made such tight fists that her knuckles turned white. "How dare you make him believe he was a murderer! He wasn't made to be a killer. He didn't have a killer's heart."

"But you will destroy his trust in me."

Merlin was pleading. Could that be?

"Trust you don't deserve."

"I will not stand here begging you." Merlin resumed his usual arrogant tone. "If I have taught you anything, it should be that you must not try to tamper with history."

"You're the only one who can tamper with it?" she asked. "Why did you let Shakespeare model Richard on Mordred? That was your fault."

Merlin shook his head. "I thought that putting Mordred in a new play would contain him. My strategy was wrong. The opposite happened."

"I don't understand," Beth said to the wizard. "If you have so much power, why can't you defeat Mordred?"

Merlin covered his eyes with his hands. "Do you have any idea what it would cost me to do that?"

"No, I don't."

"Good. May you never know." Merlin took his hands from his face.

"Why do you never confront Richard?" Beth asked.

The wizard frowned. "Can't you do it?"

"I'm a girl. You're a powerful wizard. Or at least I believed you were. Richard should be afraid of you."

"Perhaps."

"Are you more afraid of him than he is of you?"

He shook with anger. "How dare you!"

Beth folded her arms. "I dare. Richard and Mordred have to be separated, and it's your responsibility to figure out how to do it."

Merlin shuddered. "There is a way." His voice sounded hollow. "A terrible way." He groaned again and vanished.

What could be more terrible than the things that had already happened? Beth wondered.

SHOULD SHE TELL THE living Shakespeare that Merlin had deceived him, or should she tell Shakespeare's ghost? Much as she longed to ease the living Shakespeare's pain, she thought it was more urgent to tell the ghost. As a ghost, he might be able to communicate with the ghost of Marlowe, who was the immediate danger.

She spun through a forest of playbills. Props bumped into her—the moon from *A Midsummer Night's Dream*, various rings, even the dog from *Two Gentlemen of Verona*. Juliet's balcony whirled at her, but she ducked.

She landed on the bare stage where the ghost dwelt. She was herself, dressed as Ben. Beautiful Renaissance music filled the air. The blurred ghost of Shakespeare appeared to her.

He frowned at her. "Why do you invade my world?" he asked. "Leave me to enjoy the music in the air."

"I have important news," Beth told him. "I have seen the night that Marlowe was killed."

"No!" the ghost moaned. "Be gone!"

"Three of Walsingham's men attacked him and were ready to kill him." Beth spoke as fast as she could in case the ghost might vanish. "You came in and attacked one of them, but the man ducked, and that's how you killed Marlowe. You didn't mean to do it, except in a duel."

The ghost sucked in air. "Can that be? Don't deceive me, I beg of you."

"I'm not deceiving you. I saw it. That's how it happened. Please believe me. You bent over Marlowe's body. You were grieved. You were trying to defend him. You know that's what you would do if you saw him attacked by ruffians, even though you were furious at him for abandoning your sister."

"I would have." Shakespeare's ghost took a long pause. "There is a vague stirring of memory. Men grappling with Kit. But why have I remembered it so differently?"

Beth said just one word. "Merlin."

"Merlin?" the ghost moaned. "Merlin deceived me?" He put his hands to his head. "I loved that old man so much. He showed me almost more beauty and terror than my heart could bear. But such an awful grief. Can I believe you?"

"Please believe me," Beth begged him. "You need to tell the truth to Marlowe's ghost to protect your plays from him. I don't know how he could manage to rewrite them, but he will if he can because Richard said you tampered with his."

The ghost winced. "But I did kill him. You saw me do it. And he saw me do it, did he not?"

"Yes, but you struck the wrong man. You must convince him of that."

Shakespeare's ghost shuddered. "A task grievous enough to break my heart again. But I must undertake it. Take me to him, if you can. Now, before cowardice weakens resolution."

"I'll try." Beth's heart flooded with love for him. She wished she could hug him, but it didn't seem right to try to hug a ghost.

She thought of Marlowe's ghostly Thames. She hated to take Shakespeare's ghost there. It was so much more horrible than his afterlife. It would pain him to see Marlowe there.

She imagined fog, endless chilling fog, and permeating dampness. She spun through it shaking.

She dropped to the bank of the ghostly Thames, and saw that Shakespeare's ghost was with her.

"'Tis bitter cold, and I am sick at heart," Shakespeare's ghost said. "Must Marlowe hover through this fog for eternity?"

"Who spoke my name?" Marlowe's ghost appeared in the fog. "Will?" Marlowe's single eye glowed with anger; it was the only bright thing in the unnatural mist. Blood oozed from his other eye socket. He twisted his hands. "If only I could strangle you! If you were alive, I would kill you. I would tear out both your eyes."

"Peace, Kit," Shakespeare's ghost intoned. "We are both dead. I have come to make peace with you."

"Peace!" Marlowe's ghost howled. "Peace! I have no peace, and you shall have none. I will murder your heroes and ravish your heroines. I will tear your foolish clowns to shreds."

Shakespeare's ghost backed off. "Kit, the day you died I came to duel with you, not to murder you. I was trying to kill the man who held you, not you."

"You killed me!" Marlowe screamed. "I suppose you died peacefully in your bed."

"I did," Shakespeare admitted. "But I did not spy for an ungrateful crown. It was your work that led you to be killed. Be angry at Walsingham, not me. You embraced danger, and it betrayed you."

Marlowe's ghost regarded him with contempt. "You fled from danger; you just penned your worthless plays. But you cannot flee from me. I haunt you. I have always haunted you."

"You have." Shakespeare's voice was quiet, though he trembled. "But you should have haunted Walsingham, and the queen."

"Do not pretend friendship!" Marlowe screamed at him. "You destroyed my work. You made my Tamburlaine one of your milksop heroes. You made my Faustus a prattling monk."

"I never did." Shakespeare's voice was firm. "You have listened to the words of my most treacherous character, who wants only to see his own play rewritten. How could you believe Richard III? If you dislike my characters so much, why would you have listened to one of them?"

"You killed me." Marlowe wailed. "Why should I doubt that you killed my plays, too?"

"Because plays are sacred," Shakespeare's ghost said.

Marlowe's ghost grabbed him by the throat and wrestled with him.

Shakespeare's ghost struggled back. "You cannot kill incorporeal air, Marlowe. Cease this madness."

The fog began to cover them, obscuring them from Beth's vision. She moved closer.

"I would kill you a thousand times, if I could!" Marlowe cried. "I would keep you in this hideous fog rather than let you return to whatever haven where you rest." He pushed Shakespeare's ghost towards the Thames.

Beth gasped.

"I know you would." Shakespeare's ghost slipped away from him. "You know you cannot kill a ghost." His voice was calm. "You cannot change your fate or mine. Do not try to slip through worlds to distort my words. You will only make yourself mad. Avoid madness, I pray you."

"Please, Master Marlowe, listen to me," Beth exclaimed. "I am living four hundred years after you died. Your Tamburlaine is terrifying. All your characters are. No one has changed them. Richard is lying to you. He always lies. That's his nature. He succeeds by deceit, rather than by force like your Tamburlaine. That's why you used to despise Richard."

"So I must believe the word of a girl? I am reduced to that?" Marlowe's ghost said. But his voice was quieter.

"A girl brave enough to enter our dead worlds and bring me here," Shakespeare's ghost said. "You may not believe me, but do not be foolish enough to believe a consummate liar."

"If you have not touched my plays, I will not touch yours," Marlowe said grudgingly. "But go, go, and never come back." He turned away from Shakespeare.

"Fare as well as you can," Shakespeare's ghost said. He vanished.

Beth spun through fog to Ms. Capulet's office. She closed her eyes. The fog seemed to chill her even there.

She wanted to tell the living Shakespeare what she had just told the dead one. But the living Shakespeare wanted never to see her again.

Would it be fair to Merlin to tell the living Shakespeare? Would Shakespeare reject him? Would that break Merlin's strange heart? Beth knew that King Arthur had rejected the wizard but Shakespeare had not. Did she have the right to interfere, even if her interference might soothe Shakespeare's mind?

She wasn't supposed to change history. Would telling Shakespeare about Merlin change history? Did he write his story of a wizard, *The Tempest*, knowing that Merlin had misled him, or not knowing? Shakespeare's ghost hadn't known, so the living Shakespeare must not have known. Would he have changed *The Tempest* if he had known?

BETH WAITED AND WAITED, but Ms. Capulet didn't come.

Finally, the door opened. Arnie entered.

"Ms. Capulet sent me back because she guessed you'd be here," he said. "Are you all right?"

Beth jumped up. "I'm fine, but how's Kevin?"

Arnie shook his head. "As okay as he can be. He promised over and over not to try suicide again. He finally persuaded her not to tell. There was a long wait in the emergency room, but at last a doctor set his broken ankle. Kevin's parents came, and Ms. Capulet told them that he'd been pushing himself too hard and should rest at home for a few days."

Beth exhaled with relief. "Thanks for telling me. He's been hurting himself more than me."

"But you need to be protected from him. And maybe the rest of the cast does, too. Of course, I'll visit him as soon as I can. Poor dumb Connelly." Arnie shook his head. "Maybe you should go home and rest, too. I could walk with you."

Ms. Capulet entered the room. Her wrinkles had deepened. She looked as if she hadn't slept in days. "An excellent suggestion, but I think it's better if I drive her home. Thank you for everything, Arnie. You're really a trouper."

"Okay. Good night." Arnie's voice was reluctant. He looked at Beth and went on his way.

"Please stop trying to fight Richard. This fight against him is too much for you. It's too much for all of us." Ms. Capulet seemed to be summoning up her last reserves of energy. "I don't want to hear one more word about Richard. He's done enough damage."

Beth felt her own energy ebbing away. "I won't talk about him if you don't want to hear about him, but what happened to Kevin makes me more determined than ever to keep on. Evil people won't stop doing evil if we try to ignore them."

"Let Merlin fight him! He shouldn't have dragged you into so much danger. Do you have any idea how much sadder your expression is than it was a few weeks ago?"

Beth choked. "I know. Please take me home so I can rest."

"Of course." Ms. Capulet pulled out her car keys. "Let's go right now."

Beth felt as if the whole night had passed. She was surprised to walk out of the building and see that the sky was still dark.

Fortunately, her teacher didn't talk on the way home. When Beth walked in through the front door, her mother took one glance at her and exclaimed, "What's the matter? You look terrible."

Beth turned her face away. "Kevin broke his ankle at rehearsal, so the play has been postponed."

"What a shame! But a broken ankle shouldn't postpone the play for long. I'm sure Kevin will want to act anyway. Don't be too disappointed," her mother said. "We have veggie lasagna for dinner."

The aroma of lasagna reminded Beth too much of Verona, but she said, "That's great."

Chapter 32

BETH SLEPT AND DREAMED. She saw Shakespeare pacing around his room. Knowing that he couldn't see her, and wouldn't want to if he could, saddened her.

He hit his head with his hand.

"Why do these strange ideas come to me?" he exclaimed. "Why should I mutilate my plays? Why do voices tell me, 'Make Juliet a whore, make Romeo go mad and kill Juliet's parents? Take away Hamlet's finest lines, and make him run away, leaving Claudius to rule? Have Duke Theseus order Bottom, Quince, and all the other mechanicals executed for putting on a bad play? End all the comedies with bloodshed?'

"Why must I have these ugly thoughts? Is this Marlowe's revenge? Must I make all my plays as cruel as his?"

Shakespeare stopped pacing and took a drink of ale. "Be calm. I must be calm. I killed Marlowe in a duel. I had good cause to fight him. But even if that was murder, I cannot murder art. His plays will live, and mine also. The world must have beauty. We are not all brutes.

We must laugh at times. I must not listen to my demons. Demons, toy with some other poor wretch. I will not be your fool."

He sat down, took up his pen, and smiled.

Beth hoped that he found peace.

WHEN BETH WOKE IN the morning, she felt good after time traveling. That hadn't happened in a long time.

On her way to school, she saw Sita waiting to walk with her. "Hi!" Sita's voice was too perky. She wore a glittery scarf over her jacket. "How are your journeys going?"

"Well. Very well." Beth eyed her friend suspiciously. "I've been thinking. Both Cordelia and Desdemona appeared at just the right moment and persuaded their angry male relatives to stop fighting for Richard. Is that just a happy coincidence?"

Sita grinned. "That's wonderful. I guess it's a coincidence."

Beth grabbed Sita's sleeve playfully. "I think you know something about it."

"Hmm." Sita put her hand on her chin. "I did happen to see Cordelia recently. Desdemona, too."

Beth hugged her. "You're amazing. But did you do it on your own?"

"A certain lady from Scotland told me how to find them." Sita smirked. "I had to get to know Lady M. I'm going to play her part again someday, and I want to be spectacular. She approves of that ambition. Let's go see her."

"Just like that? Pay her a visit?"

"You can do it, can't you? Will you need a tune-up after a certain number of miles of travel?"

"Definitely a battery recharge," Beth said.

They whirled around with ravens, then landed in Lady Macbeth's withered garden. Beth was Mercutio, while Sita was dressed in the gown she had worn earlier.

The lady sat on a stone bench, playing with a dog that looked at least half wolf. The dog gave the girls a bored look, then went off to sniff in a corner.

"I hope he doesn't dig up too many bones," Lady Macbeth said. "That could be inconvenient."

Beth gagged even though she guessed the queen was making what was her idea of a joke.

"Lovely lady, I could stay away from you no longer," Beth said, kissing the queen's hand though doing it in front of Sita was embarrassing.

Sita mimicked Lady Macbeth's every gesture. The resemblance was eerie. Beth marveled that Sita could be so much like both Lady M and Titania.

"We came to tell you that Cordelia has persuaded King Lear to stop siding with Richard. And Desdemona persuaded Othello," Beth said.

Lady Macbeth smiled. "I thought that might work," she said. "Women can be very persuasive, as I know to my regret. Why didn't I just ask Macbeth to move to Cawdor and renovate the castle there?" She shook her head. "I am so glad that I can ask Regan and Goneril to leave. They have been such tiresome guests, but I wanted to keep them here until Lear made up his mind."

"That's why you asked them to be on our side?" Beth asked.

"Of course. I needed to keep them on the sidelines so seeing them would not encourage him to continue his working for Richard." Lady Macbeth shook her head. "They may have thought their father was a discourteous guest when he stayed at their castles, but I assure you that they are just as bad. So many ladies in waiting! Such quibbling over the food and wine! Such noisy quarrels between them! Let them keep house for themselves."

Beth couldn't help laughing. The witches had been right that women would bring peace this time. Things were working out so smoothly. Could that last?

"What of Bottom?" Lady Macbeth asked.

Beth's cheerful mood vanished.

"Later," Sita said. "We'll be late for school. And we can't disappear too long when we're standing on the sidewalk.

They spun back. Beth scraped her feet on the curb.

"Don't visit Richard without me," Sita said.

Beth said nothing. She didn't want to keep lying.

Sita gave an exaggerated sigh.

As soon as Beth got a break after first period, she went to a stall in the girls' room.

She willed herself to travel to the place she hated. Richard's hall. She was alone. She hadn't wanted Sita to come. That might have been a mistake.

Beth found herself in one of Richard's mirrors. The inside was like a box. Was she trapped? There was not enough air. Panic took away her breath. She could only gasp. She touched the walls. They were hard. The box was too strong for her to break out of. All of the sides but one were opaque. That one was clouded over with incense. That must be the way to Richard's hall.

The incense was as thick as smoke from a fire, but she forced herself to walk through it. She choked. Her eyes stung so that she could not see. She trudged on through the smoke until she saw a light—the glow from Richard's hall. She plunged on.

She tumbled into the king's great hall. The light from the torches blinded her. She heard Richard's laugh. She rubbed her eyes.

Finally, she could see.

The sight of Richard sitting on his throne and chortling was not pretty, but it was a relief after all the smoke.

"Greetings, dear Beth." He smirked. "You came the hard way. I congratulate you on finding your way out of the mirror. Welcome back. You're wearing your own face, not Mercutio's. Yours is so much prettier."

Still choking on incense, she managed to speak. "You are the same as ever," she said.

But while Richard laughed, Beth realized she had made a discovery. The way out of his mirror boxes was to follow the incense. If only she could communicate that to Bottom.

She looked in another mirror and saw the weaver, now wearing a crown.

"I am determined to prove a villain," Bottom intoned in a stage villain's voice. "No, good people, I am not. I am Bottom the weaver, and I will not kill anyone. Dear brother Clarence, don't be alarmed. I will not have you killed. Dear Lady Anne, I have killed your husband. I would kill all the world to rest one hour on your sweet bosom. No, I would not. Do not fear. I would not kill your husband."

Richard laughed at him, but his laugh was thinner than usual. "See how the fool tries to imitate me," he said, but there was a slight tremor in his voice.

Beth applauded. "Keep on, Bottom," she cheered the player. "Give us more of Richard." She willed Bottom to hear her. She cheered louder.

"What a fool," Richard said, but his gaze was fixed on the mirror.

Bottom is getting to him, Beth thought.

Bottom stuck on an ass's head like the ones actors used to play his part. He put a crown on over it. "An ass! An ass! Hee-haw!" he brayed. "My kingdom for an ass! Hee-haw!"

"Enough!" Richard yelled. "Stop this nonsense!"

Bottom looked straight at them. He could hear Richard's voice. Richard's anger had made a small crack in the mirror. The incense swirled into the crack.

"Through the smoke!" Beth shouted.

Bottom started walking in their direction. He coughed, but the ass's head seemed to function like a gas mask and protected him.

Sputtering, Bottom entered the hall. He was still an ass, with a crown on his head. "This is the winter of our—hee-haw!—discontent," Bottom chanted.

"Go back to the Midsummer world where you came from, or I'll kill you!" Richard screamed.

Bottom vanished.

Beth laughed. She believed that sunlight and moonlight would illuminate the Midsummer world again.

Richard glared at her. "Do not imagine that laughter will defeat me."

"I don't." Beth stopped laughing.

Then Richard began to laugh like a fiend. "Do you realize that I hid that foolish clown only to distract you from working against me? He is another character you have hurt through your pursuit of me. Freeing him solves nothing."

Rage choked Beth. Gasping out the words, "I hate you," she wished herself in Bethesda, and found herself in the girls' room.

She went to wash her hands. No one else was in the washroom. She scrubbed harder and harder.

Saving Bottom wasn't enough. She still needed to save Mercutio.

Chapter 33

THAT NIGHT AFTER DINNER Beth sat at her computer chair, closed her eyes, and prepared to travel. She felt a longing for Verona much greater than she had ever felt before. But she also felt afraid. She remembered that Mercutio had died there as well as having lived there.

Beth landed beside Verona's rose stone coliseum, and remembered how Mercutio had showed it to her. She had been horrified when he told her that gladiators had once fought there. Now she thought more about what it was like to be a killer. The gladiators were forced to fight, so they were less guilty than she was. She hurried away from that place to the more crowded streets. Should she go into one of the beautiful churches that Mercutio had shown her? The Duomo, still under construction, or a smaller church? That would be a mockery, she thought. She wasn't a Catholic. She couldn't go to confession.

She was Mercutio in his home city, the city he loved. The fragrance of flowers and ripening fruit wafted from the walled gardens. The scent of oregano and basil drifted out of the homes.

It was her home. She felt as if she were walking down her own street in Bethesda, transformed to a place of much greater beauty.

But it was also Tybalt's home, or it had been. Her stomach lurched. He had lived on these streets. He had smelled these smells. She had cut short one of his lives.

Beth hoped that she wouldn't meet any Capulets. She could never tell Juliet what she had done. Juliet would be angry that her cousin had been killed again. And what if her father, Lord Capulet, heard that she had killed Tybalt? Would he try to kill her to avenge Tybalt, in the endless cycle of violence?

Some urchins waved at her and called, "Ho, Mercutio!" She waved back, but hurried on.

A young woman with uncovered fair hair curled her finger and beckoned Beth. The woman winked. "Ah, Mercutio. I was just longing for you."

Beth gulped. "I am so sorry, but I have no time at the present."

The woman pouted. "You know that you have nothing to do but play. You have found another girl to play with. I am so sad." She sauntered closer to Beth.

"Don't be sad. You're the prettiest girl in Verona," Beth said. "I am running an errand for my cousin, the Prince."

"That is a poor excuse. I must make you remember me." The girl threw her arms around Beth and kissed her on the mouth.

Beth realized she had to let the woman linger for a moment. Yes, the woman's mouth was soft, but she smelled of garlic. Beth pulled back and squeezed the woman around the waist.

"It gives me great pain to pull myself away from you, lovely acolyte of Venus, but my cousin will be angry with me if I do not do as he says. Perhaps I can visit you tonight." Beth touched the woman's cheek, then moved away from her.

The woman pouted again. "Only perhaps? You are cruel. Go serve your pompous cousin. I don't care."

"I am cruel to myself, not to you. Thank you for permitting me to tear myself away." Beth bowed to the woman and walked off, not too fast because that would be insulting. Thank goodness she'd had practice as Viola.

Being Mercutio was wearing her down. She felt jealous of the woman. Mercutio had kissed her, but he had never kissed Beth because she hadn't let him. Beth suspected that his relationship with the woman was nothing she should envy, but she did anyway. It was ridiculous to fall in love with a guy like Mercutio. She would stay away from guys like him in her own world.

But if she could save Mercutio, she wanted to kiss him. Just a kiss, nothing more.

At least meeting the woman had made her forget about Tybalt for a minute. Beth remembered him again. She walked in the opposite direction from the Capulet mansion.

She turned a corner and found Romeo. The luckless lover embraced her.

"Mercutio! I thought you were dead." Romeo's huge eyes teared.

"Take me to a safe place and I shall explain everything, you old fool," Beth squeezed Romeo's shoulder. She feared that she would give herself away. How could she deceive Mercutio's friend? But she had fooled Tybalt, so why not Romeo?

"Good. Let us go to the olive grove." Romeo hurried on. "Do you have some wine?"

"Am I Mercutio? Am I not a devotee of Bacchus almost as much as of Venus?" She proffered her flask.

Romeo drank. "Very fine. Wherever you've been they have good wine."

Beth drank also. "You know that Richard III had me killed by Tybalt."

"Yes." Romeo gritted his teeth. "I avenged you. And then what happened?"

"I cannot reveal all that I know. But Richard is plotting to change the endings of all Shakespeare's plays, and I am gathering characters together to oppose him. He has already brought together a formidable band."

Romeo stared at him. "And you truly oppose changing the endings?"

"I must. If Shakespeare's plays are altered, the whole world could change."

"I had heard that there was a man posing as Mercutio, and I heard truly." Romeo glared at her. "Mercutio wanted our play changed. He wanted to live." He drew his sword. "Die, imposter!"

"No!" Beth cried. "I can't fight you. Stop."

Romeo slashed into her chest.

Beth collapsed. The blood seeped out of her. "Don't trust Richard, I pray you, my friend," she gasped out.

"How dare you call me friend?" Romeo stabbed her again.

Beth hurt so much that the wounds must be real. She groaned. The groan gurgled in her throat.

"I will bring them back to life. Juliet, Mercutio, even Tybalt," Romeo declared. He stalked off, leaving her alone under an olive tree.

Tears of pain streamed down Beth's cheeks. She had never guessed that Romeo would be the one to kill her. She hoped she could live again as herself after this was over. But did she deserve to live, now that she was a killer?

She thought of Merlin, but he had sent her to die. The orange juice hadn't been enough to save her. She wished that it had given Arnie magical powers. Arnie would want to save her. Maybe Arnie would be grossed out by her Mercutio body, but he would save her anyway. How funny. She loved Mercutio, but she thought of Arnie.

Mercutio, she thought. I am you. Where is my other body? Where is Mercutio? We must be linked. I must be able to see where you are.

She saw a room hidden away somewhere in Verona. Of course, his body had been held in Verona all the time. He was in a tower, not the tomb where Romeo and Juliet had been. She saw a staircase.

She dreamed that Arnie climbed the staircase and found a large wooden door. He tried to open it, but it was locked. Of course. Was it a magical door, or an ordinary one? There was no keyhole. He looked as if he were trying to puzzle out the problem. She willed him to solve it.

Beth groaned with pain. Would it never stop? She should cease struggling and die. That would end the pain.

She saw Arnie stare at the door. "The spell must be something Shakespeare wrote about doors," he murmured. "The porter's scene in *Macbeth*? 'Here's a knocking indeed.' The door opened, but all it showed was a second door. 'Let the doors be shut upon him, that he may play the fool nowhere but in his own house,'" Arnie said. "*Hamlet.*"

The door creaked open, revealing yet another door. It was pointed at the top and was decorated with a stained-glass window.

"How fortunate that the spell's so simple," Arnie said. "Mercutio's own line. 'Tis not so deep as a well nor so wide as a church-door.'"

The door flew open. Mercutio, or his body, was lying on a bed.

The body twitched.

Arnie rushed over to him. "You must be Mercutio. Wake, Mercutio. Please wake." He shook Mercutio. "You must wake to save Beth. She's dying to bring you back to life. You're able to move now only because she's dying in your body. Bring yourself back before she dies."

Mercutio's eyelid flickered.

"Wake! You must wake to save Beth!"

Mercutio's head moved just an inch.

Arnie pumped Mercutio's chest as he would to revive a drowning person. "Wake! Wake!" Arnie cried. "Beth needs you. She's dying for you."

Mercutio's eyelids fluttered open. "Beth? Queen Mab? Dream?"

"Yes, Beth! Get up, get up!" Arnie grabbed Mercutio's arm. "Save Beth, save Beth!"

"Beth?" Mercutio's hand grabbed Arnie's arm.

Beth felt the blood seep out of her. Would her life pass before her eyes?

It did. There was a woman, holding her, and she was struggling to get out of her arms and pick a flower. Then she was running along a marbled hallway carrying a sack of something wriggly. Frogs. She ran into a bedroom and put a frog under the sheets. It was Mercutio's life she was reliving, not her own.

She was climbing trees with a young Romeo and some other boys. They stole apples.

She tried not to think. She was sure there were parts of Mercutio's life she didn't want to revisit.

She saw a girl winking. No, she tried to put the picture out of her mind.

She saw herself, but through Mercutio's eyes. She looked prettier than she was.

She saw Tybalt. She felt her blood surge with rage.

Her blood. There was less and less of it. Cold seeped into her.

She could hear her breath gasping and rattling. Everything was going dark.

Beth woke. Her breath had stopped rattling, and sounded almost normal. Someone put a pomander to her nose. She smelled oranges, roses, and cinnamon. She opened her eyes. She raised her head. She was in her own body. Still cold, but alive.

Mercutio moved the pomander away from her nose. He was good-looking as ever, but his face was pale and his forehead was lined with worry. "I thought I was seeing my own body!" His voice shook. "But now you've turned back into Beth!"

Tears streamed down her eyes. "I didn't die," she said. "I'm afraid you won't be able to live."

Mercutio bent over and kissed her on the mouth. "Beth, dear little Beth," he said. He stroked her hair. "You have brought me back, for however long. You are brave beyond description. Who tried to kill you?"

So this was what it was to be kissed. It felt nice, but his lips were cold, and so was his hand. Mostly she was glad to be alive. And she wasn't some princess in a story. His kiss had come after she woke up, not before. She rubbed her eyes.

Arnie stood behind Mercutio.

"Hi, Beth," he said. He sounded as if he had aged fifty years.

"Hi. Did you bring Mercutio?"

"Yes."

"Thank you." She smiled.

"Beth, who tried to kill you?" Mercutio repeated. His hand touched his sword.

"It was Romeo."

"No!" Mercutio gasped.

"Don't blame him. He could tell that I wasn't really you." She enjoyed the sound of her own voice. She was in Verona, but she no longer sounded like Mercutio. Mercutio had kissed her, so she must be in her own body. She looked at her hand. It was a girl's hand.

"That fool! I'll batter his addled head." Though Mercutio's voice was angry, he took his hand off his sword.

"Romeo believed Richard, who said that there was a man posing as you. It was I. Merlin put me in your body to die and bring you back to life," Beth explained. Though her voice was her own, it was weak. She struggled to speak clearly. "We must help Shakespeare. There's so much to tell you."

"Richard!" Mercutio spat out the word. "I will do anything I can to oppose his schemes. Forgive me for ever believing him. Forgive me for deceiving you."

Beth remembered her anger and pain at learning Mercutio had deceived her for a long time. He had been Richard's agent. He had helped Richard gain access to her brain. Glad as she was to see Mercutio living, the thought of how much suffering he had brought her made her catch her breath. "I forgive you," she said, but she knew she could never forget. She loved him, but if she had ever been in love with him, she didn't think she was any longer.

"Thank you for your generosity." Mercutio kissed her hand.

The touch of his lips didn't thrill her. She had kissed hands herself, and thought it was a stupid custom. "I was you, or almost you," Beth said. "I nearly lived inside your brain."

Mercutio's face flushed. "What thoughts you must have seen there!"

"Some, fortunately not all," Beth replied. "I'm glad to see you, but I want to go home now." Saving Mercutio filled her with pride, but she felt more tired than heroic. She had wanted to see him for so long, but now she just wanted to sleep and know it was not the sleep of death. "We can discuss Richard later."

"And Tybalt." Mercutio's face flushed with anger. "If he ever lives again, I must kill him this time."

"He did come back. I killed him." Her voice broke. She fought back tears.

Arnie gasped.

"You killed him?" Mercutio clenched his fists. "I had no chance to fight him, and he was killed by a girl. I am disgraced."

Beth shook her head, which felt heavier and heavier. "I killed him as you. So consider yourself avenged."

"Nooo." Mercutio's exclamation was something between a groan and a growl.

"Didn't you hear Beth say she wants to go home?" Arnie asked. "Worry about your manly pride later."

The tenderness returned to Mercutio's face. "You have been through so much for me," he said, eyeing Beth tenderly. "Of course you must go home."

"Home," Arnie said. He grinned wide as a Halloween pumpkin.

She turned to Arnie. "Yes, let's go home now."

Chapter 34

WHEN BETH FELL BACK into her computer chair, she shook herself to make sure she was alive. She pinched her arm. Yes, it hurt. That pleased her.

She felt an uncontrollable urge to go downstairs and hug her mother.

She rose with difficulty from her bed and staggered down the staircase. The staircase looked beautiful. The cluttered living room looked beautiful. The faded sofa looked beautiful. It all looked so solid, so real.

Her mother was bent over the dining room table grading papers. Her mother's back looked beautiful. Beth put her arms around her mother and hugged her.

"How sweet!" her mother exclaimed. "Thank you, honey." She turned and looked at Beth. "Are you all right? Your face is pale and your eyes are red."

"I'm fine." Beth backed off, though she didn't want to. Too much affection would be too unusual.

"Have you been crying about that boy again? Or are you sick?" Her mother put her hand on Beth's forehead. "You feel colder than normal."

"I'm not sick." Beth forced herself to speak in a petulant tone though she didn't feel petulant in the least. "I'm not still upset about him. I believe he's in a better place."

"Do you, honey?" Her mother smiled. "I'm glad." She paused. "Would you like some hot chocolate to warm you up?"

"Yes, thank you."

Beth followed her mother into the beautiful kitchen. The graying linoleum floor was beautiful. All the appliances were beautiful. The hot chocolate smelled and tasted better than anything Beth had ever tasted before.

When Beth went upstairs to go to bed, Merlin was sitting at her computer.

"Well done," the wizard said, giving her a brief nod. "I hope you're ready to work against Richard tomorrow."

Beth shook with anger. "You don't worry much about life and death, do you? I almost died as Mercutio and brought him back, but Richard is still a problem. What is Mercutio supposed to do stop him?"

Merlin raised his eyebrows. "Nothing. Bringing Mercutio back to life will do nothing to stop Richard. I never said it would. I asked you to live and die as Mercutio because I knew that would persuade you to return to the fight against Richard. You were the one I needed, not Mercutio."

Beth fought to contain her rage. "So you used my caring about Mercutio against me."

"What do you mean, you unreasonable girl?" Merlin looked at her as if she had asked him to turn Bethesda into Disney World. "You got what you wanted. You brought Mercutio back to life in your time. You still intend to fight against Richard, don't you?"

"Do you have any idea how much I've suffered?" Beth's tone was sharper than his. "Of course you don't. Human pain doesn't even register with you. Yes, I'll keep on opposing Richard, but I'm tired of you. Go away."

"Gladly." Merlin vanished.

When Beth went to bed, she feared she would slip off to death. She knew the fear was irrational, but closing her eyes was difficult. She pinched herself again. She was alive. She would just sleep, not die.

Finally, she fell asleep.

When she woke in the morning, there were tears in her eyes. She was still alive. It was too early for the sun to come up, but she could see street lights through her window. The world was normal. Her life was pretty good. She didn't want to leave it. She was safe. Mercutio was safe. But she had killed Tybalt. Had Tybalt felt the same way when he died that she had when she died as Mercutio? Had his life passed before his eyes? Had he felt the blood seep out of him? Did she deserve to live? She wanted to, whether she deserved it or not.

She wondered why her mind had called out to Arnie, not Sita. Was it because she wanted to be saved by a boy? Was she being sexist? Was she fonder of Arnie than she thought she was? Or was it because her jealousy of Sita's relationship with Amelia was even deeper than she had realized?

BETH THOUGHT SHE HEARD someone calling her. She slipped into Verona and saw Mercutio in an orchard. He glowered. "I will kill Richard." The lines of Mercutio's face tightened, showing what he would have been like if he could have lived to be old. It occurred to Beth that he was a slightly older Peter Pan. She should have seen that long ago.

"I swear . . ."

"Don't swear," Beth said. "I'm sure you are an able swordsman, but fighting has only brought you death. Richard couldn't bear hearing Bottom make fun of him. I think the way to defeat Richard's plots is by jesting. You excel at that."

Mercutio sighed. "Moonface, you talk nonsense. Queen Mab has touched you with stardust. Jests cannot stop murderers."

"But showing how grotesque their villainy is may stop others from joining them. We are contending not just with random violence, but with plotting. Conspirators need other conspirators. I've met so many characters whom Richard has beguiled. We need to show them how idiotic it is to try to destroy Shakespeare's plays."

He shook his head. "You are young and innocent."

Beth drew a deep breath. "You forget that I lived as you. The longer I did, the more I felt emotions like yours. I killed Tybalt as you, but also as myself. I nearly died as you. I am neither innocent nor inexperienced."

Mercutio grabbed her arm. "If I could have prevented you from doing all that for me, I would have. I wouldn't have wanted you to experience dying, nor killing neither."

Beth shook her head. "I did what I had to do."

"You love me." He clasped her hand. "We should marry."

The words didn't sound particularly sweet to her. "I love you, but I wouldn't want to be your wife, or your sweetheart either." She tried to make the words gentle. "I belong in a different world. But please listen to me, and jest."

"I will jest as long as you like." He ruffled her hair. "I will jest to put a smile on your face. I fear that you are a chaste Diana, not a Venus. So I shall worship Diana, and sing her praises. Di-aanna, Di-aanna." His voice slid from high notes to low.

Beth smiled. She couldn't manage a laugh. When she thought of Tybalt, she still longed for a basin of water to wash her hands. Her hands twitched.

He took hold of her hands and rubbed them. "Are your hands cold, Moonface?"

"No." She didn't want to say that they were blood-stained.

Mercutio kissed them, one after the other.

"Do I love the left hand most, or the right?" he murmured.

Beth repressed a sigh. This was not the kind of jesting that she meant. It wouldn't defeat Richard.

"We died for each other, like Romeo and Juliet," Mercutio said. "Does that mean we are sealed together forever?"

"We are true friends to each other." She wondered why her heart wasn't racing. Having nearly stopped once, would her heart always be cold?

Cold. It wasn't her heart that was frozen, it was a wind that blew around them, sweeping them away.

They landed in a fog.

Rain poured down on them, then turned into pellets of hail. They struck Beth's cheeks as if pebbles were being hurled at her.

Mercutio tried to wrap his cloak around her, but the wind whipped it away.

"Hail!" called out three cracked voices. "All hail Beth! All hail Mercutio!"

The witches' dim figures appeared in the storm. Beth thought their jest of making hail fall was unfunny in the extreme.

"Who are you?" Mercutio drew his sword.

The hail disappeared.

"They are the witches from *Macbeth*, of course," Beth said. "They have generally given me good clues. Hail, awesome hags." She could tell from Mercutio's breath that he was afraid.

"Fear what is ancient," the first witch said in a crackling voice.

"Age gives power," the second witch chanted.

"A life for a life," the third witch sang.

The fog covered not the witches' heath, but a battlefield strewn with corpses. Crows pecked at the gore-covered bodies of men in chain mail, and dogs gnawed at them.

Beth shuddered. Mercutio made the sign of the cross.

"Who are these soldiers?" he asked.

"They are the men of Arthur the just, Arthur the good, Arthur the great king," chanted the first witch.

"Slain by each other, all slain," chanted the second witch.

"See who remains," chanted the third witch.

A large man in fine armor bedecked with dragons lay near them. He clutched his chest.

"Still alive," whispered a slender man who lay near him. Painfully, he moved his sword, apparently to finish off the larger man.

Out of the shadows, a figure covered with a cloak and hood emerged. The hooded man dropped down beside the large man and tried to cover him. The hood fell off, revealing white-bearded Merlin.

"Arthur must not die." Merlin's voice cracked. "He must go to the Isle of the Blessed."

The man with the sword drew himself up. Blood dripped down his body. "Weak though I am, I am stronger than you, Merlin. I will finish killing him."

"No. I will bargain for his life, Mordred," the wizard whispered.

Mordred sneered. "What can you give me, now that I am dying? Can you give me immortality, like yours? That is the only thing I want."

Merlin scowled at him. "You do not deserve that. You will only do more evil."

Mordred pushed the old wizard away from the king's body. "Then I will cut his body to ribbons."

"No!" Merlin cried. "I do not know whether I have the power to give immortality as well as to have it myself, but if I am able, I will let you share mine. As long as I live, you will live ... ."

"Done!" Mordred exclaimed. He gave out a hideous laugh, and collapsed in death.

". . . . in words," Merlin said. "You will live someday as a character in another tale. Ha! He's dead. I've fooled him."

Arthur's breath rattled.

"No!" Merlin cried. "Arthur!" He cradled the man in his arms.

Arthur died.

Tears poured down Merlin's cheeks.

The scene faded.

Beth felt her own tears fall. "Poor Merlin," she choked.

"Poor Merlin!" the witches chanted. "Poor Merlin."

"What does this mean?" Mercutio asked. "Why should we care?"

Beth shook her head. She didn't want to say what she had just realized. Mordred would die if Merlin died. She feared that if Mercutio understood, he might want to hasten Merlin's death. "Just be glad that you weren't one of King Arthur's knights, dying on a battlefield, with no one to bury your body," she said. "Be glad that you are Mercutio." This time, she was the one to clasp his hands.

The witches made a maniacal sound that might have been laughter, and disappeared, leaving Beth and Mercutio back in Mercutio's Verona.

Beth shuddered. Now she realized why Merlin feared Mordred. Merlin loved immortality. How could she want to take that from him?

"I am angry at the witches for showing you that terrible sight," Mercutio said. He put his arm around her. "Poor little Moonface. Only men should have to see such dreadful things."

"Why shouldn't girls and women know what battles look like?" Beth tried to keep from pushing his arm away. "Shouldn't we know that they are horrible?"

"You should know only sweetness," Mercutio proclaimed.

"So should you," Beth told him. "So should everyone." She wondered how she could keep her new knowledge from Sita, who would want Merlin to die.

"Dear little Moonface." Mercutio touched her cheek. "Why couldn't we have been characters together in a comedy?"

Beth summoned a smile. "That would have been nice." Then she frowned. "But how could I love such a worthless layabout, who lives only to deceive women with honeyed words and to waste his time fighting in brawls?"

"How could I love a girl who is such a prude?" Mercutio shook his head. "She is a common scold. I would rather lie dying on the street than be tied to a girl who is as cold as a March wind."

Beth put her hands on her hips. "You are the one who is full of wind. I would rather live single all my life than be tied to a braggart who believes that because he is the cousin of a prince he has no need to open a book or do an honest day's work."

Mercutio grinned at her. "You see, we are perfect for each other."

"But we cannot write our own play." Beth's voice softened.

Happy that she could see Mercutio, though she thought she no longer was in love with him, she returned home.

BETH LOOKED OUT OF her window to see the dawn, but instead she saw rain drip down. She had been back in her room for only an hour, but she wanted to see Mercutio again.

She moved from Bethesda's early morning rain to Verona's sun.

Verona looked less friendly since she had been killed there, but she tried to tell herself that she was safe. She now looked like Ben, an innocuous boy.

She saw little children running and tossing a ball back and forth. A small, barking dog dashed around them. Birds chirped in the trees. And the delicious smells of Italian cooking came from the doors.

Beth stood near the river's ancient Roman bridge. Mercutio crossed it and she hurried towards him.

But Mercutio didn't see her. He was looking at another young man who was as well dressed as he.

"Romeo!" he called out, hurrying to his friend.

Romeo stared at him. "Is this the true Mercutio?" he asked, holding back.

"It is me, Prince of Fools," Mercutio exclaimed. "The one you killed was no evil man, but a friend of mine whom Merlin disguised as me to bring me back to life. When my friend nearly died from your wound, I woke. I am glad to be alive, but I am angry that you were the one who killed my friend. How could you slash my body? How could you look at me and do that?"

Beth remembered the feel of Romeo's sword entering her body. She could never like Romeo again. The sight of him made her chest ache.

Romeo put his hand on his sword and frowned at Mercutio. "How do I know that you are Mercutio and what you say is true?"

"I remember the prank we played on your tenth birthday," Mercutio told him. "Your parents were angry when we stole the Capulets' banner and put it in their garden. We were spanked because our jest could have led to someone's murder."

"That was your foolish idea," Romeo said, moving his hand from his sword. He shook his head. "I should never have let you persuade me to try it. You are Mercutio, and a wild man." He reached out to clasp Mercutio's hand. "I am glad to see you again."

Mercutio did not clasp Romeo's hand. "Dying twice has sobered me more than I want to be sobered. The friend who chose to take my body made a noble sacrifice and was sorely hurt by your hand. You and I have been friends for all of our short lives, and always will be, but I am not yet ready to embrace you. It is time that you ask questions, instead of acting as rashly as ever I did. Richard III and those who work with him mean to do evil, and if they can change our play, they will turn it to even more of a bloodbath than it is, with friend striking friend. Do not let them make you their pawn."

"A plague on them!" Romeo flushed. "I am still fortune's fool. I should have learned never to kill again."

"We both died too young to learn wisdom." Mercutio's tone was bitter. "May Queen Mab send us dreams of wisdom, but I am not sure I shall know it when I hear it."

"Drink with me, good friend," Romeo pleaded, taking out his wine flask. "We have lost too much. We must not lose each other."

"I shall drink with you anon, just not today." Mercutio gave Romeo a faint smile.

Beth ached in the places where Romeo had cut her. She hated the thought of Mercutio being friends with him. But after all, Romeo had been Mercutio's friend since they were children. She could forgive her own friends a great deal. She forgave Kevin. But she didn't want to see Romeo and Mercutio mend their friendship. She wished herself home.

Back in her bedroom, she cried again. She was tired of crying. She was tired of dying. She was tired of Mercutio.

She realized that saving Mercutio didn't solve the problems in Shakespeare's world. She had killed and she had almost died, but she still hadn't defeated Richard. She buried her head in her pillow. There was still a little time to cry before the inevitability of school.

Chapter 35

AFTER CLASSES HAD ENDED, Arnie asked if he could walk home with Beth. She didn't want to be rude, but she was worried that he wanted to become her boyfriend. She said yes, but was careful to keep her tone casual and not look into his eyes.

The day was so cold that they could see their breath.

Beth didn't speak until they were a block away from the school. "Thank you for helping me when I was dying as Mercutio," she said, though she wondered what thanks could possibly be adequate.

"I was glad to. What a terrible experience for you. Seeing you like that was terrifying." His voice trembled.

"How did you manage to get to the other world to find Mercutio?" Beth asked. "I wanted you to come. Did I pull you in?"

He shrugged. "You must have. I felt that you were dying and knew I had to help you."

"Thank you." She found it strange that he could have felt what was happening to her, but then everything was strange.

After they had walked another block, Arnie said, "Excuse me, but I have calculated the way to defeat Richard."

Beth stared at him. Her stomach lurched. "How?"

"It's simply logical. Merlin has to die," Arnie said, as if he were talking about how to win a game.

"What!" Beth could hardly believe he had spoken those words. She wished he hadn't figured out the answer.

Arnie continued. "Consider," he said. "Merlin is the most powerful person from Mordred's world. Merlin perpetuates that world. If Merlin dies, Mordred will die, and Richard will be only Richard."

"Kill Merlin?" Beth gasped. "I couldn't do that."

"Of course you couldn't. But you might be able to persuade him to die," Arnie explained.

"Persuade the world's greatest egoist to commit suicide? Impossible. And I don't even want to." Beth shuddered. "I don't want to have anything to do with anyone dying. Especially now that I know how it feels."

"He's a character. He says he's immortal, but that's because he's a character."

"Death feels awful even to characters. No. I couldn't."

"Then Mordred will live forever." Arnie looked her in the eye. "What more terrible things could he do?"

"Don't mention that idea again. I always thought you were a gentle person." Beth shivered from more than the cold. She remembered feeling as if she were fading into oblivion. "And don't tell anyone else."

"I've already told Sita."

"You haven't!" Beth put her hands to her face. "She'll agree with you."

"Yes, she does."

"And she'll be waiting for me on my doorstep." Beth raised her voice.

"I believe she will be." Arnie spoke with a calm that disconcerted Beth.

"Neither of you know Merlin." She shook her head. "I know him. It's not just an academic question to me."

"It isn't to anyone who knows what's been happening." Arnie's voice was sharper than usual.

Beth remembered the witches saying two minus one is one. Mordred had to be severed from Richard. But at what price?

Beth looked down her block and saw that Sita was indeed on her doorstep. Never had the sight of her friend been more unwelcome.

The three of them entered the house.

"If you won't summon Merlin, I will," Sita said.

"How can you be so cool about it?" Beth chided her.

"What am I supposed to do? Wait to see whether Kevin gets you killed before he kills himself?" Sita looked like a doctor telling a patient there was only one chance to save her life. "I care more about my friends than about a wizard character."

Beth sat on the sofa and tried not to think about Merlin.

The wizard walked in through the kitchen door. He was dressed in fine Renaissance garb, with a large ruff and a brocade doublet.

Sita stepped up to Merlin. "We know your secret."

"I have many secrets." He looked down on her.

"But you have one in particular."

No, no, Beth thought. Don't say that King Arthur betrayed him and exiled him. That would be too cruel. That was Merlin's deepest secret, hidden even from himself. Shakespeare had told her about it, but she was the only one who knew. Surely Sita hadn't found out.

"Your energy keeps Mordred alive outside King Arthur's stories. You are the only character who is able to live in any world you want. You must have shared that power with Mordred. You are perpetuating Mordred's reign of terror," Sita accused the old man. "You are by far the most powerful character from his world. If you no longer lived, Mordred would fade away, and Richard would be just an ordinary villain like Macbeth."

"What a contemptible lie!" Merlin whitened as usual when he was angry. He advanced on her, as if to intimidate her.

Sita stood her ground. "It's the truth, and you know it."

"You would murder me?" the wizard asked.

"I'm not talking about murder." Sita was implacable. "I'm talking about self-sacrifice."

"Then sacrifice yourself. Don't sacrifice me." Merlin glared at her. He turned to Beth. "What do you think, Beth? Do you want me to die? You might not be able to time travel if I died. Even when you seem to be traveling under your own power, you are still using my energy."

"Don't insult me by saying the only reason I would want you to live is selfish," Beth told him. Her heart pounded. "I wouldn't ask you to die. I couldn't ask anyone, human or character, to do that."

"Not even to save Shakespeare's world?" Sita asked. "Think, Beth. Don't just feel."

"I can't ask anyone to die!" Beth insisted. "Isn't there some other way? Merlin, do you know any other way to stop Mordred?"

Merlin said nothing.

"He doesn't," Sita said. "Listen to me, Merlin. You care about Shakespeare. If there was a choice between your living another thousand years and Shakespeare's work, which would you choose?"

Merlin looked at Sita as if she were a demon. "You know the answer," he said.

The wizard focused his gaze on Beth. "If I die," he said, "you'll never see Mercutio again."

Beth bit her lip.

"That's unfair," Sita said.

"True, nevertheless." Merlin's smile was smug. "Did it ever occur to you very intelligent young people that if I died, Mordred might be even more uncontrollable?"

Sita didn't back down an inch. "He isn't controllable now. You're lying."

"So you have decided that I am expendable?" Merlin stared into their eyes.

Sita stared right back at him. "I don't want my friends to die. You're a character. They are human. Yes, that's my choice."

"But is it Beth's choice?" Merlin asked.

Beth shook her head. "No. I can't make that choice."

"I can," Sita repeated.

Arnie finally spoke. "So can I."

"I shall consider your request," Merlin said.

"No," Beth said, reaching out to him. "Think of another way."

Merlin sighed so deeply that the sigh turned into a groan.

Beth glared at her friends. "You don't understand anything about death! You're almost murderers."

"Oh, please." Sita rolled her eyes. "You have to remember the difference between characters and people. We can't let characters hurt people in the real world."

"I'm sorry about this, Beth," Arnie said, looking at her sorrowfully. "What else can we do?"

"I killed Tybalt! I've killed a man!" Beth screamed. "I never will again. Never!" Her whole body shook. "You don't understand anything about life and death."

Merlin put his hand on her shoulder. She stopped screaming. Merlin had never touched her before.

"You were enacting Mercutio when you killed Tybalt," he said in a surprisingly gentle voice. "Did that hurt you so much?" He sounded as if he cared. "Tybalt will live again. It's true that characters and mortals are different." He disappeared.

"Did you really kill Tybalt when you were Mercutio?" Arnie asked.

"Yes," Beth choked. "I'm a killer."

"You weren't yourself," he said.

"Please go away," Beth implored Sita and Arnie.

"OK," Sita said. She and Arnie went to the front door. They took a long look at her, and left.

Beth slumped in an armchair. Not more death, she thought. Please, no more death.

Chapter 36

THE NEXT MORNING, BETH saw Sita on the way to school. Sita turned and waited.

"Hi," Beth said, dreading what would come next.

"Hi, yourself. What a nice day." Sita smiled. "A nice day to go to Ms. Capulet's office before classes."

Beth paused. "Okay, I guess," she said. The winter sunlight did nothing to cheer her, and neither did the sparrows chirping in the hedges. Dragging her feet was no good. She knew what she had to do.

When they entered the drama teacher's office, Ms. Capulet nodded to them and gestured for them to sit in the chairs.

"Good morning, girls," she said. She looked into Beth's eyes. Ms. Capulet's looked as if she wanted to cry. "Beth, I've heard that you died as Mercutio. I'm sorry for your pain. I wish I had never encouraged you to time travel."

Beth winced. "I'll be all right."

"I certainly hope so! Is there anything I can do to help you?"

"No, thank you." Beth paused. "I suppose I have to time travel now to finally get rid of Richard."

"That's your choice," Sita said. "Or shall we call Kevin and ask how he's doing?"

Ms. Capulet put out her hand as if to restrain Sita. "Don't pressure her. She's been through so much."

"Please leave me alone with Ms. Capulet," Beth said. She didn't want to see how happy Sita would be if Merlin sacrificed himself and ended Mordred's life.

Sita hugged her and left, closing the door behind her.

"I suppose I have to save Kevin by any means necessary?" Beth asked her drama teacher.

"Have you figured out how to do it?" Ms. Capulet asked. "I don't want you to suffer anymore, but by saving him, you would also save yourself and all your friends."

Beth remembered the sight of Kevin holding the noose. She forced herself to think of Richard.

She spun past torches glittering in mirrors. She felt that she never wanted to see a mirror again.

Richard sat on his throne. His crown glittered in the light. Incense swirled around him.

"Greetings, dear Beth," he said. "To what do I owe the honor of this visit?"

"I know who you fear," Beth told Richard.

In one of his mirrors, a figure appeared. A white-bearded man wearing long robes.

Richard shrank back in his chair, but he said, "No one can hurt me."

Merlin strode through the mirror, into Richard's great hall that looked like a film set.

"If you persist in trying to enter the twenty-first century, I will force you to stay in it." Merlin's eyes bored into Richard. "I will turn you into the real Richard III. I will make you lie with his bones. You will be in the coffin at Leicester Cathedral, trapped with him for all eternity!"

"You can't do that." Richard attempted a laugh. "I am Shakespeare's Richard. The real Richard would have nothing to do with me."

"I do hesitate to desecrate his grave," the wizard said. "But I wouldn't hesitate for long. If I sever Mordred from you ... ."

Beth gasped. Would Merlin let himself die?

"You would not dare to do that." Richard tried to glare as fiercely as Merlin. "You know what that would mean for you. You'll never agree to die."

"If I sever Mordred from you," Merlin repeated without flinching, "you will lose your powers. But I will still have mine for a moment. I would not hesitate to send you to Richard's grave when I send Mordred to his. Be Richard in your own play, or be nothing."

"You can't take my play from me." Richard's hand grasped his sword. "It is mine."

"Then stop sharing it with Mordred," the wizard commanded. "Stop trying to enter other minds and other eras. Your play could live just in pages, as most people believe it does, or you could continue to be a thinking Richard and live in your world, as the other characters do. You must choose your own play, or oblivion. Cut yourself off from Mordred."

Richard's voice changed. Mordred cackled. "He'll never do that, any more than you will agree to die. Without me, he's just another Shakespearean character who grabs a throne but cannot hold it. No one loves Richard."

Merlin stood his ground. "Leave Mordred or die."

"Farewell, Mordred," Richard said. "I can do very well without you. Leave me."

"No, you fool!" Mordred screamed. "You will lose your powers. Think. If Merlin dies, the boundaries of all the plays will close. You will no longer be able to talk to characters from other plays, but will be eternally marooned in your own play. No more alliances will be possible."

Richard shook his head. "Impossible. I can't accept that."

Beth ventured. "I think you killed Mercutio not just because he threatened you, but because he was witty. You tried to turn him away from his wit, to make him a soldier. But what you really wanted was to destroy him. That's why Bottom was your other prime target. You want to kill humor."

Richard chortled. "Oh, you're too clever by half, but that won't do you any good. I'll destroy what characters I please."

Merlin glared at him. "You should have power only over the characters you kill in your own play. Not any others."

Richard sneered at Merlin. "Don't pretend you cared about Mercutio. You thought he was expendable. You detest comedies. You never wanted Shakespeare to write them. So you should have no problem with my destroying them. You especially hate *A Midsummer Night's Dream* because it makes magic seem cute. So surely you wouldn't stop me from destroying that play and turning it into a tragedy?"

"You mean a bloodbath!" Beth cried.

"Why not?" Richard shrugged. "I can tear the fairies' wings to shreds. I can make Bottom's fellow players so angry at him that they kill him."

Merlin raised his hand. "No." His tone was cold and sharp as an ice pick.

"No?" Richard laughed. "No? Why not?"

"Shakespeare's words are immortal. No one should destroy them." The wizard voice softened. "I will do everything in my power to prevent that. Everything."

"Everything?" Richard laughed again. "No, you won't. Shakespeare is not so precious. He is not an immortal like you. Or like Mordred."

"Everything." Merlin repeated. "I helped Shakespeare. We made a pact. His works, even those I dislike, are like my children as well as his. Bastards, perhaps, but still my children. I must support him, regardless of the cost."

"Regardless?" Richard laughed and spoke in Mordred's tone. "Now you jest, Merlin. Go join the fairies and gambol through the woods and become a comic character."

"I never jest." Merlin took a step towards Richard. "I am resolved."

"I call on Mercutio," Mordred's voice intoned. "Yes, Beth I am using your power to summon him."

Mercutio appeared. When he saw Richard, he put his hand on his sword hilt.

"No," Beth said, putting out a restraining arm. "He is both Richard and Mordred. You can't kill him. His powers are too great."

Mordred's face floated over Richard's. He laughed. "What do you say, Beth?" Mordred asked in his smoothest voice. "Will you let Merlin die? Will you destroy the one who brought you to see Shakespeare and Mercutio? Mercutio, will you let her do it? If you let Merlin live, and let me live, you can be together. Beth, you could have the best of both worlds. You could have Mercutio's love, in whatever form you want, and also have whatever life and love you want in your own century. All you have to do is beg an old man who has befriended you to live. Is that so difficult?"

Beth covered her face with her hands. "I don't want him to die. I won't ask him to die, no matter what. So I want him to live, for his own sake."

Merlin put his hand on her shoulder. "Thank you for that. Take your hands off your eyes. You have said that nearly dying was so painful for you that you wouldn't ask anyone else to do it." He paused. "Would you do it again, to save a friend?"

"Yes," Beth said without hesitation. "But I would never ask anyone else to die."

"Ah. I looked back and watched you nearly die. I saw your pain, every moment of it. But nevertheless, you would do it again to save a friend. Watching your almost death has changed me." Merlin's features softened as much as it was possible for them to soften after a thousand years of being set in firm expressions. He looked at her as if seeing her for the first time. "There can be nobility in mortals. Can I be less noble than you are?"

"Persuade her to beg him to live, Mercutio," Mordred said. "Don't you want to continue seeing her? Don't you want to kiss her?"

Beth shook her head. She looked Mercutio in the eye. "He'll have power over the plays. What can we do? Mordred will never stop trying to intrude in my brain, and other young people's brains, and Shakespeare's brain."

"I can see that, Moonface," Mercutio said, his voice grimmer than she had ever heard it. "He would try to make me a cat or a rat, a villain or a fool. No, Mordred, you will never deceive me again. You will make Queen Mab give us all dreams of bloody war. I no longer want to fight in wars. I laugh at your ugly schemes. Let Beth and Merlin decide what they will."

Iago emerged from one of the mirrors and strode into the hall. "Think, Beth. Think, Mercutio. You cannot possibly want Merlin to die. Neither of you will be able to visit the Forest of Arden again. You will never again see Macbeth's castle and plot with the queen. You will never be able to speak with Hamlet. You will never be able to see the Midsummer World you are so fond of. True, Verona is beautiful, but do you want to spend your whole life there, Mercutio? You have become accustomed to so much greater freedom. And Beth, do you want only your humdrum world, with no chance to live in others?"

"I would give that up to preserve those worlds from Richard's schemes." Beth took a deep breath. "I won't try to hold onto Mercutio. I won't try to hold onto Shakespeare's world. I won't try to hold onto Merlin. But the decision is Merlin's to make. I won't make it for him. I must warn him that death is painful."

"You are brave, Moonface," Mercutio said, taking her hand.

"Your death as Mercutio was painful because you were killed by a sword. Mine wouldn't be," Merlin said. He turned to Mordred. "It's time, Mordred. It's time for us to go back to our deaths in Camelot and to die in all other eras."

Mordred scoffed. "I know you don't want to die, old man. That's why you've lived so long. You're a coward, afraid to die. You've used most of your magic to prolong your life."

"You must leave Richard and go back to the battlefield where you died, and were left unburied. And I must return to a cave." Merlin's voice was solemn. Not loud, but terrible. "Come, Mordred."

"No!" Richard screamed. "You'll divide me in two. You can't do that."

His voice changed, and Mordred said, "He won't do it. Merlin will never agree to die. No immortal would."

"Only because of you, Mordred," the wizard said. "Now," he intoned.

Merlin clutched at his heart.

Beth gasped. "No!" she cried. Could she bear to see the old man who done so much for her die?

"It must be," Merlin choked. "Everyone must die." He sank to the floor. "Perhaps I'll be reunited with Arthur."

Richard screamed and tore at his chest. Mordred emerged, kicking and yelling. "Merlin, you fool, don't do this!" he cried.

Merlin's eyes closed.

The slim man collapsed beside him. "No! Power will keep me alive," he insisted, but his voice broke.

Mordred's eyes closed.

Beth felt tears for Merlin drip down her cheeks. She had never imagined that he would sacrifice himself.

Richard bent over Mordred's body. "No, don't go!" he cried. "Don't leave me alone."

The bodies disappeared.

The hall began to change. Its mirrors dissolved, revealing bare stone walls. It became an ordinary fifteenth century castle.

The throne remained, and the boar pendant.

"You are just Richard III, no more and no less," Beth said.

"I am still terrifying," he insisted, glaring at her. "Plots have I laid. I am determined to be a villain."

"You are a villain," Beth said, "but only in your own play. You have no power elsewhere."

Iago stepped forward. "I am in charge now. Richard has as good as abdicated. I am the only one who is rational enough to control Shakespeare's world."

"No," Beth said. "You'll have to go back to your own play, and the wife you killed."

"Traitor!" Richard yelled. He drew his sword and fought Iago, killing him quickly.

Richard wiped his sword. "It was tiresome waiting to see when Iago would betray me. How pointless to wait until the last possible moment."

Iago's body melted away.

"You should have no power ever again." Mercutio strode up to Richard and confronted him. "You had me stabbed in the back. Now you must fight me in single combat."

"No!" Beth cried. "Please don't, Mercutio."

"I must, Moonface." Mercutio's mouth was rigid and his eyes were cold. "Come, pig king. Fight me if you dare."

Richard smirked. "I can easily defeat you, little Veronan."

Mercutio drew his sword, and Richard drew his.

"No!" Beth exclaimed.

But Mercutio slashed forward and Richard lunged at him. Steel struck steel.

Mercutio pushed Richard back towards the throne. Richard tripped.

"Stay in your own play, boy, and I'll stay in mine," Richard said. He fell back into the throne and began to disappear, throne, pennant, and all. Richard laughed his hyena laugh.

"Pig! Coward!" Mercutio shouted.

Beth sighed with relief that Mercutio had not been hurt, but she still wept over Merlin's sacrifice. It had been hard for her to risk her life, and she imagined how hard it must have been for him to give up immortality. Of course, as a character, he would be immortal like other characters, in all the books written about him, even though he had lost his special ability to appear in all eras.

Mercutio sheathed his sword. "I should have known that Richard had no interest in fair fights," he said with disgust.

Beth exhaled. "I'm glad he didn't hurt you," she said.

The incense smell disappeared, and the scents of flowers and rich, garlicky food filled the air.

Mercutio's brow furrowed. "Verona is approaching. We may never be able to see each other again."

Tears formed in Beth's eyes. "I'm so glad I've known you."

Mercutio put his arms around her and kissed her on the mouth.

She pressed her lips against his. The kiss was wonderful. Just what a kiss should be.

The aromas of Verona became stronger. Mercutio pulled away. "Farewell, my Moonface," he said in the tenderest of voices. "Queen Mab will bring us dreams of each other."

She clasped his hands as if that could keep him with her. "Good-bye, dear Mercutio." Her voice cracked, but she tried to smile.

Then he disappeared. Beth moaned. She seemed to fly over England and Italy, rivers and cathedrals, lakes and mountains. Then she spun through flying mirrors. She dodged them and refused to look in their glaring light.

Beth sat in a messy office. She shook her head as if she had just emerged from a swimming pool.

"Richard has been defeated." Beth felt dazed. Her voice was hollow. "But Merlin had to die to defeat him."

Ms. Capulet bit her lip. "We shall miss Merlin." Tears dripped down her cheeks and she rubbed them away. "But if Richard can no longer harm you or my other students, I am grateful."

"It's over. It's all over." Beth was almost too sad to appreciate the victory over Mordred. No more seeing Merlin. No more seeing Mercutio. No more witches offering clues. No more seeing Shakespeare. She was exiled from his world. Banished.

She bowed her head. The loss felt too great.

"Your career is just beginning." Her teacher's tone was brisk and hearty. "You're a good actor. If the problem with Richard is resolved, I think you should go to Kevin's home and tell him. I'll text Sita and Arnie so they can go with you."

"Sure, I'll tell Kevin." Beth remembered the sight of Kevin with the rope. She jumped up. It was important to tell him as soon as possible. That was the only thing that could make her feel better.

She walked through the halls. They looked the same, but everything was different. No one would try to injure her on her way to class or in the auditorium. Her muscles relaxed. Only then did she realize how tense they had been in the past weeks.

At the main entrance, she found Sita and Arnie, both beaming at her. Frank stood with them.

"This is my show, too," he said. "I want to say hello to Connelly without worrying that he's going to get me thrown into a pit or sent to prison for something I didn't do. I used to like the guy. I can give you a ride."

"Sure, let's all go," Beth said.

Sita hugged her. "I'm so proud of you," she said.

"Thanks." Beth tried to smile, but her chest felt hollow. She had lost something that none of the others had experienced, so how could she expect them to understand?

The temperature was around forty degrees, but the wind tossed the branches. In a few weeks, spring will be here, Beth thought. A year ago, she could never have imagined that she would meet Shakespeare or Mercutio. She could live without them. She just wished that she didn't have to.

Kevin's house was Tudor-style. It even had a little turret. Beth thought he was lucky, at least in his home.

Kevin answered the door himself. His face was pale and there were circles under his eyes. His ankle had a bandage and brace.

"What's up?" he asked in a strained voice. "I hope you haven't come to escort me to a mental hospital."

"No way," Frank said. "Your troubles are over." He gave him a high five.

"Everything's OK, Connelly." Arnie smiled his widest smile.

"Let Beth tell him," Sita said. "Sit down, Kevin."

Beth still felt nervous around Kevin, but she tried to make her voice sound warm. "Richard has been defeated. I don't think he has the power to affect any of us anymore."

"Really?" Kevin blinked. "Is it safe for me to come back to school?"

"It's safe," Beth said, hoping that was true.

"Come back tomorrow," Sita said. "We're finally going to have the real dress rehearsal. The show must go on. The audience can believe that Sir Toby's ankle is bandaged because he has gout."

WHEN SHE GOT HOME, Beth went to bed as early as possible.

"Are you feeling sick?" her mother asked.

"Everything's fine. Kevin's better and the show will go on. I just need to rest," Beth told her. "I'll have lots of late nights with the new dress rehearsal and the performances."

She went up to her room and sobbed silently into her pillow. Now she had killed Merlin. She hadn't begged him to live, which was almost the same as killing him.

She didn't want Queen Mab to bring her dreams of Mercutio. They would be too painful. No, wait, she did want the dreams. She did and didn't.

Was seeing Mercutio a few more times worth killing and dying? No, Beth thought, it wasn't. But giving him a chance to enjoy life, even if she couldn't see him, probably was worth it.

She reminded herself that her real purpose was to reduce King Richard's power by separating him from Mordred, maybe saving Shakespeare's plays. Perhaps that was worth all her pain. Merlin believed in that task enough to die for it.

THE NEXT AFTERNOON, BETH walked to the auditorium. She took a detour to the bathroom and scrubbed her hands. No, she couldn't be Lady Macbeth today. She tried to put herself in a Viola mood. She had been lost at sea, and now she was in Illyria. She had met a man and fallen in love at first sight, but she was disguised as a young man. She tried to walk like a guy. Fortunately, she'd had practice. She would be the best Viola ever.

The lights were on, transforming the auditorium to a real theater. She would have a chance to be on stage. Her favorite place. She would show her love of Shakespeare by acting in his plays.

As Beth walked to the stage, Sita began to sing, "A great while ago, the world begun, with a hey, ho, the wind and the rain. But that's all one, our play is done, And we'll strive to please you every day."

THE END

ACKNOWLEDGEMENTS

I WANT TO THANK Debra Doyle for editing this book and encouraging me. I thank Sherwood Smith for reading an early version of the manuscript of *Merlin's Shakespeare* and for her frequent encouragement.

Rose iStrode's reading of the manuscript and her excellent suggestions helped me immensely.

I am grateful to L.M. Elliott for her suggestions regarding the first chapter of *The Mercutio Problem* and to the Society of Children's Book Writers and Illustrators (SCBWI) for providing a space for critiques.

I am grateful to Viable Paradise for providing a wonderful atmosphere for learning about writing fantasy.

I thank all my friends for encouraging my writing, especially Ned Cabot Sr., Susan Carrigan, Virginia Cerello, Tacie Dejanikus, Beth Eldridge, Daniele Flannery, Julie Harris, Marlene Howell, Sue Lenaerts, Kate Leonard, Mary Leonard, Vickie Leonard, Tricia Lootens, Elizabeth Lytle, Colise Medved, Trudy Portewig, Luanne Schinzel, John Schmitz, Dolores Smith, Betty Jean Steinshouer, Liz Quinn, and Judith Witherow. I also want to thank the women of the Writers' Circle at Carefree, especially Dana Finnegan, for their encouragement.

I thank John Appel, Catherine Lundoff, Catherine Schaff-Stump, and Mary Anne Yarde for publishing advice and support. I'm very grateful to Gabriella Eriksson for her beautiful graphics and to Terry Roy for formatting this book. Many thanks to Liz Quinn for proofreading the galleys.

ABOUT THE AUTHOR

CAROL ANNE DOUGLAS HAS loved Shakespeare since she was introduced to *A Midsummer Night's Dream* when she was a child. She identifies with the character Nick Bottom because she wants to play every part, which only a writer can do. She has written the novels *Lancelot: Her Story* and *Lancelot and Guinevere*. She is an avid reader of Arthurian and Shakespearean lore and writes plays as well as fiction. She was born in a suburb of New York, grew up in Los Angeles, and lives in Washington, D.C. When she isn't reading or writing, she spends as much time as she can in the national parks hiking and observing wildlife.

Visit her website:
www.CarolAnneDouglas.com
Follow on Twitter:
@CarolAnneDougl1

Made in the USA
Middletown, DE
05 June 2022